DEATH ROUND THE CORNER

THE DEPARTMENT Z SERIES

DEATH ROUND THE CORNER

DEPARTMENT Z

JOHN CREASEY

OPEN ROAD

INTEGRATED MEDIA

NEW YORK

ISBN: 978-1-5040-9187-9

This edition published in 2024 by Open Road Integrated Media, Inc.
180 Maiden Lane
New York, NY 10038
www.openroadmedia.com

DEATH ROUND THE CORNER

PROLOGUE

1930–1935

I N the Spring of 1930 the hotels of London were full to overflowing, peopled by a host of distinguished gentlemen from all corners of the world, with their secretaries, legal advisers, personal servants and, with a few exceptions, their wives. Those people whose memories take them back to that year will remember the influx, and will remember the cause of it. The World Economic Conference was widely reported in the daily papers, some organs of which poured ridicule and derision over the object of the Conference, while other and more sober journals helped with encouragement and a good Press.

No sane man could have failed to support the object, but many, while regretting the biting leaders in some of the yellowest of the Yellow Press, could only foresee failure. Failure came, for in 1930 the world was not ready for a united effort to combat the problems confronting it. The prosperity of some countries compared with the poverty of others so favourably that idealists claimed the prosperity should be and could be shared equally, but only the unhappy and parlous Powers agreed. The failure, foreseen by many, regretted by most but heralded as a triumph for common sense (or insularity) by those papers which had viewed the Conference as impracticable, and which had launched a vitriolic campaign against it from its inception, was hidden in a smoke-screen of words; a month after their descent on the Metropolis, the economists and their advisers made their way back to their own countries wiser but sadder men. Prosperity was still a national, not an international, consideration. War was too costly, but Power would still fight Power on economic grounds, and fight until the weakest nations were no more than semi-independent.

No one had watched the Conference more eagerly than a gentleman who for some time had been increasing his monetary power in England and overseas. Mr. Leopold Gorman was a shrewd man. Some years before he had become obsessed with an idea, the fruition of which could not be contrived by himself alone, but which was possible if he had the help which he needed from powerful enough sources. In the World Economic Conference Leopold Gorman saw a way of finding this support. He spent a great deal of time at the meetings, suffering the rendering of each and every speech in five different languages, intent only on picking his men.

The first qualification in such men was strong antipathy towards the subject under discussion—the more equal distribution of wealth throughout the world. Secondly, their standard of economic morals must be low. Thirdly, they must be content to leave the managing of the scheme which Gorman had in mind to him, without question. It was in his search for the third qualification where Gorman found most difficulty, but one evening in May, ten days after the wind-up of the Conference, he met five men, all of different nationalities, all powerful financiers or industrialists, whom he considered would meet his requirements. He did not say so, but if any one of them had shown reluctance to fall in with his scheme, that one would have been dead within an hour of leaving his Park Place house. Having once broached his idea,

Gorman dared not risk the chance of it becoming public knowledge.

But Leopold Gorman had chosen his men well. None of them turned a hair after they had heard him talk. Holstein, the German iron and steel magnate, and Yushimuro, the Japanese cotton dictator, were only lukewarm in their reception of the proposition, but it was more native caution and doubt as to the eventual success which would be met than moral reluctance which prevented them from being enthusiastic. Higson, the American motor and aeroplane king, was openly jubilant, and Miccowiski the Russian was as keen (although Gorman had not doubted his ability to persuade the Soviet of the advantages of working with him). Leugens the Dane, whom Gorman had selected because of his world-wide shipping influence and his virtual control of food exports from Europe to tropical countries, spoke first after Gorman had stopped talking and while the other four magnates were mentally digesting the Englishman's strong meat.

"Five of us are not enough," said Leugens. "We want five—even more—in every country."

"We shall get them," said Gorman, "or, what is better, we shall buy their interests in their own countries."

"That will mean big money," grunted Holstein.

"That," said Leopold Gorman blandly, "is why I did not attempt to handle the proposition entirely by myself, gentlemen. We six together are rich enough to make the scheme successful—providing, once we have started, we do not back out."

"How long will you give us to make a decision?" demanded Yushimuro.

Gorman eyed the Japanese thoughtfully.

"Will twenty-four hours be enough?" he asked.

"More than enough," grunted Higson. "I say yes, and I don't need to think about it."

"Me too," said Miccowiski.

"You?" Gorman looked at Holstein.

The German hesitated.

"How are we to know," he demanded, "that we can rely on you, Mr. Gorman?"

"That is not important." Gorman shrugged his shoulders impatiently. "We can discuss ways and means of making each one of us secure against any possible neglect on my part or yours. In principle you are with us?"

"*Ja*." Holstein lapsed into his native tongue unconsciously.

"Leugens?" Gorman looked at the Dane.

"Yes," said Leugens slowly.

Gorman turned again to Yushimuro.

"Do you still want twenty-four hours?" he asked.

The Jap shook his head suddenly.

"No. I will be with you," he said.

The smile on Leopold Gorman's face betrayed little of the triumph which he felt.

"Gentlemen," he said, "we shall do what the Economic Conference failed to do. We shall secure the more equal distribution of prosperity—amongst ourselves. Shall we dine, gentlemen?"

His five visitors laughed at his joke, and said that they would dine.

In the early Spring of 1935, Leopold Gorman told himself that the plans which he and his five backers had made were near maturity. By the end of the year he anticipated complete success, and that without creating a suspicion of his plans in the mind of any member of the English Government, or, for that matter, of anyone but those who were directly interested.

There had been throughout those five years only one man who had caused Leopold Gorman anxiety. That one man was the Chief of the British Intelligence, Gordon Craigie. Craigie numbered some of the most brilliant Intelligence men in the world amongst his agents, and Leopold Gorman told himself that his safest policy to draw Craigie's teeth was to kill his men. One by one, Gordon Craigie's best agents "disappeared", but that was the way of things in the Intelligence, and the Chief knew no more than that more men than usual failed to return after he had sent them on various missions.

It was in the May of 1935 that Leopold Gorman, completely satisfied with the way his plans had worked, decided that the next man on his list would be one Tony Beresford. It was about the same time that Gordon Craigie decided that Leopold Gorman needed even closer watching than he had had in the past, and that the only man he could trust with the job was the same Beresford. The Devil and Destiny laughed at their joke.

CHAPTER ONE

SOME PEOPLE AND THEIR PLEASURES

MAJOR GULLIVER ODELL, D.S.O., M.C., O.B.E., sat in the fourth row of the stalls of the Emblem Theatre one night in May, staring and grunting with unbridled enthusiasm at the stage. Major Odell was a man of medium height who looked short because he was fat. That evening, his clothes stretched tightly across his shoulders, under his arms and at other places; his butterfly-collar—for he was in evening-dress—gripped his red neck so that a bulge of flesh hovered about the edge, and both coat and collar looked likely to give way under the excitement which possessed him. His straw-coloured moustache bristled, his full lips pursed or gaped to show immaculate dentures, his clean-shaven face shone multi-coloured from the reflection of the spot-lights on the stage. Major Odell, in fact, looked and was obsessed by what he saw, by what he had visited the Emblem Theatre to see.

In justice to the Major it must be said that seven hundred others gazed with the same rapture, and shared similar emotions.

They stared at a shimmering black curtain made, if the truth was known, by row upon row of black-painted shells, and at the one superb woman in front of it. They watched breathlessly as she twisted and turned, vivid white against the background so cunningly chosen: they saw the great white fans which she held in each hand, fans which were never still, were always covering or revealing, suggesting, exciting; and subconsciously they heard the low, haunting music to which she danced, little knowing that it was as much part of the display as was Adele Fayne herself.

They saw the dance grow faster, fiercer; they heard the music quicken, throbbing like the blood in their veins; they saw the flurry of those white fans and then, with a suddenness which startled them, they heard the orchestra crash out its *finale* and saw Adele Fayne motionless in the centre of the stage, alabaster against the shimmering black curtains, fans held high above her head, superb body poised, small head rigid between her slender, lovely arms.

And then the curtain dropped. For a moment there was a complete silence; then came the murmur of seven hundred people taking breath, a sudden, low-voiced thunder of applause.

"Gad, sir!" Major Gulliver Odell turned excitedly to his companion, his bright blue eyes starting from his head. "Did you ever see anything like it? Did you ever, Craigie? Damme, the woman's superb! She's—she's wonderful, Craigie! And you say she's going to marry that young pup Lavering—lucky young devil, that's all I can say. Damme, if I were half my age I'd cut him out, devil me if I wouldn't!"

The rather gaunt face of the Major's companion was twisted in a smile which could only be called sardonic. Gordon Craigie was taciturn by nature and observant by practice, while he possessed that rare thing, a sense of the ludicrous. The thought of fiery, portly Major Odell clamouring for the hand of Adele Fayne, that sensation in London in 1935, had its fair share of the absurd, but that evening Craigie's appreciation of the joke was marred by his disgust at Major Odell's general level of intelligence.

"Why not have a shot now?" demanded Craigie.

Odell looked at him suspiciously, and was about to remark

that some comments were uncalled for when Adele Fayne reappeared to take her curtain. The thunder of applause increased, helped in no small measure by the handclapping of the Major, while Gordon Craigie stared at the dancer, completely unmoved by her beauty or her figure. It was his business to know things, and he knew that Adele Fayne's success was due almost entirely to the genius of her manager-producer, Solly Lewistein. Take Solly away from her, Craigie thought, and she would have dropped into the second row of the chorus. But while Lewistein continued to hoodwink the censor, Adele Fayne would go from height to giddy height.

Perhaps Craigie was unwontedly bitter that night. He had cause to be, for he had hoped to get information from the Major, and Odell was as barren of information—and ideas—as Adele Fayne had been innocent of clothes; both had just enough to get them through.

Craigie went through that evening in his mind.

At six o'clock he had met Odell, recently arrived from the British Embassy in Paris, where the Major was Military Attaché. He had put to Odell a question which he considered of considerable importance, while the soldier had shown his deftness in shaking a cocktail. The place of their meeting had been Odell's temporary apartment at the Hotel Éclat.

"What do you think," Craigie had asked, "that Leopold Gorman was doing in Paris, Major?"

Odell had stopped shaking for a moment to glare.

"What was he doing? What do most people do in Paris, Craigie—ask yourself? He was on the loose for a couple of days—told me so himself, begad!"

Craigie had accepted his cocktail in numb silence. It had become a habit with him to disbelieve anything that Leopold Gorman—landowner, theatre-owner, and financier—said, and the discovery of someone supposedly intelligent who had taken his words on their face value was a shock. It had almost convinced

Craigie—whom many will recognize as the Chief of that ever-active but little-known Intelligence Department called Z—that Odell could tell him nothing about Leopold Gorman. But Craigie wanted to learn things of Gorman's recent Paris trip, and wanted to learn quickly. So he had suffered Odell for the rest of the evening, hoping that the Major would let something drop, if only by accident.

But Odell had been, bluntly, dumb. Craigie sighed to himself. He knew that Gorman was working on something big, and something that was probably crooked. He knew that chance had thrown Odell—who had been on a short vacation and had stayed at the Hotel Splendide instead of the Embassy during Gorman's visit—and the financier together, and he knew that Odell had been asked, in a discreetly worded note from the Foreign Office, to take careful stock of Gorman's activities and conversation. If Odell had been sharp, and Gorman had let slip an accidental word about his plans, Craigie might have been helped in his efforts to find the nature of Gorman's latest financial operations. As it was, Odell had believed that the financier was in Paris to shake a leg, and Craigie sighed.

As Adele Fayne disappeared behind the curtain, the Intelligence man gripped Odell's arm.

"We'd better be moving," he said.

Odell pulled his arm away, and looked sheepish.

"I say, Craigie, would you mind if——"

Craigie chuckled grimly.

"You'll never get near her room," he said.

Major Odell spluttered and bristled.

"Won't I, then—won't I? I know Solly Lewistein. He'll fix it for me. Care to come?"

The invitation was reluctant, and Odell was frankly pleased with Craigie's dry, "No, you can have her all to yourself." Odell pushed his way back-stage, while Craigie sought his hat and coat and reached the cool night air of Coventry Street with a sigh of relief. He walked briskly towards Whitehall, where he spent sixteen out of every twenty-four hours, and told himself that if nothing was reported about Leopold Gorman during the next forty-eight hours he would send one Tony Beresford to France.

Major Gulliver Odell saw Adele Fayne that night, but it was not because he knew Solly Lewistein. If Lewistein, short, fat, oily-skinned and temperamental, had had his way, he would have spent five minutes in telling the Major what kind of fool he was and another five in telling him that he was the hundredth-and-one acquaintance who had begged an introduction to Adele Fayne during the past week without getting it, and one tense moment in telling Odell just where he could go. Instead, Lewistein screwed his plump face into a smile and led the Major into the star's dressing-room.

Adele Fayne made Odell breathless, but not too breathless to prevent him from telling her so.

The dancer was swathed in a shapeless white dressing-gown, a precaution against catching a chill after her exertions on the stage which Lewistein insisted she should take. The silver wig which she had worn for the Fan Dance was on her dressing-table, and her own luxuriant black hair coiled about her lovely face, emphasizing the creamy whiteness of her skin. To the Major she was the height of beauty; to a keener student of human nature her smile would have seemed artificial, her sloe-black eyes lustrous but lacking in intelligence. The student might not have been able to deny the physical perfection of her features, her warm Latin beauty, but he would have said, like Tony Beresford of Major Odell, that she was dumb. He would have been right, but Odell didn't know it.

Odell suggested supper, but was sweetly refused. He suggested supper some other night, and was made happy by vague promises. He offered his tentative congratulations on her coming marriage with one Robert Lavering, and was politely thanked. He was ushered out of the dressing-room by Solly Lewistein (whose temperament was such that he pulled a face at the stout Major's back and banged the door to). He went back to the Hotel Éclat and talked of Adele Fayne to everybody from a bellboy to the manager, who wished heartily that he had not visited the Major's apartment to make personal inquiries as to that august gentleman's comfort.

When Lewistein banged the door behind the Major, he in turn talked of and to Adele Fayne, but in less glowing terms.

"Vun of these days," said Solly, glaring at the dancer, "you vill do somethings silly like you tried to-night, an' ve vill vind ourselves both in the gutter. Ven vill you learn to do vot Leopold Gorman says, Adele, viddout being obshectionable?"

The dancer leaned back in her chair, her eyes closed and dark with grease-paint, her red, ripe lips set thinly together.

"Don't keep on about Gorman," she said lifelessly. "I did what he wanted, didn't I? I saw that fool of a soldier and made myself pleasant to him. Now forget it."

Lewistein pursed his lips. His anger evaporated. In its place there was pleading, a pleading inspired by fear.

"But, Adele, ve must not forget Leopold Gorman! He owns the theatre, his money pays for everyt'ing, Adele. Eef he turns against us he vill break us. He is too beeg for us, Adele, an' you must have the patience. Vun day, perhaps, he vill not be so important as he is, an' then ..."

The dancer laughed again, unpleasantly.

"One day, perhaps! You've been saying that for years, Solly—as long as I've known you. Oh, for heaven's sake get out, and let me dress!"

She swung round towards her mirror. Lewistein stood with his back to the door, a fat little bundle of greasy flesh, looking at her as she started to clean the paint from her eyes. Then, with a little dejected sigh, he went out.

As he walked along the passage towards his office, he thought of the man whom he knew as Leopold Gorman, and he wished that the man was dead. He had hated Leopold Gorman for years, but he feared him more than he hated him. Everyone who worked for Gorman's money hated and feared and obeyed him, because his money gave him power, and there were times when he used his power in ways which made Solly Lewistein shudder.

Lewistein reached his office, locked the door behind him, and dropped heavily into his padded chair. From his vest-pocket he took a visiting-card, inscribed on the one side with:

Leopold Gorman
5, *Park Place, W.*1

and with a message in Gorman's thick, back-sloping handwriting which said:

A Major Odell is coming back-stage. Treat him well.

The Jew took a match from a stand on his desk, struck it viciously, and held the card over the flame. As the card burned, he dropped it into an ashtray, then stubbed the ashes into black powder. That was how he treated all messages from Leopold Gorman—on Gorman's instructions. Gorman knew well enough how to look after small things.

Lewistein swore suddenly.

"Vun day," he muttered, "vun day, Gorman, you vill vind someone who iss not afraid of you."

CHAPTER TWO

TONY BERESFORD AND OTHERS

THE size of Tony Beresford was such that it made him a man to look at once, twice, and then to marvel. Six feet three he stood, with a shoulder span of a yard, biceps approaching eighteen inches, and a chest which was at once the admiration of his many friends and the despair of Blunt, his tailor. Fortunately, Providence had made him comely. His skin was tanned deeply by summer sun and winter storm, his forehead was broad, his eyes grey and usually smiling with lazy good humour, wide-set on each side of a well-bridged nose. His lips were full and generous but well-shaped, and his chin square without being ostentatiously aggressive—unless he was in a bad temper, which was rare.

Like many big men, Tony—or Anthony Charles—Beresford was light on his feet, and he was demonstrating his ability on the crowded floor of the Two-Step Club that same evening in May when Craigie and Odell went to the Emblem Theatre. His companion was the incomparable Diane Chester, tall, slim, slender Diane who had once adorned the stage of the Emblem Theatre with as much beauty and infinitely more wit than Adele Fayne. She had, let it be said at once, left the stage when she had married Aubrey, Lord Chester; the only people who regretted it were those theatre-fans who viewed their stars as their own private property.

"Where's Aub?" asked Beresford, steering Diane past a portly Cabinet Minister and an angular spouse. The Two-Step Club was at once exclusive and reputable.

"At our table, glaring at you," said Diane. "Haven't you seen him?"

Beresford eyed her reproachfully.

"Don't you know me enough," he said, "to know my eyes are only for you?"

Diane's eyes sparkled.

"You get a bigger fool than ever," she said frankly. "One day some poor married woman will believe you when you talk like that and——"

"If I may interrupt," said Beresford coldly, "and answer your first accusation first, I don't. I weigh fourteen-stone thirteen pounds and seven ounces, and I am half an ounce lighter than I was a year ago. And when I say things to any woman, married or spinster, who might believe me, goldfish will be drawing the Lord Mayor's coach. Did you tread on my toe?"

"I don't know. I meant to kick your ankle."

"Thank you," said Tony. "This is my night out. Why did you tread on my toe?"

"To attract your attention and stop you from talking."

"You could have poked me in the ribs," said the big man, "and gained your object while giving me a thrill."

"And he would have seen me," said Diane.

Beresford widened his eyes.

"So-ho! Little Aub's getting green eyes, is he?"

"I didn't mean Aubrey," said Diane Chester, with a frown. "I——"

Beresford whistled under his breath.

"If you're starting to talk about the obvious," he quizzed her, "I'm going to retire. Go on. I know you didn't mean our Aub, because you can see him ogling that brunette girl from Boston——"

"That's his cousin," said Diane indignantly.

Beresford grinned and sniffed.

"All right with me, sister. Carry on."

"Thank you," said Diane with some sarcasm. Then, as she went on, Beresford saw her eyes lose their humour, and saw a frown puckering her forehead.

"It's funny you mentioned green eyes," said Diane, "because his eyes *are* green—greenish-grey, anyhow."

"You mean the 'he' who stopped you from poking me in the ribs?"

"Yes. You'll see him in a minute—that big man with the sloping shoulders."

Beresford glanced about the crowded floor.

"The feller dancing with Adele Fayne?"

Diane Chester looked intently but with seeming carelessness at the partner of the man with sloping shoulders. Her eyes glistened with a natural interest.

"Yes, that's right—Adele Fayne. I didn't recognize her at first. She hasn't lost much time getting from the theatre."

"And the past shall always be jealous of the present," grinned Beresford. "Oi! My ankle's six inches lower down than that, to the right and left of my shin. What's the matter with the man with green-greenish-grey eyes, anyhow?"

"He was looking at you," said Diane simply.

Beresford lost a step as he stared at her.

"And is all this because a man with sloping shoulders, green eyes and Adele Fayne was looking at me?" he demanded with some heat. "Darn your pretty face, men often look at me. Boxing promoters wonder if I'll turn pro, retired colonels think I ought to join the Army, and——"

"He's looking again," said Diane Chester, with a superb disregard of Tony's fine flow of words. "I don't want to scare you, Tony——"

Beresford laughed, and his eyes creased attractively at the corners.

"Thanks a lot," he said. "You're good to-night, Di."

"All the same," said Diane Chester, with a seriousness which made Beresford frown, "it was a dirty look, Tony, and he's a man I wouldn't like to meet without a large escort."

"Seriously?" Beresford demanded.

"Honest-to-goodness."

"Well, well, *well!*" drawled the big man. "If I knew what a cock-fight was like I'd say this beats it. Beautiful Diane warns Big Beresford of Villainous Look. Let's get out of the crowd, old girl. I'd like to take a peek at this man, and when I'm dancing with you that bump on the end of your nose always fascinates me. *Touche!* Dead centre of the ankle that time, my angel, and my bump's bigger than yours."

Beresford guided his companion skilfully towards the side of the restaurant-room, dancing the while and nodding his big head to the rhythm of the music. He was smiling at Diane, telling the world that he was completely satisfied with life, that he had no care in the world. A hundred revellers at the Two-Step Club that night saw Beresford and envied him. Half a hundred nodded or smiled at him, recognition which he acknowledged with a beam or a cheery wave of his hand. He had, they thought, money to spare— which was true—freedom in the sense that he was single—also true—just enough intelligence to enjoy himself, but not enough to get himself into one of those emotional tangles which the intellec-tuals imagine are mind-states known only to themselves.

About Beresford, men and women danced, ate, drank, talked and, for the most part, took pleasure in the amenities so plenti-fully provided at the Two-Step Club. The sober oak panelling, tables and chairs lent a solid, comfortable impression, while the lighting effects, mellow and pleasant and coming from the ceiling, created a slight but intriguing sense of the unusual.

As a night-club, the Two-Step was certainly unusual. Its management employed no stunts, its waiters were dressed in black and white, its drinks were of good vintage, good value, and wholly legal, its music was straightforward, coming from two bands set at each end of the restaurant-cum-dance-room, bands which were in full view and whose members might have slipped from their seats and masqueraded as waiters unobserved by any but Palluski, the director of music, or Anton, most famous of head waiters, both of whom reflected the high standard set by the Two-Step Club. The Two-Step was a night club not because it catered for those thrill-starved souls called the Bright Young People, not because it was under surveillance from the police, but for the simple and ample reason that it opened and provided recreation by night.

Normally, night-life had little attraction for Tony Beresford. He liked day to be day and night to pass unnoticed while he slept. In summer he played cricket seriously, and no serious cricketer can gain a reputation on less than eight hours' sleep, some of it before midnight. In winter he liked the touch of a horse between his great legs, the roar of the wind in his ears, the exhilaration of an early-morning gallop over good country which provided jumps in plenty, the pleasing rumble of the horse's breath when he dismounted to give that noble beast a rest. In his pleasures Beresford was a simple, likeable soul.

But there were times when he broke out of his shell, and the occasion of the return of Aubrey and Diane Chester from America, with Valerie Lester, Aubrey's cousin, was one of them. The Chesters had been back in England for two days, after three months abroad while Aubrey had played tennis. On the morning of the second day—that morning in short—Aubrey had telephoned Beresford—an Aubrey in trouble. He had been charged to see that Valerie Lester's visit to England was an uneventful—or at least non-scandalous—one. He did not approve of the B.Y.P., but he knew that Tony Beresford was solid and safe, yet at times amusing, and would he like to make a fourth at dinner, the Palladium and the Two-Step? Beresford had said that he would try it, and say whether he liked it later.

He was liking it.

Valerie Lester was young, vivacious and interesting. One of those intriguing brunettes whose blue eyes darkened in laughter, she was slim and supple but exquisitely formed, while contriving not to notice the sudden interest with which men looked at her for the first time. Few would have called her beautiful, and only the unimaginative could have called her pretty, for prettiness suggests children or dolls or paint and powder. Her smooth, creamy skin was without blemish, her lips were a trifle large, but curved and shapely. Her nose was short and straight, her chin square but delicately moulded. Men being men, they saw the lovely roundness of her slender neck, merging into flawless shoulders, and all but one of them would wish for the thing that could not be.

Beresford wished for nothing that evening. He was enjoying himself, and he was content to admire.

As the big man and Diane reached the table at which Aubrey Chester and his cousin were sitting, Aubrey complained.

"Twenty minutes you've been on the floor," he said. "It's n-not fair, Toby, old scout, when it's c-crowded. I-it's only a s-small floor——"

"If that was meant to be a humorous remark anent my size," grinned Beresford, sitting down and proffering cigarettes, "it's a proof that America sharpened your grey cells, my Aub."

"Th-they were always p-pretty sharp," admitted Chester modestly.

Diane broke in with a *moue* of annoyance.

"I thought you were going to look at the man with Adele Fayne, Tony."

Beresford grinned, and the others looked interested.

"I was and am," he said. "A tough-looking customer I'll grant you, lass. Funny how he looks lopsided—shoulders, eyes, lips, everything. Don't stare round the floor like a day-old gazelle, darn you, Aub."

Valerie Lester laughed—she had a low-pitched laugh and a husky voice which suggested rather than declaimed that she came from America—and asked whether Tony always talked just like that.

"Always," said Aubrey bitterly. "He's got no sense, so he tries to be funny. What are you two talking about?"

Beresford chuckled.

"Diane saw a man with green eyes dancing with Adele Fayne and looking hard at me. So she dug me, metaphorically, in the ribs, and we came over to take a peek at the gent." He grinned at Valerie. "I think she thinks he thinks I'm a rival."

Aubrey Chester grunted suddenly.

"F-funny thing she's over h-here so soon," he said—Aubrey Chester had a stammer which one grew used to quickly; "the show at the Emblem doesn't finish till el-leven, and it's only a-about twelve now."

Beresford winked at Valerie Lester.

"Proper soul-mates, these two," he said. "Diane said the same thing just now."

"If I'd thought you were going to be as bad as this," said Diane, "I'd never have asked you to make the four."

Aubrey looked indignant.

"S-steady," he protested. "T-Tony was my idea."

Beresford wagged a large forefinger.

"Now, friends, no quarrelling, or you'll disillusion us. What I think is funny," he added more seriously, "is that the great Fayne isn't with Bob Lavering. Usually you can't see 'em apart."

Valerie Lester looked interested.

"Bob's engaged to her, isn't he?" she asked.

Beresford eyed the girl from Boston with fresh interest.

"Yes," he answered. "Of course, you came from the same home town. D'you know Bob Lavering well?"

There was an expression in Valerie Lester's eyes which might have meant anything. Beresford, whose sense of observation was abnormally keen, noticed it and told himself that the girl was not altogether happy when thinking of Bob Lavering of America. But his own eyes were smiling as he spoke.

Valerie nodded, without smiling, and Beresford told himself that the occasional gleam of her teeth as she talked was well worth looking at.

"I wouldn't say I know him well," she said, "but I do know him. I've had more to do with his father than with Bob himself."

"Jonathan Lavering?" said Beresford. "What's that man doing these days? Still piling up the oof?"

"For Bob to spend. Yes, he's still working."

Beresford grinned, but was thoughtful. He had told himself before that Lavering, Senior, was not likely to look on his son's coming marriage with any favour. But that was a matter purely domestic. For his part, Beresford was sorry for the younger man. Anyone who married Adele Fayne needed a fortune all right, but he needed the patience of Job and a charity far above the human if he was to be happy when married. Adele Fayne was famous—or notorious—for the quantity, quality and brevity of her friendships. And Beresford liked Bob Lavering, although he knew nothing of his father beyond the fact that he was one of the biggest landowners in the U.S.A. and that his reputed fortune was comfortably past the seven-figure mark in sterling.

Aubrey Chester proffered cigarettes.

"D-didn't I read in the *T-Tatler* that Bob's been to P-Paris?" he asked as he struck a match.

Beresford chuckled.

"Paris, eh? That's an original one, even for Bob, who's got some funny habits. He's disporting himself in Paris while his beloved enjoys herself in London. When are they getting married? Did the *Tatler* say that too?"

"It said sh-shortly," said Aubrey. And then he thumped his hand on his thigh, his eyes gleaming. "I-I've g-got it! I knew I'd s-seen the c-cove before."

Beresford's eyes went up.

"You mean the lopsided customer?"

"Y-yep!" said Aubrey. "It's G-Gorman—the m-money merchant. D-don't see him about m-much."

Beresford looked again, casually on the surface but with considerable interest, at the man whom Diane Chester had noticed viewing him with disfavour. It was true enough that Leopold Gorman was rarely seen in public, and his photograph never appeared in the papers. But Beresford, whose job it was to know things, just as it was Craigie's, knew that the landowner-financier had more than one black mark against him.

"Gorman owns the 'Emblem', doesn't he?" asked Diane.

Beresford nodded.

"Yes. He's just bought it, with the whole mid-country Play-house Circuit," murmured Beresford thoughtfully. "That explains why he's dancing with Adele Fayne, anyhow."

As he spoke, Gorman and the dancer whirled nearer the table. Beresford, still appearing to interest himself solely in his three companions, thoughtfully surveyed the couple.

Adele Fayne was dressed in a startling creation of silver lamé, cut to a peak at the front and suspended by a buckle attachment to a skin-tight necklet of glittering diamonds. The back, Beres-ford afterwards said, was not; certainly there was little enough of it above the waist. The dancer's raven-black hair and milk-white complexion made her the cynosure of many eyes, frank and covert. But the discriminating looked at the man, whom a few knew as Gorman.

Gorman was a man of more than medium height, but he looked shorter because of his enormous breadth of shoulders, a size exaggerated by the fact that the right shoulder was a full two inches higher than the left. The face was heavy—swarthy skin, dark with pregnant stubble, heavy jowls of solid flesh, his chin massive, nose prominent yet flattened at the bridge—and every feature had that peculiar lopsidedness which characterized the man. His deep-set, black-browed eyes were built curiously below his high forehead, the right well above the left, and the colour of them was green, jade-green. Beresford judged that Gorman wore a wig of black hair, although few people would have thought it unnatural. But all men must have thought that Leopold Gorman was a fish out of water amidst that glittering gathering of celebrities and monied nonentities.

Diane apparently sensed that Beresford was sizing the couple up. Not until they were hidden by the crowd of dancers swaying to the never-ceasing music—the band at each end of the room ensured that rhythm never stopped at the Two-Step Club—did she break the brief silence at the table.

"It may explain why he's dancing with that woman," said Diane, "but it doesn't explain why he glared at you."

"Glared now, is it?" Beresford wagged a large finger. "Say what you mean, my Ugly One, or . . .".

Diane wrinkled her nose in a grimace.

"I hope he sticks a knife in your back," she said with feeling. "If you want to be taken for a fool, try it with someone who doesn't know you so well."

Tony Beresford grinned his attractive grin, and winked at Valerie Lester.

"That's her way of paying me a compliment without letting Aubrey know," he said. "Let's dance, Miss America, and give Gorman a chance to look at me again."

Valerie stood up, laughing.

"Conditionally," added Beresford suddenly.

"All right," said the girl. "Name it."

"Whatever you do," warned Tony, "don't say that green-eyed

Gorman glowered. Diane's got the copyright on that little word. I can see it hovering on the tip of her tongue."

He grinned, and Valerie Lester, from America, told herself that she had rarely seen a more attractive grin. It illuminated Beresford's already pleasant countenance and made him a man whom one instinctively liked, trusted, and guessed to be capable of many things. She knew, now, that when Diane had said, in effect, that Beresford was no fool, she had been right.

For the next ten minutes the big man and the girl from America danced easily and pleasantly together, talking of trivial things and liking it. But as he talked, Tony Beresford wondered whether Diane had been right when she had imagined Leopold Gorman had looked at him with something more than curiosity. Unlike Aubrey Chester, who knew Gorman to look at but not his reputation, Beresford thought chiefly that the financier and theatre-owner was a man of many parts, few of them reputable.

CHAPTER THREE

DEATH PASSES BY

L EOPOLD GORMAN, Beresford knew, was not viewed with any favour by the Intelligence Department—or Z—nor by the police. His financial interests in England were considerable, and it was well known that he had other interests, on as great a scale, abroad. As with most men with fingers in the financial and economic pie, Gorman did most of his dealing through agents, and in person he was not a well-known figure. But his activities often ruled the markets. When he started to buy stock—any stock —buyers went mad and prices leapt up. When it was rumoured that he was selling, the market came down with a rush, and at times reached zero. Yet Leopold Gorman contrived to buy when others were selling low, and sell when others were buying high. In short, he rigged the market.

Rigging the market in itself is not a crime. It is the age-old game of making a fool of the other man and profiting by it. But the border-line between honest dealing and fraud which divided Gorman's activities was so faint as to be decipherable only by those who knew the tortuous working of the Company Laws— and the evading of them; a fact which the police had known for a long time. The authorities believed that Gorman was crooked from top to bottom, and believed that he was riding for a fall. They knew, too, that if Gorman did crash, half financial London would go with him. In consequence, powerful influences guarded and sheltered him—influences which had always been formidable enough to prevent the police from taking action, but not strong enough to keep the financier away from the watchful and hopeful eyes of the Yard and the Intelligence, who at times worked hand-in-hand.

Beresford knew that Gordon Craigie was doubtful of Gorman. He reasoned, as he walked home that night from the Chesters' Regent's Park home, and when he had dispersed the pleasant thoughts of Valerie Lester which had at first filled his mind, that it was possible that Gorman guessed he was being watched, and as possible that he knew the identity of several of Department Z's agents, including his humble self. It was conceivable, he thought, that if the financier was half-fearful of being tripped up by the police or Department Z, he would naturally look on the Department agents with keen disfavour; thus he might have looked, glared, or even glowered at the big man that night.

Tony Beresford, apart from being no fool, and something of a judge of character, had known Diane Chester for many years. She was not easily scared, and she was not unduly fanciful. She would not, in fact, have drawn attention to Leopold Gorman's apparent interest in Beresford unless it had been there. The thing to learn, then, was whether Leopold Gorman knew that he was Number Two—or any old number—on Department Z's list.

It was not a problem, Beresford told himself, which could be worked out by a process of heavy thinking. In the morning he could call on Gordon Craigie, and ways and means could be worked out. Meanwhile he was tired, and he turned into Auveley Street, at Number 7 of which he had a second-floor flat, with pleasant visions of his general factotum, one Tricker, being still up and awake and ready with coffee.

An old trick with a new variation nearly caught even him.

If he had been three inches shorter, and his line of vision consequently lower, his interest in Department Z and Leopold Gorman would have been brought to an abrupt close. But he saw the thing move that vital fraction of a second before it dropped, and he threw himself sideways, banging himself against the railings but unconscious of the sharp pain they caused.

As he moved, a block of stone dropped from the portico of the house, smashing against the doorstep into a hundred pieces!

Beresford stayed there, pressing against the railings, staring at the stone, possessed by a cold, intense anger. The squeak of a hurriedly opened window and a gruff voice broke the tension.

"Hey, there! Anything hup?" demanded Samuel Tricker.

Beresford found his voice, but it was harsh and unnatural.

"No, but there's something down, Sam. Slip here quickly and bring a torch, will you?"

"I'm on me way," said Samuel Tricker, who was a regular patron of the cinema.

The window squeaked again as Tricker closed it, and Beresford looked up and down Auveley Street, mildly surprised that no one else had heard the crash. The street was empty, however, and in the near vicinity of Number 7 no lights glowed.

"I suppose not," Beresford murmured to himself, "seeing that it's nearly two. Now I wonder . . ."

What he wondered was simply whether Leopold Gorman, who was very much in his mind that night, knew anything about the loosened stone which had crashed. He kept an open mind, and even told himself that the thing might have been accidental. When Tricker arrived, however, complete with a bull's-eye lantern and a lead-weighted strip of leather called a cosh—Sam Tricker was always hoping for the worst—Beresford knew that it had been no accident. It was murder attempted; and it sent a peculiar quiver up and down Beresford's spine.

The fallen stone had been the centre-piece in the roof of the porch. It had been carefully loosened, and kept in place by two wedges of chiselled stone. The wedges had been tied round with strong twine which ran down both sides of the porch and was stretched across the top step, on which Beresford had trodden. Now that the stone had crashed, the twine was lying on the ground, but it was still connected with the two wedges, which helped Beresford to reconstruct the affair without much trouble.

He had trodden on the cord, noticing nothing more than he would have done if he had trodden on a matchstick, and the leverage on the wedges had jerked them out of place, so that the slab had fallen. If, Beresford reminded himself with a sudden return of that cold rage which he had felt after the first shock, he had not noticed the slab move, because of his height, it must have crashed, fifty-six pounds or more of solid stone, on his bare head.

Beresford cursed suddenly. Sam Tricker, who was sound if slow in thought, was fingering the twine round one of the wedges, and the meaning of it came suddenly to his mind.

"Blimey!" he gasped, his rugged, honest face stiff with astonishment. "The dirty, murderin' lot o'——"

"Have you been in the front room all the evening?" Beresford demanded abruptly.

"Fer the larst coupla hours, Mr. B."

"Heard anything unusual?"

"Not ter say I noticed it."

"Humph," grunted Beresford. "Let's see—the top flat's empty, isn't it?"

"Since Monday," said Sam, moving pieces of the broken stone towards the side of the porch with his foot.

"Is Williams in downstairs?"

Tricker stopped his clearing-up to whistle. It came to him suddenly that the occupant of the ground floor flat—one Nicholas Williams, a middle-aged widower with an interest in fine art and highbrow literature—had left Number 7 Auveley Street that morning after receiving a wire. Sam said as much.

Beresford's eyes widened.

"Are you sure about the wire, Sam?"

"Sure's my name's Tricker," asserted Sam. "I 'eard a rat-tat abart ten this morning an' I 'appened ter be looking art of the winder, Mr. B., when the boy wot brought it went orf. Mr. Williams went art abart an hour arterwards."

"That means," said Beresford thoughtfully, helping Tricker in a fresh assault on the débris in the porch, "that the house has been empty all day, except when you and I were in. I was out from ten to half past four, and you—"

"I went ter the Regal," Tricker said, "just arter twelve, Mr. B., and got back 'alf a nour afore you did."

"So this," said Beresford, jerking his head at the roof of the porch, "was worked between twelve and four o'clock. You haven't been out this evening, have you?"

"Not even fer a quick one, Mr. B."

"Humph," grunted Beresford. "Well, it's a funny business, Sammivel—but it's time we went in. I can see a Robert coming this way, and somehow I don't feel like talking until I've settled down a bit."

Sam slipped rapidly into the hall of Number 7, and Beresford followed suit. The servant closed the door quietly as a red-faced beat-policeman looked curiously towards the debris at the sides of the porch, sniffed, reminded himself that the big man Beresford lived at Number 7, and that Beresford had been known to associate with gentlemen of importance at Scotland Yard, and then passed on forgetfully.

Beresford, naturally, forgot nothing. The stark fact was that he had been within a split second of being brained, or as near brained as made little difference. The trap had been carefully rigged in the porch, obviously while the house had been empty, and it was a hundred per cent. certainty that the man who had rigged it had been waiting near by when the intended victim had turned into Auveley Street. In the few minutes which it had taken Beresford to walk the two hundred-odd yards (he had entered the street from the Bond Street end, and Number 7 was near the Park Lane end), the would-be murderer had slipped into the porch, set the twine so that Beresford would work the trap by treading on it, and, Beresford thought, had hovered near by, ready to dart forward and remove all traces of the wedges and twine before investigations started. The fact that Beresford had dodged the slab had urged the man to make himself scarce, quickly and certainly thoroughly. It would have been useless, Beresford told himself, to have started looking round the neighbourhood for a large or small specimen of vermin.

But there were other things to look for, and think about, concerning both the ground-floor tenant of Number 7 and Mr. Leopold Gorman.

Samuel Tricker took his employer's hat and coat—Beresford bowed to convention by carrying a topper in his hand when clad in the full if ridiculous regalia of evening-dress—and hovered solicitously about the big man as he dropped into a chair and lit a cigarette.

"Feel like a black corfee, Mr. B.?"

"No," said Beresford, "I feel like black murder. Whisky, Sam, in large glasses."

"Soda, sir?"

Beresford said he would have a little soda, and that Sam could have a lot.

As he measured the drinks out, Sam Tricker's face was twisted in frustrated anger. It was slowly dawning on him that tragedy had knocked on the door of Number 7 that night, and Sam loved Tony Beresford with that fierceness typical of a disciple and his master. To Samuel Tricker, Beresford was as near perfection as the world could show; to Sam, the most heinous crime in the world was an attempt to defraud, catch, or threaten bodily harm to his Mr. B.

As Beresford tossed his drink down, he saw the scowl on

Tricker's face, and spluttered, for even he could not laugh and drink at the same time with success.

"Worried, Sam?" he demanded, as he recovered.

Sam sniffed.

"Not so worritted as them vermin 'ud be if I got me 'ands rarnd their froats, Mr. B. Any idee 'oo it was?"

Beresford nodded.

"The vaguest of vague ideas, Sam. Er—hop down into the front hall, will you, and squint round for that telegram. Williams might have left it about."

"O.K.," Tricker said, and departed.

Beresford grinned as the door closed behind his servant. Tricker was—or had been—a champion light-heavy in the pre-war period. The holocaust of hell in Flanders had put the prize-fighter out of fighting action, but Sam had started, and for some time had prospered with, an Academy of the Boxing Art. At that school, and from Sam's shrewd tuition, Tony Beresford had learned nearly all that there was to learn about using his fists. The University and All-England Amateur Championship titles had been his, and Sam's, reward. Soon afterwards, pneumonia had put Sam in the ring for the biggest fight of all. He had won, but only on points. The Academy had suffered while he was ill, and he had not the strength to put it on its feet again. Sam had been perilously near to down-and-out.

Beresford had discovered his plight and remedied it. For five years prior to the affair of the dislodged porch-stone Sam Tricker had been what was loosely termed 'Beresford's man'. There had been times, early on, when Tony had despaired of making the boxer a valet, but perseverance and patience had gained its reward. To Beresford, life without Sam Tricker would have been dull. To Tricker, although he could not have put the thought into words, for speech was not his medium of expression, life without Beresford would have been impossible.

That might sound like sentiment, but it is—and was then —true.

There were things, however, which Beresford kept from Sam; his association with Department Z was one of them. Sam knew that the big man went at times on mysterious missions, but he knew not where nor why. Nor was he ever present when Beresford put one of his rare calls through to Whitehall six threes, the then number of Department Z's office. As the ex-fighter went downstairs, Beresford climbed to his feet and hurried to the telephone in the corner of his room. It was late for a call, but not necessarily too late for Gordon Craigie.

The Chief's dry voice greeted the big man after a brief pause.

"Still at it?" asked Beresford, grinning into the mouthpiece.

"Always at it," said Craigie, with truth. "What's your trouble, Tony?"

"You'd be surprised," said Beresford. "Can I come over?"

"Yes. I was going to call you in the morning, anyway."

Beresford's brows arched. For some weeks past he had been 'off duty'; Craigie's words suggested that things were beginning to stir, somewhere between London and Timbuctoo, and that Craigie was going to find the whys and wherefores of them.

"I'll be over in twenty minutes," said the big man. "Which entrance?"

Craigie hesitated. His office was walled by steel-lined partitions, any one of which could open to serve as a door, and it could be approached by a dozen different routes.

"Use Number Three," he said at last.

Beresford said, "Oke"—an expression which he only used when talking to the Chief, because Craigie detested it, and replaced the receiver. With a thoughtful grin on his face, he moved across the living-room, which was furnished with an eye to comfort and usefulness. There were three large armchairs, a small sideboard, two revolving bookcases, an oak bureau which was Beresford's especial pride because of the number of pigeon-holes and drawers which were covertly or openly built in it, and a sizeable oak dining-table with its complement of four stiff-backed chairs. He went into his bedroom, which was furnished with the same purpose, possessing a suite of magnificently carved walnut, an outsize in beds, a third bookcase filled with a motley of yellow-backs and classics, the latter well-thumbed, and a cupboard-cum-table by the bed.

Beresford went to the wardrobe, and pressed a slight protuberance in the carving of the bottom drawer. The drawer itself did not move, but a false bottom slid silently out of the wardrobe, revealing an apparently solid block of wood, its area akin to the wardrobe's base, and some three inches in depth.

The big man ran his thumb along the edge of this uninteresting piece of work, and a soft whirring sound revealed the seemingly solid surface to be a lid operated on the roll-top principle. The things that rested on the green baize lining of the hidden drawer would have astonished anyone in the world with the exception of Tony Beresford.

It was a veritable armoury! Two Webley .32's, fitted with Maxim silencers, were cheek-by-jowl with two small grey automatics. Three sheathed knives of varying sizes were thrust through two pairs of up-to-date handcuffs. Two gas pistols were packed, with grim humour, in two gas masks of the latest Siebe pattern, and round the sides of the drawer were packets of ammunition, for both guns. To himself, Beresford called it his 'gathering of friends'. There were times when he had used them all, to kill to save being killed; and he hoped that there would be many times again.

Memories of a hundred tight corners flashed through the big man's mind as he opened the drawer, but he had no time to dwell on them. He took one of the automatics, loaded it, and slipped it, with a spare box of cartridges, in his coat pocket. One of the knives, still sheathed, he slid into a place made for it on the inside of his waist-band—Blunt, his tailor, thought that the slots were made to hold a stiffening for relaxing stomach muscles, but Blunt didn't know everything. In faith rather than hope Beresford dropped a pair of handcuffs into his other coat pocket, and then he stood up, replaced the shutter, pushed the secret drawer into position, and left the room.

Tricker was still downstairs. Beresford wondered absently why his man had been so long on the search for the telegram, which would almost certainly be futile, and slipped into his overcoat, for that May morning was cold. This time, scorning his hat, he fortified himself with a tot of whisky, and went downstairs to tell Sammivel what he thought of him.

But he told Samuel Tricker nothing of the kind.

The ex-fighter was sprawling on the hall floor, his legs doubled queerly beneath him, his grizzled hair showing very grey in the dim light of a street lamp which filtered through the frosted-glass panels of the door; and on his forehead, spreading to the hair on his head, was a dark, ominous patch which Beresford knew instinctively was blood!

CHAPTER FOUR

HELP FROM THE UNHOLY TWINS

A T a crisis some men swear, others are speechless, and some simply act. Beresford belonged to the last category. For a split second he stood on mid-stairs, staring down at the inert body of his man, and then, his mind numb and cold, he raced towards the hall, on his toes and noiselessly. That instinct which made him Department Z's safest agent also made him duck his head, and he bent almost double as he reached the level of the floor. He stepped over Tricker, and reached the door, keeping close to the wall as he flung it open.

Nothing happened. Beresford waited for an ever-lasting second, and then looked into Auveley Street. Nothing was there, but from some distance off the sound of a heavy tread echoed dully through the silence of London's night. It was a comforting sound, the thud of a policeman's reputed nines. Beresford's expression eased. The sound grew nearer, and he knew that the man was approaching Number 7, which was just what he wanted.

Beresford turned to the unconscious Tricker, satisfied himself that his man was alive, and moved his legs into a more natural position. The policeman's shadow loomed in the doorway, and Beresford called out softly:

"Don't look this way, constable, and don't stop. Tell me if there's anything or anyone in the street."

The policeman seemed intelligent. He walked past the open door of Number 7, and spoke softly but clearly.

"There's a couple of gents getting out of a car twenty yards along, sir. What's the trouble?"

"Getting out or getting in?" insisted Beresford.

"Out I said and out I meant. They passed me as I came out of Bond Street. You know 'em, Mr. Beresford—they're the Arrans."

Beresford thought rapidly that here was a constable who knew him by his voice and the Arrans by sight, and who kept his head in trying circumstances. He made a mental note to say as much to Superintendent Miller when he saw him next—Superintendent Miller will play a prominent part in this narrative—and stood up from Tricker's body.

"All right," he said; "you can come in and give me a hand now, Robert. My man's been laid out."

"Laid out?" The policeman echoed the words incredulously.

"With a gun, or the bullet from one," said Beresford grimly.

The policeman said something not allowed for in police regulations, and bustled into the hall. He grunted as he saw Tricker, and pushed his thick woollen gloves under the unconscious man's head.

"Lucky it's you, sir," he said grimly, "or I'd want to ask some questions."

"Meanwhile I will," said Beresford.

He took a thin flask from his hip-pocket—emergencies were made to prepare for, Beresford always told himself—and while the policeman held Tricker's head, he forced a trickle of spirit between the clenched lips. As he acted he asked:

"Did you see any other car, or anyone walking?"

"No one walking," said the policeman. "A Daimler passed me just before the Talbot with the Arrans. It came out of Auveley Street, going pretty fast."

"Did you take its number?" asked Beresford.

"Can't say I did," said the patrolman.

"Can't say I blame you," said Beresford.

Tricker groaned suddenly, and turned his head. In the better light, for the door was open and the street lamp shone more fully, the wound could be plainly seen. Beresford pushed back a lock of blood-sticky hair, and peered at the wound, a two-inch long score starting over the left eye and reaching to the centre of the forehead.

"It's not deep," he said thankfully, "and I don't think the bone's broken."

"He's stunned," said the policeman, "but he's lucky to be alive. There's a doctor at Number Fifty, Mr. Beresford. I'd better knock him up."

"I'll go," said Beresford, getting up and starting for the door. "I know him well enough to wake him from his beauty sleep, and I'd like a word with the Arrans."

"Please yourself," said the man in blue, still intent on Tricker's broken head.

The Arran Twins—sometimes called the Unholy*—were at that time Number Six and Seven of Department Z. Beresford knew it, and was thankful. He felt that to work single-handed for that mad night was beyond him. Too many things were happening with a rush, and more were likely.

"You'll get the doctor first?" asked the policeman.

"Of course," said Beresford over his shoulder.

But as he spoke he experienced a sudden revulsion of feeling towards the policeman. The man was too cool, too matter-of-fact, Beresford thought. He should, intelligent or not, have reacted differently to the discovery of an unconscious man, knocked out by a bullet. He should have shown more surprise; he should have asked questions; he had not, in fact, acted like a policeman.

And then Beresford had a mental shock, as a forgotten fact dropped into his mind. A quarter of an hour before he had seen a policeman walking along Auveley Street, manifestly curious about himself, Tricker and the fallen slab of stone. The policeman had been stout and red-faced; the man at Number 7 was lean and pallid. Two different policemen would not, normally, be patrolling the street at the same—in effect—time!

Beresford felt a clammy sensation at the pit of his stomach. He was not easily scared, but he had known fear, the fear which comes less from the grin of approaching death than from uncertainty—the knowledge that death might come out of the blue. And as he strode along Auveley Street he had the peculiar fancy, which comes to all men at times, that he was being watched by unseen eyes. The stillness of the night added to the mystery of it. The street lamps and the twin orbs of the sidelights of the Arrans' Talbot outside their door heightened it. There was more shadow than light, and nothing moved, only the wind which his body stirred as he hurried. His right hand was in his coat pocket, gripping the automatic, and he kept his head half turned, so that he could see behind him.

Suddenly something moved in front of him, and Beresford breathed with real relief. A man walked out of a house opposite the Talbot; Tony recognized the lean figure of Timothy or Tobias Arran—the twins were of a height with each other, distinguishable only by their faces, one of which was classic and the other reputedly the ugliest in London. Beresford was twenty yards from the twin when he called out quietly, throwing his voice with a trick he had learned years ago.

"Oi, there, Timothy!"

The man in front stopped and stared along the street.

"Oi yourself," he called, in a whisper which carried as far as Beresford's. "Toby is my name——"

"Hop over to Doc Little," said Beresford, "and send him to my place. Where's Tim?"

"Laughing because he won the toss," muttered Tobias Arran tartly. He spoke and acted in a series of assumed jerks, just as his brother affected to linger in his movements and drawl his words. "Third time I've garaged the bus this week."

Beresford grinned; the tension of the night eased. He turned into the doorway of Number 57—the Arrans' house—as Toby Arran obeyed him unquestioningly and hurried across the road to Number 50 and one Doc Little. It was part and parcel of a Department Z agent that he acted without thinking first but thought hard while he acted.

The Arrans had the ground-floor flat. Timothy, the other twin, stepped into the hall as Beresford crossed the threshold.

"Did I, or didn't I, hear you calling?" he demanded softly.

"You did," said Beresford. "Listen, Tim. You can get round to the courtyard back of my place from yours, can't you?"

"Sure I can," drawled Timothy, turning as he spoke. Beresford obviously meant business.

"Take a gun," said Beresford, "and look for a policeman."

Timothy Arran grunted and dived into his rooms for a gun. Beresford swung round towards the street, and saw Tobias Arran silhouetted against the red lamp of the doctor's house. He jerked his thumb towards his own flat, and Toby's low-voiced "I'll be there" came softly across the street. Then Beresford turned grimly towards Number 7. That strangely unemotional policeman, he told himself, was going to have a shock before he was much older. If he was a genuine Robert, Beresford thought, with a grin, he would have something to say about the Arran Twins, who at times were unreasonable. If he wasn't . . .

Beresford's thoughts were broken suddenly as he reached the still open door of Number 7 Auveley Street. The one thing which he had not expected was to see the policeman walking down the stairs from his—Beresford's—own flat, carrying a towel over his arm and a bowl of water in his two hands. But that was happening.

"Well, well, *well!*" said Beresford to himself. "This is what the

41

Arrans will call a disappointment." Aloud: "Well, Robert, how's the patient?"

The policeman looked first at Beresford and then at the bowl of water.

"He'll be all right," he said in that voice which might have belonged to anyone but a London bobby. "And so will you—if you don't catch a cold."

Beresford gaped.

"If I don't——" he started incredulously.

And then the policeman's sense of humour was displayed at its best. For as Beresford stared at him, the man heaved the bowl, water and all, into the big man's face. Beresford staggered back, stupefied by the cold douche, and as he hit against the wall the policeman pushed past him and, in the words of Toby Arran who saw him, "greased along the street towards Park Lane like the devil dodging his conscience". Toby Arran had been too startled to swing in pursuit until the man had reached Park Lane; after that, pursuit was useless. The man in the blue uniform might have taken any one of three different directions—right, left, or through Hyde Park.

Beresford spent those few minutes which he had to spare during the next half-hour in wondering whether, and if so where, he had seen the pseudo-policeman before.

"And that's that," said Beresford, looking ruefully at the lean face of Gordon Craigie in the Chief's office at Whitehall. "It stands to reason, Gordon, that the man who shot Tricker, probably in the assumption that he was shooting me, wouldn't have gone so far down the scale as to drench me with water. Don't it?"

Craigie nodded, and drew at his meerschaum—a massive-bowled creation filled with black twist.

"You mean your bogus policeman didn't shoot Tricker."

"How bright you are!" said Beresford, who was in no very good humour that night. He had changed his coat for a loose jacket before journeying to Whitehall, but he had not changed his shirt and he was damp and uncomfortable.

Craigie grinned. Clad in an open-necked shirt, a once brilliant but now drab dressing-gown and a pair of new carpet slippers, his face looked positively gaunt—'hatched-faced', men had called him —and his grey eyes gleamed with a humour occasioned by Beresford's story of his drenching.

"All right," he said. "I'll grant you that the man who shot Tricker wasn't your policeman. Then who was he?"

Beresford growled.

"If you're going to ask questions like that, I'm going to resign, drat you. How the blazes do I know who he was? What the devil's gone wrong to-night, anyhow? And——"

"Let's analyse it," suggested Craigie mildly.

Beresford's face split in a grin.

"Carry on," he said.

Craigie tapped the stem of his pipe against his firm teeth.

"To start at the beginning," he said; "the first idea you had that things were—getting warm, shall we say?—was when Lady Chester told you about Gorman's interest. Yes?"

Beresford nodded, but was dubious.

"I don't say definitely that Gorman's connected with to-night's circus, mind you."

"I'd fire you if you did. Keep quiet a minute. The Gorman incident made you curious, but it didn't prepare you for the porch trick, which was a straightforward attempt to kill you. It failed. The men who engineered it knew that it failed. So they—we can assume, I think, that there were two in it—hung about Auveley Street, and kept near enough to your house to see Tricker's shadow when he went downstairs, and shot him through the letter-box or a broken panel of glass in the door. That's reasonable, isn't it?"

Beresford said it was. He was watching Craigie intently, and yet the Chief of Department Z had an idea that the big man was thinking about something other than his careful summary of the night's events.

"So," said Craigie patiently, "Leopold Gorman had been looking daggers at you at the Two-Step Club, and then there were two separate but connected attempts to kill you——"

"What are you doing?" interrupted Beresford, still looking preoccupied. "Trying to make me nervous?"

Craigie ignored the sally.

"Now then. Your attackers saw, or heard, the Arrans' car as it turned into the street. They decided to give up the idea of getting you out of the way——"

"Only for to-night, mind you," encouraged Beresford.

"Maybe only for an hour or two," said Craigie sardonically. "Anyhow, they went. And as they went, so your policeman came along——"

"It might have been the bogus bobby who scared 'em off," interrupted Beresford.

"Someone scared 'em, anyway. All right. Now the policeman was interested in you, not enough to——"

"Kill me," said Beresford, *sotto voce.*

"I almost wish he had," said Craigie with feeling. "Now we've got three problems. Why was Gorman interested in you? Were the efforts to——"

"Kill me——"

"Connected with Gorman—he's capable of anything, and you might be treading on his toes somewhere—and what part does the policeman play? It'll take some thinking," said Craigie, stuffing black twist into the meerschaum, "to work those out."

"You've forgotten the telegram to the man Williams, on my ground floor," Beresford pointed out. "We can trace back on that, and if whoever sent it's connected in any way with Gorman, we can guess the porch trick and the shooting was engineered by our

Leopold. You'd better telephone the Yard to get on to the telegram right away, hadn't you?"

Craigie nodded, and stood up. As he walked across the office—a large barely furnished room, with only a light oak desk, a portable typewriter, a dictaphone on its stand, half a dozen steel filing cabinets and three hardwood chairs at one end of it—Beresford leaned back in an armchair by the fire, and looked thoughtful.

The office of Department Z needs further description. The walls, it has been said, were made of sliding steel partitions, grained like oak. Three parts of the large room was furnished as an office, but the fourth part, near the fire, might have been taken completely from the living-room of the laziest and most untidy bachelor in London. About the fire were two armchairs, old, disreputable and comfortable, a portable cupboard containing an assortment of eatables and drinkables in half-empty pots, tins and bottles, loose and packet tobaccos, cigarettes, magazines and yellow-backs, and near the cupboard were the rumpled pages of two daily papers, a fine dust of tobacco-ash and an assortment of matchsticks. On the tiled hearth a pair of poplin pyjamas rubbed shoulders with a bath towel and odds and ends of clothing. To anyone who did not know that Gordon Craigie spent most of his time, sleeping and waking, in his office, the fireplace end of the room would have been a thing seen in a nightmare.

But Tony Beresford was used to the room, and he had no eyes for the paraphernalia about him. Actually he leaned back in his chair with his eyes closed, his great legs stretched out in front of him, his lips moving regularly as he inhaled or exhaled smoke from his Virginia 3. He heard Craigie telephoning Scotland Yard on the matter of the wire to Williams at Auveley Street, and heard the Chief replace the receiver, but still he kept his eyes shut.

"Tired, or just thinking?" asked Craigie as he walked back to his living quarters. Long association with young men whose humour was bluff and whose comments were usually sarcastic had made him fall into their ways when he was with them.

Beresford blinked.

"Neither," he said. "I was trying to see something, Gordon."

"Try opening your eyes," suggested Craigie, sitting down.

"In my mind's eye," said Beresford with dignity. "Listen. As I came downstairs looking for Tricker, I saw him sprawling on the hall floor, and assumed that he'd been shot from the front door. I looked at the front door. I saw the glass panel—a frosted one—and there was no break in it. I saw the coloured glass at the top of the door—and I'm sure all the sections were there. So——"

"Tricker must have been shot through the letter-box," said Craigie.

"That's just it," said Beresford, and Craigie saw that the big man's eyes were bright with excitement. "Tricker was shot in the head. If the bullet was fired through the letter-box it was while he was stooping down. *But if he was stooping down, he couldn't have been seen at all!* The glass panel only goes half-way down the door. So it was either a lucky shot through the letter-box, or——"

Craigie leaned forward, his muscles tight.

"Or from inside the house!"

"Exactly!" Beresford boomed the word. "Williams is away, and the top-floor flat's empty. 'Phone my place at the double, Gordon, and put the Arrans wide. I'll get the Yard on another line."

Just twenty minutes later two police cars drew up opposite Number 7, Auveley Street, and eight plain-clothes men clambered out. At the same time another carload of policemen drew alongside an alley which led to the courtyards at the rear, the odd numbers of Auveley Street, and went quietly, like ghosts of the night, towards Number 7. By the time the cordon was complete, Beresford and Gordon Craigie had arrived with Super-intendent Horace Miller—a big, bluff, blond man who would have looked completely at home amidst sacks of flour and the rumble of a mill, and therefore looked his name—in a third police car.

One by one, the rooms in the house were searched, in the empty flat upstairs, in Beresford's apartment, and in the rooms rented by the absent Williams. There was, remarkably enough, only one door that was bolted on the inside, thus defying the efforts of a police expert with a skeleton key.

"I suppose it's asking too much to expect to find anyone now," muttered Beresford. "All right, Horace—I'll bust it."

Miller motioned his men away from the door which led to the front room from the hall. Beresford stepped a couple of yards away and then hurled his great body against the wood. The door creaked, groaned, and the top bolt was torn from its sockets. A second heave sent Beresford tumbling into the room beyond. Miller and Craigie followed him quickly but more gracefully.

"Empty," muttered Craigie, sniffing the air.

"Empty," concurred Beresford, recovering his balance and looking round as a policeman switched on the electric light. "But someone's been here lately, drat it, and they smoked. Damn me for a lunatic! If I'd kept my head and thought harder before, we'd have had the birds."

Craigie granted as he picked up a spent match, one of several on the floor, and the butt of a cigarette.

"Can't be helped," he said. "Whoever it was smoked Player's, and that's as useful as if he'd smoked Woodbines. I wonder if that wire's about? Better have a look in the desk by the wall, Miller."

Superintendent Miller looked about to demur, but changed his mind. After all, there had been grievous bodily harm and attempted murder—ample excuse for making a thorough search without a warrant.

"Open that desk," said the Super to one of his men, "but treat it gently."

The man stepped towards the desk, but his efforts were not necessary. From the hall there came the sound of voices, some gruff and low-pitched, one of a higher cadence and indignant to an extreme.

"It's an outrage," asserted the man with the high-pitched voice, "a positive outrage, and I shall complain. Am I to be kept out of my own rooms while a flock of muddle-headed——"

Beresford chuckled.

"That's our Mr. Williams," he said, "of the ground-floor flat."

Miller raised his gruff voice.

"Let Mr. Williams come in," he called to the policeman on guard at the door.

"So I should think," said Williams, hurrying along the passage and turning into his room. "I——"

And then he saw the wreck of the door, and stood in spluttering indignation, marshalling words which somehow would not come in the presence of the portly Miller, the lean but somehow impressive Craigie, and the grinning Beresford.

"Afraid we had a spot of bother," said Beresford.

Williams snorted and snapped his fingers.

"It's a disgrace," he said. "I'm surprised to find you here, Beresford—I could understand the police, but when a gentleman sinks to this level I——"

Miller's back went up, and he opened his lips.

"Steady," cautioned Beresford. "No fighting, sons. Listen, Williams. ..."

He gave a brief résumé of the affairs of the night—the porch incident and the shooting of Tricker. Williams, a thin, lean-faced man with academician written all over him, let his face drop into lines of incredulous surprise. As Beresford finished, Williams looked at the red-faced Miller.

"I beg your pardon," he said. "I withdraw my remarks unconditionally, gentlemen. And these—these outrages serve to explain the remarkable hoax I had played on me to-day. You see this?"

The scholar flourished a buff-coloured envelope which he drew from his pocket. "The wire," Beresford thought, and knew what was coming. "Yes," he said aloud.

"I received it this morning," spluttered Williams—"a telegram purporting to come from Mieklejohn, the Oxford Mieklejohn, gentlemen. It asked me to attend a lecture at Trinity College this afternoon—you can read it for yourself——"

"And there was no lecture," murmured Gordon Craigie.

"There was not!" snapped Williams, who had a habit of speaking in italics and exclamation marks when he was annoyed. "And Mieklejohn knew nothing about the wire! It was a senseless hoax, gentlemen, and I hope the police will do all they can to trace the perpetrators of it."

Beresford grunted.

"They'll do that," he said. "But I wouldn't call it senseless, Williams. It was intended to get you away from here this evening——"

Williams widened his eyes, weak blue eyes hidden by big-lensed, horn-rimmed glasses.

"Bless my soul!" he said. "Of course—I didn't think——"

Beresford grinned to himself, and told himself that learning meant little compared with common sense. And then he stopped grinning. For the academician claimed that he hadn't thought of that possibility; yet a few moments before he had suggested that the outrages served to explain the hoax!

"Now, why," Beresford demanded of himself, "did he lie?"

CHAPTER FIVE

THE STRANGE ILLNESS OF BOB LAVERING

"BUT did he lie?" asked Craigie. "From the look of him, Tony, I'd say he was a harmless old soul who forgets one moment what he said the last. Do you know him well?"

"He's lived here for three years," said Beresford, lighting a cigarette. "It was a funny thing to say, harmless old soul or not, but I know he's a queer cuss. And it was a funny wire, too."

"How'd you mean?" asked Miller, eyeing not Beresford but a whisky-and-not-much-soda thoughtfully.

The three men were in Beresford's living-room, and for the first time since the arrival of the police at Auveley Street were able to talk freely. Hitherto, Doc Little, that giant of a man famous for his treatment of the foibles of London's rich, had been fussing about the flat, ordering this and ordering that for the comfort and well-being of Tricker, who was conscious now and acutely aware of the fact that he was resting on Beresford's big bed instead of his own truckle. Beresford, well pleased with the minor nature of Tricker's injury, which Little predicted would be healed within a week, had told his pale-faced valet not to be chuckle-headed, and had outraged Sammivel by demanding Little to send a nurse for the rest of the night; Sam, said Beresford, wanted attention. While

Little had been fussing, Miller had sent the police-party back to the Yard and the protesting Arrans packing, while a fingerprint expert was at that moment going through the still palpitating Williams' rooms for the prints which were there in abundance. Nothing would be left to chance, but the three men in Beresford's flat knew that the odds against catching the attackers (they assumed the plural) were heavy.

Beresford pushed his hand through his hair.

"I mean," he said quietly, *à propos* the telegram, "that if I'd wanted to get Williams out of the way for twenty-four hours, I'd have sent him a telegram from the Scottish Universities, not from Oxford. Our intellectual might have been back here by seven or eight o'clock."

"I don't know," demurred Miller, who was a ponderous man both physically and mentally, but who knew his job from A to Z. "Put two dons together, and they'll talk for hours. Whoever sent the wire probably relied on that."

Beresford looked dissatisfied.

"Funny thing to take a chance if they reckoned they would have their shot at me late in the evening, and obviously they were prepared for that. What do you think, Gordon?"

Craigie was smoking a Virginia 3 and wishing for his meerschaum. He wrinkled his nose.

"I'm inclined to agree with you," he said. "The telegram should have sent Williams a couple of hundred miles away, not fifty or sixty. But that's incidental. It kept the man away while it was necessary. The puzzle is, Tony, why did they go for you? You haven't been up to any tricks, have you?"

"What, me?" Beresford looked a picture of outraged innocence. "You ought to know me better than that, old son."

"Might be someone with a grudge," suggested Miller, who had worked several times with Beresford and Craigie, and knew a little of the operations carried out through Department Z.

"Too elaborate," said Beresford decisively. "If it'd been a knife in the back or a bullet out of the blue, I'd have said that someone who remembers the past well was trying to get me. But this thing's been carefully worked out—and then there's the bogus bobby to account for. No"—the big man sent a perfect smokering ceilingwards, watching it lose its formation in a grey haze—"no, it's something new, sons, and something nasty, and somehow I don't think it'll be long before we know more about it." He broke off suddenly. "That's the front door," he went on, as a piercing ringing sound shrilled through the room. "I'll hop down."

The caller, however, was none other than Samuel Tricker's nurse, a middle-aged matron who proved to be sharp-tongued, lynx-eyed and uncompromising in her attitude towards Tricker, who wanted to go to his own room.

"Keep him under your thumb," grinned Beresford, as he left the bedroom, "and don't let him get saucy, nurse. Be good, Sammivel!"

When the big man returned to the living-room, Miller was putting on his coat, a rejuvenated British Warm, still eyeing the whisky thoughtfully. A very thoughtful man was Horace Miller on things alcoholic. He was always asking himself whether he could carry just one more.

Beresford, who had opened a fresh bottle of Shortt's XX, thumbed the cork into the neck and handed the bottle to the Super.

"Take it with you," he said affably, "and make up your mind when you get to the office. Good night, Horace, and don't forget to ring me about those fingerprints in the morning."

Miller grinned, making his rosy face more cherubic than ever, and bade them a gruff good night.

As the door closed behind the policeman, Beresford looked inquiringly at his Chief.

"Didn't you say, earlier on, that you wanted to see me?"

Craigie, still fidgeting and wishing for his meerschaum, nodded and accepted another Virginia 3.

"Yes," he said. "I wanted to talk to you about Leopold Gorman."

Beresford opened his eyes.

"Oh-ho! That man's in the news to-night."

Craigie frowned.

"I'm worried about him, Tony. He's been over to Paris on some job or other, and I can't find out what it is."

Beresford laughed suddenly.

"So's Bob Lavering," he said. "Perhaps they're both shaking a leg. Even the great can laugh and have their pleasures."

Craigie grimaced.

"I asked Odell——"

"The gallant Major?" asked Beresford.

"Yes, drat him. He was staying at the Splendide and Gorman was next door to him. I asked Odell to keep his eyes and ears open, and he told me to-night—last night that is—that Gorman told him he was spending a couple of days and nights on the tiles."

Beresford chuckled again.

"And Gulliver believed him. So we can take it conversely that whatever Gorman was doing, he wasn't just having his fling."

"We can," said Craigie grimly. "I knew that, anyhow. Gorman's staging something big, but I can't figure what it is."

"How did you get on to it in the first place?" asked Beresford.

Craigie leaned back in his chair.

"Nevillson, of the Ministry of Transport, told me that half a dozen big North Country road services have changed hands, but he didn't know whose money was behind it. Nevillson wanted to find out——"

"The Intelligence," said Beresford, without much humour, "is going up in the world."

"I'd asked Nevillson to keep me in touch with anything that he couldn't fathom," said Craigie, "because I don't like the way Gorman's interests are spreading. He's just bought up the Mid-Country Playhouse Circuit, and he bought Rundle's Chain Stores less than a fortnight ago."

Beresford pursed his lips.

"After all," he said, "Gorman's a big-money man, and he's not the first money-merchant to grab all he can get."

"I know," said Craigie. "But Gorman's not the type to have too much say in public services—and if he goes on as he's been doing over the past month, he'll have ten per cent. of the country's food stores in his pocket, a third of the amusement houses, and a substantial part of transport services before the end of the year. And that," said Gordon Craigie grimly, "means that he'll have a lot of power and even more influence than he has now."

"He'll be big enough to be dangerous, will he?"

"Yes, more than big enough. And he's exploited the stock markets in a way that we don't want him to start in other things, Tony. Imagine what will happen if we have a really severe winter, say, and Gorman's controlling a large percentage of available foodstuffs——"

"The chain stores only sell it to the public," Beresford pointed out. "He's got to buy his stuff from abroad, and if he can, others can."

"Now we're getting somewhere," said Craigie. "Gorman's clever, and he's getting this monopoly in different parts of the country for foods, transport and amusements. That's definite. But he's not the man to work from the wrong end. If he's got a monopoly for selling—like he's bought with Rundle's Stores—you can be pretty sure that he's got a monopoly for buying too."

Beresford lit another cigarette from the butt of his first. Watching Craigie, and hearing the Chief's quiet statement of Gorman's recent activities, he not only sensed Craigie's concern, but he felt the stirring of anxiety himself. Gorman had virtually controlled the stock markets for years. He had widespread interests in shipping, and his companies owned a good third of the merchant services of England. So much was known. How much more, Craigie was wondering, did Gorman control?

Craigie snapped his fingers suddenly.

"It's worrying me," he said unnecessarily. "I don't like it a bit, Tony. It's not as if everything was split up among a thousand or so individual firms. Everything's run—food, clothes, shipping, coal and petrol, to mention a few of them—by syndicates. The petrol ring's as tight as an oyster; four firms control petrol supplies in England, and there aren't more than two dozen big combines in the world. You can imagine what would happen if a man like Gorman, concerned solely with making money, gets control of petrol."

"Up goes the price," muttered Beresford grimly.

"And up goes everything," said Craigie. "Prices are controlled by expenses, and the petrol expense is a big one. The general increase wouldn't be big, of course, but it might not stop at petrol. Well"—the Scot looked at Beresford with a sudden smile, that smile which made Gordon Craigie a man loved by all who worked for him—"how do you feel about it, Tony? I must find out what Gorman's doing, and I'd like you to tackle the job. It might not give you much of a thrill," he added, with a chuckle.

Beresford thought suddenly of the events of the past three hours, and there was a gleam in his eyes as he answered.

"If to-night's any criterion, it'll give me a long box, old son. I'll tell you what, Gordon."

"All right. What?"

"I'll wager you a month's supply of my Virginias to a year's supply of your black twist that Gorman was behind the porch trick and the shooting."

"No, you won't," said Craigie decidedly.

And each man knew, as the Chief of Department Z picked up his hat and coat, that the other believed Gorman was trying to make sure that the tentative inquiries from Department Z stopped; and they knew, too, that the world would stop before that happened.

* * *

Two days went by, dull days to Tony Beresford, save for a spin into Surrey with Valerie Lester as a companion and a *tête-à-tête* lunch with that refreshing young woman of the New World. The vitality of Valerie Lester made Beresford admire her, and her vivacity made him laugh. It did not occur to him then, but twice Diane Chester laughed at him, and he wondered why, not knowing that the ways of fate with a man and a maid were like an open book to Diane, who above all things was a woman, beautiful by accident.

The Arran—or the Unholy—Twins had spent one riotous hour in Beresford's flat, demanding to know what had happened and what was going to happen and whether they couldn't have a share in it. Beresford was tempted to rough-house them, but Tricker's nurse, christened Maria by the exuberant Twins, sent them packing. Maria looked, Beresford said, like becoming a fixture. Samuel Tricker had overcome his early repugnance to womanly care, and seemed reluctant to admit that he need not be bedridden. Beresford grinned, and persuaded Doc Little to certify that Tricker was suffering from nervous shock and light concussion. After that one mad night, the Auveley Street flat was becalmed.

Beresford arranged with Craigie for the Arran Twins to be detailed on the Gorman job, and then visited the Twins' flat. This was towards the evening of the second day after the attacks, a Wednesday of bright May sun and cool winds.

"Work, boys," he said simply as he dropped into a chair.

The Arrans looked at him with disfavour.

"We can't work to-night," drawled Timothy, smoothing his shiny hair. "We are engaged."

"Got a friend of a cousin from America," jerked Toby, "and we've——"

"Promised to entertain her, Tonee-ee," drawled Tim.

For the first time that he could remember, Tony Beresford went red.

"Work, I said," he insisted, "and lay off the funny stuff, darn your eyes, or I'll get Craigie to cut you out of the Service."

Timothy looked at Tobias and Tobias looked at Tim, and they nodded, their faces masked with mock-seriousness and their right hands on their chests.

"He's got it—got it bad," said Tobias.

"And so that he may entertain the wench," drawled Timothy, "he's pushing his job on us. We won't stand for it, old son, we won't stand for it."

Beresford eyed them in silence, and his refusal to rise to the bait took the edge off their so-called wit.

Tobias, the dark one, took three glasses from the sideboard, while Timothy, the fair one, opened a bottle of Shortt's. The Twins did most things together, and despite their physical dissimilarity held the same views on sport, politics and women. When they were not being offensive by trying to be funny they contrived to be amusing.

"Whisky before dinner," said Beresford, "means drunk before midnight. Here's how, sons, and now listen."

The Arrans grew serious and attentive.

"You, Tim," said Beresford, "had better get over to Paris and see what you can find about Bob Lavering. He went over there five days ago, and his man's heard nothing from him since."

"That's a police job," protested Timothy.

"I don't want it to be a police job," said Beresford. "The *Sûreté* isn't all it could be these days, and I want to learn something quick, without letting anyone know we're inquiring."

"What's Lavering done to deserve the interest?" asked Toby, lighting an inevitable cigarette.

"Nothing yet," said Beresford. "But he's engaged to Adele Fayne, and Adele's been seen several times with Leopold Gorman lately, and——"

"Gorman, is it?" muttered the Twins in unison.

"Gorman it is, so be careful. How are the 'planes running from Croydon, Tim?"

"There's a Paris 'bus at seven-thirty or thereabouts."

"You'd better catch it," said Beresford. "You've two hours or more to pack a brush and get to Croydon. Toby——"

"Sir," said Toby Arran.

"Do you know Oxford?"

"I know how to avoid being sent down from," grinned Toby.

"Know Mieklejohn, the Trinity don?"

"You forget," said Toby gently, "that Trinity was once my home from home, and Mieklejohn my foster-mother."

"I don't," said Beresford, whose cricket blue was a light one. "I wanted to make sure there is a Mieklejohn at Oxford. Do you know him well enough to visit him?"

"Well enough not to want to," grimaced Toby.

"Swallow your pride and look him up to-night," said Beresford. "Don't ask him point blank, but find out whether he had a visit from a Nicholas Williams on Monday afternoon. Telephone me what he says, and then follow Tim to Paris, and check back on Major Odell's visit last week."

"The Gulliver Odell?"

"Yes. Do you know him?"

"Not well. I heard this morning that he's been hanging round Adele Fayne's skirts for the last couple of days."

"Has he, then!" Beresford reflected on this item of social chatter, and passed on. "Well, I want to know just how much Odell saw of Leopold Gorman last week—they were in Paris together. Both of you can telephone me from Paris, and if I'm not in, get through to the office. All set?"

The Arrans said that they would be, in a brace of shakes, and Beresford left them, very thoughtful as to Odell's devotion to Adele Fayne. Was there anything behind it? Was Gorman watching Odell because the Major had let slip the word that he had been asked to keep a careful eye open?

He didn't know, but he hoped that the Arrans' investigations would lead towards knowledge, not only on the subject of Major Gulliver Odell, but on the matter of Bob Lavering's absence from London.

There was nothing, of course, to suggest that Lavering was being forcibly kept away, but Beresford sensed that things were a long way from being straightforward where the son of America's foremost landowner was concerned. For a month, Bob Lavering—who had been at Cambridge with the big man, and who was one of the few Americans who could hold a cricket-bat as though born to it—had been at Adele Fayne's beck and call. He thought he was in love, and Beresford, while hoping that he would get over it, had admitted to himself that Lavering had been thoroughly smitten. Yet, without warning, Lavering had gone to Paris, and stayed there for the best part of a week, while Major Odell and Leopold Gorman—which latter gentleman was appearing in public much more often than was his wont—played ducks and drakes with Adele Fayne. Or so it seemed.

Yes, Beresford told himself, the Lavering business was funny. And his theory was confirmed at half past ten on the following morning, when Timothy Arran telephoned him from Paris.

"I've found Lavering," said Timothy. "He's staying at a third-rate hotel near Montmartre, and he's in a darned bad way, Tony. Ptomaine poisoning, according to the doctor bloke."

"I'll be right over," said Beresford swiftly.

"Half a mo'," said Timothy Arran. "There's more in it than that, but I can't say too much, because I fancy I'm being overheard. Only be ready——"

"What for?"

"Anything, any time, anywhere," said Timothy. "I'm staying at the Royale, but you'll find me with Lavering at a place called the Hôtel Divante."

CHAPTER SIX

OF AN ADVENTURE IN PARIS

BERESFORD reached Croydon in time to catch the twelve-o'clock 'Air France' liner. He squeezed in a two-minute telephone conversation with Gordon Craigie while the great engine was warming up, filling the air with a deep-toned roaring, and while the last of the mails were being put on board.

"Yes, go over to Paris," said Craigie, "and keep me in touch. If you can find the slightest thing to catch Gorman on, grab it. I'd like to feel that he's under my eyes for a day or two."

"Any developments?" asked Beresford.

"He's bought Harridges," said Craigie simply, "and he's bought a controlling interest in the Orient-Western Oil Company."

Beresford whistled over the telephone, and Craigie's next comment was terse and unlike that gentleman's usual idiom. The big man grinned and said good-bye as he replaced the receiver, but as he sprinted for the quivering air-liner there was a grim expression in his grey eyes.

Harridges, he knew, was the biggest departmental store in London, with a chain of lesser brethren throughout England. The Orient-Western was the biggest petrol combine by a long chalk. Gorman was buying big, as Craigie had expected. Why? Was he trying to corner the commodity markets just as he had cornered stocks, to sell at an abnormal profit when the opportunity presented itself? Was he playing a lone hand, or was he being backed by a powerful syndicate?

Beresford couldn't know. But he shared, with Craigie, an overwhelming conviction that if Gorman's interests spread much further, the financier would be in a position similar to that held by the bankers in a previous era, when the banks held and owned the money and dictated policy far more effectively than the Government. And with Craigie, he knew that Gorman was not only crooked; he was bad, through and through. He could do an incalculable amount of damage by wielding his influence— damage which would increase as his holdings grew stronger and more varied.

So, as Craigie said, there was only one thing to do. They must prove that Gorman's activities in some quarters were illegal, then hold him on a charge which would enable thorough investigations to be made. Once contrive that, thought Beresford, and the job was done—or his part of it.

Being of a philosophical nature, he told himself, when he was inclined to chafe at the hundred-odd miles between the airliner and Paris, that a year or two back he would have been forced to travel by steamer. A good airman, although he had never handled a 'plane of his own, Beresford suffered not at all by the bucketing of the giant of the air. Several of his fellow-passengers looked, felt, and said, however, that they wished they were dead. Airsickness being more violent, but also more brief, than *mal-de-mer*, Beresford cheered them, and tried to point out that the gale which had sprung up, accompanied by distant rumbles of thunder and an occasional flash of lightning, unusual in May, created a sky panorama which would probably be unsurpassed in their naturals. While he talked, he wished that he was in the third-rate hotel which was sheltering the sick person of Robert Lavering. While he talked, also, he was manoeuvring to converse with a ruddy-complexioned man at the far end of the cabin.

Beresford, who was interested in gadgets of all kinds, was as near the controls as he could be, and the ruddy-faced man was as far away from them as possible. That, Beresford told himself thoughtfully, just about agreed with the relative position of himself and Ruddy Face for the past two hours.

The big man had noticed a closed Daimler saloon as it had followed his own touring Hispano into the Croydon airfield, and he had seen Ruddy Face climb out. Then his mind had kicked back to the pseudo policeman's statement, two days before, that he had seen a Daimler saloon moving rapidly from Auveley Street.

Daimlers were popular, Beresford reminded himself, and were struck as frequently as coincidences, while the policeman's word was not reliable. It was not, in fact, until Beresford had fancied the man was surveying him covertly that the closeness of Ruddy Face's arrival at Croydon on his own heels was properly noted.

Beresford stood up eventually and sauntered to the rear of the saloon, ostensibly to look back across the Channel to the vague mass which was England. He turned away, and opened his cigarette-case, proffering it casually to Ruddy Face. The little man looked surprised, but accepted a Virginia 3 very much as a rabbit would take a present from a genial fox; he looked, Beresford told himself, frightened out of his life!

"Rough journey," said Beresford pleasantly, striking a match.

Ruddy Face agreed, in a high-pitched voice which reminded Beresford of Nicholas Williams, the tenant of the ground-floor flat at Number 7, Auveley Street. It was just one word 'yes' which was similar; when Ruddy Face spoke again his voice was lower-pitched. "Isn't it?" he added nervously.

Beresford looked out of the window.

"Funny time of the year for thunder," he added, still casually.

"Isn't it?" repeated the red-faced man, parrot-like.

And then Beresford said a strange thing.

"Thunder and lightning rather interferes with your transmitter, doesn't it?"

Just for a moment he thought that Ruddy Face was going to strike him. And then the little man sank back in his seat, his complexion tinted a pale green, his blue eyes blinking fast.

Beresford, smiling as if in gentle amusement, sat next to him, and surreptitiously touched the small suitcase which Ruddy Face had insisted on taking with him in the cabin.

"Neat little contraption," he said. "I just caught sight of the wires leading from your coat to the ear-gadgets, my son, otherwise I wouldn't have noticed it. You've got the transmitter in there, haven't you?"

Ruddy Face said nothing; he seemed paralysed. Beresford grinned.

"It's highly irregular," he pointed out, still touching the case, "for a man to come on an 'Air France' machine with a private wireless. It's even more irregular to operate it. Who or what," he added, with a hardening of his voice, "are you communicating with? Faraday House?"

The little man's colour had returned to normal, but he was still staring at Beresford with frightened eyes. Those eyes intrigued Beresford. They were a very bright blue, and they blinked a lot; rather like, the big man told himself, a man who was accustomed to wearing glasses, but had been caught short. Altogether, Ruddy Face seemed a weak-livered customer—the last man in the world to be trailing Beresford. Yet that, Beresford assured himself, was what was happening.

The man with the red face had followed him from Auveley Street to Croydon, had succeeded in smuggling a wireless-transmitter of the portable variety into the liner's cabin, and had been sending messages to someone unknown!

"What—what are you going to do?" asked the little man, shrinking still further into his corner. "I—I——"

He broke off, completely at a loss for words. Beresford, who had come across many varieties of opponents in the course of his existence with Department Z, regarded him as something unique, and yet as something infinitely dangerous.

For the red-faced, plump-looking little man with the weak but bright-blue eyes was also Nicholas Williams, the scholar from Auveley Street! And Beresford knew, now, why the bogus policeman had seemed somehow familiar. He had had these same blue eyes, even though his manner had been different, and his confidence that night superb.

Nicholas Williams, alias a policeman, alias Ruddy Face, wireless pirate! The possibilities behind those aliases were infinite. Beresford, thinking rapidly, told himself that he was on something hot, but that it must be handled carefully, even brilliantly. This man was an unknown quantity, and he had once used water as a weapon instead of lead. He was, too, a consummate actor. He aped fear so that he looked fear-stricken. Even the cheeks of his padded face—rubber pads reinforcing the teeth created the main difference in Ruddy Face's appearance compared with Williams the scholastic—seemed to sag. But all the time, Beresford told himself, he was sizing his adversary up, reading, or trying to read his, Beresford's, thoughts. So, thought Tony, with that twisted humour which occasionally seized him, the thing to do was to kid Mr. Williams, to lead him a long way up the garden.

Beresford swung his arm, with an exaggerated gesture, to look at his watch. Ruddy Face flinched. Beresford grinned.

"It is now," he said, "ten minutes to one. In twenty minutes, barring blooming accidents, we shall be in the Paris airfield. Twenty minutes after that the 'plane will go on to Lyons. I," went on Beresford, emphasizing his words by poking Ruddy Face in his middle, which was so resilient that Beresford knew it to be reinforced by an inflated rubber cushion, "shall alight at Paris. You will go on to Lyons—without your little gadget. Do you follow?"

"But——" began Ruddy Face.

"No buts and no nothings," said Beresford grimly, but patting himself on the back because of the unquestioned look of relief in his victim's eyes. "I know you're after me, and I think I know why, and if I had time, I'd fake up a charge of some kind at Paris and turn you and your precious crowd upside down and inside out. But I haven't got time, only an appointment. I can just spare the twenty minutes to see you on your way, minus the suitcase, which I shall take with me as an interesting memento of the yellowest spot of humanity I've ever met in my life."

"I——" began Ruddy Face.

Beresford swept his words away, well satisfied with the self-congratulation evident in Ruddy Face's eyes. The man was sure, now, that his disguise had not been penetrated. He might not be able to send his precious messages to that mysterious recipient whom Beresford was itching to identify, but at least he would be undetected in yet another guise—or so Beresford guessed at his thoughts.

Beresford let himself go.

"When I say yellow," he said, "I mean a deep orange. I've met some rabbits in my young life, but you're the rabbitiest of the lot. You make me want to lose my faith in human nature. You nauseate me. Whoever sent you to watch me ought to shoot himself, back and front. You couldn't deceive a traffic-cop, and you wouldn't have the guts to say goo to a two-year-old. When I find out who's paying you for air flights and Daimler limousines, I shall send him my sympathies for being the biggest mutt on earth. Do you," demanded Beresford, with a sudden scowl, "follow me?"

"Y-yes," said Ruddy Face.

"You have more intelligence than I gave you credit for. However—that's five minutes gone, and we'll be dropping soon. Let me just warn you, Rabbit, not to move out of my sight at the aerodrome, or I shall pulverize you on the spot. In fact, you'd better keep in the 'plane until she starts off again."

A quarter of an hour later the liner swooped on to Paris, and Beresford, complete with his own and Ruddy Face's luggage, climbed down to *terra firma*. Inside the scheduled twenty minutes, the 'plane went up again, and the man of many aliases went with it. Beresford watched it, dark against the sky, and chuckled loudly and at some length. Then he turned towards the Customs shed, and, knowing that all Frenchmen were not excitable by habit, told a dour official a joke which was saucy without being salacious. The bearded veteran laughed, and for a moment appeared to be taken in by the quick interchange of suitcases which Beresford manipulated, in order to get the wireless contraption through the Customs. But it was only for a moment. The man's beard stopped quivering, and his sharp eyes searched Beresford's big body from head to foot. And then, although Beresford had already spoken to him in fluent French, he burst into a flow of broken English which made the big man go hot and cold!

"Tiens!" stuttered the Frenchman official. "But I suspected, when you shoke, yes. Zat ozzer case—it has not been open, *n'est pas?* But now—*voilà!* The wireless, just as ve haff been told! You zink you haff been so clevaire, m'sieu——"

For the moment Beresford was incapable of thought. He hardly noticed the Frenchman's sudden, *"Pardonnez moi, m'sieu,"* and saw without heeding the little bunch of high officials bearing down on his counter. The realization that he had been completely fooled by Williams, the man of many aliases, was like gall. For Williams, or Ruddy Face, was even at that moment speeding towards Lyons, laughing at the ease with which Beresford had been duped. And Beresford was in one of the most awkward predicaments of his life! It would be hours before he could convince the French authorities that he had no evil intentions with the portable transmitting set which he had tried to smuggle into France, which set had been deliberately planted on him.

The next ten minutes of discussion with the more important officials confirmed the worst. A message, they said, had been tele-phoned from Scotland Yard advising that a dangerous criminal was making for France, carrying with him the portable wireless set. That said criminal, a very large man, must be held until Scotland Yard officials followed him to France. Every Customs shed had been warned, every official was lynx-eyed for an exceptionally big man with one or more suitcases.

Wouldn't they, asked Beresford, telephone Scotland Yard and confirm that the message had been sent from there?

No, certainly not. The wireless was all the confirmation needed by intelligent Frenchmen.

Would they permit him (Beresford knew better than to try to bully his men) to contact with the British Embassy? His business was urgent and his passport in order.

That was a matter for even higher authorities.

Would they permit him to telephone Inspector Piquet, at the *Sûreté?* (Beresford knew Piquet well.)

No, Inspector Piquet was engaged on a matter of importance out of Paris. M'sieu Bere'ford had broken the law by smuggling, and moreover by smuggling a wireless transmitter. He must wait for the law to deal with him.

But the thing was a hoax, a ridiculous hoax!

That was for the law to decide.

Beresford shrugged his shoulders hopelessly. He was caught in the mesh of French officialdom, probably the worst in the world. With luck and perseverance he might be released before nightfall, but time was precious, and Robert Lavering, with Timothy Arran, was waiting for him. Anything might happen in the intervening hours.

He played with the idea of making a break from the flying-field, but rejected it as impracticable. He might get away, but the whole of the French police force would be on the look-out for him, and he was an easy man to see. If he could only persuade these obstinate devils to let him telephone the Embassy, he could get clear; anyone there would have vouched for him. But there was no mule, he told himself grimly, as obstinate as a Frenchman on duty. Williams, damn and blast him, had won his trick with a vengeance!

Timothy Arran, debonair and immaculate and afflicted with his affected drawl—the affliction was mental—was also clever. He had reached Paris at ten o'clock or thereabouts on the previous evening, to seek Bob Lavering with no knowledge other than that American's name and appearance. He had set out, there and then, on a tour of hotels, from the Magnifique downwards. His seventh shot had been the lucky one. Lavering had stayed at the Hôtel Royale from the Friday until the following Monday. Thereafter Lavering had disappeared. The word was necessary, because Lavering hadn't paid his bill, nor had he brought much luggage with him. But the management was not concerned, because the American had stayed at the Royale several times during the past few years, and in Paris there were attractions which the young and rich could not resist, and which might—er—delay them for several days. Was M'sieu ...?

"Timson," Timothy Arran had supplied for a name.

The management was honoured to know M'sieu Timson, and hoped one day to be honoured with a protracted visit. Was he very anxious to discover M'sieu Lavering?

Timothy had said very anxious indeed. A domestic matter.

Ah! The management was full of understanding. It would willingly provide M'sieu Timson with a guide who could take him to the Rue des Coronnes, in Montmartre, where there was a certain attraction which had intrigued M'sieu Lavering. In fact that gentleman had been seen in the Côte d'Or, a little establishment so popular with visitors. Did M'sieu Timson so desire?

"Providing," Timothy had said with the air of a conspirator, "*M'sieu le directeur* will promise absolute discretion."

"But *certainement, m'sieu.* Discretion of the very *highest,* and a guide who could be trusted with one's life!"

The guide, a ferrety-faced man of middle age who looked as if he could be trusted to save no one's skin but his own, led Timothy to the Côte d'Or, after a circuitous journey through the Soho of Paris, Montmartre. Timothy, who knew the district as well as he knew Piccadilly Circus, suffered in silence, because he wanted to be taken for a very green Englishman looking for a misbehaving friend.

The Côte d'Or, however, surprised him. It was a comparatively new establishment, it was clean, it was brilliantly lit, and its wine was as good as its cabaret, which was excellent. The star of that particular firmament was a snake-charmer of ability and considerable beauty. Her name was Corinne, and she fondled her snakes with soft, painted hands while eyeing her patrons, until they felt that their own skin was being subjected to those entrancing caresses.

"Is this who M'sieu Lavering came to see?" demanded Timothy Arran of his guide.

"Oui, m'sieu. A gentleman of excellent taste was M'sieu Lavering. Corinne had liked him, it was said."

Timothy ordered white wine, sat at a corner table for twenty minutes, with his eyes glued to the sinuous body of the dancer, and finally sighed, so heavily that the French guide from the Hôtel Royale smirked.

"I shall ask Corinne to see you?" suggested the Frenchman.

Timothy looked dubious and a little awkward.

"Well—er—she mightn't like it perhaps. I'll tell you what, Albert. You go back to the hotel, and if I'm not back in three or four hours, come back for me. *N'est pas?"*

Albert grinned again, and said yes. Whether he was amused by Timothy's sudden outburst into execrable French, or whether it was because he had fallen so quickly and so obviously to Corinne's charms, worried Timothy not at all. He wanted the guide to think him a fool, and the guide did so, more especially after a tip worthy of a mad millionaire.

"M'sieu is a gentleman of the highest," congratulated the guide. "He has but to call and I serve. *Bon soir, M'sieu Timson.*"

"*Bong jour,*" said Timothy absently.

He gave his guide ten minutes to finish his drink and wend his way towards the Royale, and then absent-mindedly opened his wallet in full view of the company. It was well filled, and it attracted Corinne's dark eyes like a magnet. The snake-charmer had finished her turn and she disappeared for a while; but when she returned, semi-clad, she made for Timothy's table with a disarming directness.

Timothy winked. It was an English habit, reckoned to install confidence in the fluttering heart of the dancer.

"M'sieu has enjoyed to-night?" Corinne's voice was soft and pleasant.

"I'm about to," said Timothy, in flawless French. "What do you drink, *ma chèrie?*"

"I do not drink—I eat, m'sieu." Corinne's smile was ravishing.

"Better still," said Timothy, still in flawless French. "It takes longer."

An hour later, it took considerable tact on Timothy's part to convince the dancer that his business only partly concerned herself. Overcoming Corinne's disappointment, he led the conversation cunningly into the realm of dancing, and told Corinne that he believed she was better—much better—than the renowned Adele Fayne. Timothy Arran knew that a fundamental difference between the French and the English was that the former responded easily to flattery and the latter for the most part laughed it off.

"And I know Adele Fayne," he said, toying with his wineglass and looking quizzically into Corinne's eyes. "She is to marry Bob Lavering——"

He paused, ostensibly because his cigarette stuck to his lip, but actually to watch Corinne's reaction to the name of Lavering. He saw the sudden contraction of the dancer's nostrils, the tightening of her rosebud lips, the narrowing of her eyes. For a split second Corinne the dancer stopped breathing. When she went on, her breath came quickly, as it might after unexpectedly running a few yards uphill. Timothy Arran felt exultant and yet sorry; mention of Lavering had made this girl afraid!

"But yes? *La Fayne* is to marry?" Corinne's words dropped into the temporary silence tensely, spoken for the sake of saying something, anything at all.

Timothy Arran, alive to the temperamental reactions of the Frenchwoman, knew that if she was frightened money would not bribe her to talk. A greater fear than she already had would loosen her tongue more effectively than the contents of his wallet, although a few *mille* notes might help, afterwards, to compensate her for her fear. Timothy Arran leaned forward, touching Corinne's slim arm with his hand and pressing hard. His face was no longer genially smiling, and his eyes were narrow and hard as steel.

"Corinne," he said, "you are playing with bigger things than you know. Lavering is missing. He is an American of great importance, and his country is demanding the Government to find him. The *Sûreté* is looking, secret agents are looking, every *gendarme* you see is searching for M'sieu Lavering. And I am looking for him, and I know what the others do not—you can tell where M'sieu Lavering is!"

Timothy did it well. Inflexion, expression, the pressure of his hand, all had a telling effect. The fear which he had seen in the snake-charmer's eyes increased until it was sheer dread. Corinne opened her lips, but the words would not come. She passed her painted hand across her forehead, worried, alarmed.

"Where is he?" Timothy demanded, pressing home his advantage.

Just for a moment he thought that she would defy him, deny

all knowledge of Lavering's whereabouts. But the grimness of the Twin's eyes and the tightness of his lips seemed to sway her. She leaned forward, her voice unsteady.

"Come with me," she said. "M'sieu Lavering is ill, but if you ever say who told you, it will mean my death!"

"Corinne," said Timothy, using the colourful expressions of idiomatic French with a gusto, "your secret shall go with me to the grave, and for your trust you shall be rewarded. But quickly, Corinne!"

"You cannot visit the Hôtel Divante like that," Corinne said, with a quick glance at his immaculate serge suit. "The hotel is being watched, m'sieu. Your friend has powerful enemies. Will you trust yourself with me?"

"With my life!" said Timothy with relish.

Nevertheless it was not without a tremor of apprehension that he followed the dancer from the cabaret house. He was surprised, too, when she led him quickly into the Côte d'Or by a back entrance, and introduced him in rapid French to the manager, a formidable-looking Frenchman capable of giving even Tony Beresford a run for his money in a rough-house. A man to dislike and distrust, Timothy thought.

"M'sieu my friend," said Corinne, "would look round Montmartre without being seen as an Englishman. M'sieu Franchot will permit him to disguise, *n'est pas?*"

M'sieu Franchot, the manager, would, for a consideration. A *mille* note changed hands, and Timothy Arran followed the snake-dancer and her manager to a dressing-room bestrewn with costumes for all shapes, sizes and sexes.

"*Tiens!*" Franchot exclaimed twenty minutes later. "You are an *apache* to the life, m'sieu. No one would dream!"

When Timothy surveyed himself in a full-length mirror he was glad that no one would dream. A check cloth cap pulled low over his eyes hid their colour, and grease-paint had turned his face a sallow, thin-cheeked countenance full of villainy. A dirty muffler comprised his neckwear, a ragged coat and a pair of black, soiled trousers his suiting. His shoes were a bright yellow, pointed and down-at-heel.

"Charming," said Timothy, with a villainous grin.

"*Vilement!*" urged Corinne, flinging a heavy coat over her shoulders and slipping her small feet into a pair of low-heeled shoes. "And whatever you do, m'sieu, say nothing in English. Speak as little as you can."

Timothy did not reveal the fact that his argot was equal to any emergencies, but followed Corinne through the labyrinth of streets and alleyways leading, he hoped, to Bob Lavering and the Hôtel Divante. Throughout the journey, which lasted for over half an hour, they passed a dozen furtive figures, prowling vermin looking for easy money, and twice they passed the majesty of the law—two pairs of *gendarmes,* who knew better than to patrol that district singly. The smell of garbage reeked through the night air, and the cobbles of the roads were strewn with refuse and covered with a greasy slime—the mixture of dirt and a light rainfall. Timothy had thought he knew his Paris, but without Corinne he would have been lost a dozen times.

"How much further," he asked, as they dived down the hundredth—he thought—turning since leaving the Côte d'Or.

"Soon, now," muttered Corinne, glancing covertly about her. "But we are being watched, m'sieu. I am afraid . . ."

"What of?" asked Timothy.

"A knife in the back," said Corinne simply.

Then, for the first time, Timothy Arran showed her the small automatic he was holding in his right hand. It glinted blue-grey beneath the dim light of a wall-lamp, and the dancer gave a little exclamation of surprise.

"But, m'sieu! You expected trouble?"

"I always expect trouble," said Timothy.

Certainly he was expecting it that night. The darkness was unnerving, each corner offered the possibility of sudden attack.

Those few prowlers whom they had seen had disappeared. Only the quick tap-tap-tap of Corinne's small feet and his own more deliberate footsteps broke the silence of that dangerous corner of Montmartre—a silence which seemed pregnant. The misty light from occasional wall-lamps—in those back streets there were no lamp standards—heightened the gloom rather than increased it. Shadows loomed in front, behind and all about them, vague shadows and unnerving. Timothy guessed that they had made a long detour from the cabaret house to reach the Hôtel Divante, and he sensed that Corinne was trying to shake off pursuers, who might or might not be figments of her imagination. That the dancer was afraid Timothy was a hundred per cent. sure.

The attack came out of the blue!

They turned another corner, and they were hardly round it when something glinted in front of them, silvery-white. Timothy saw it when it was a yard in front of his eyes. He ducked instinctively. The knife whistled over his head and clattered against the wall behind him. A second followed it, tearing through his loose-fitting coat as it went. Corinne stood dead still, her face livid with fear. Timothy flung his left arm round her waist and lifted her bodily round the corner, out of the range of knives, which might come again at any moment.

"Where's this place we're after?" he demanded. "Are we near it?"

"It is in that street, m'sieu." Corinne's voice was quivering with fright. "The house with the red sign."

"Fine!" said Timothy. "Get back, Corinne, and go to the Hôtel Royale. Tell them M'sieu Timson sent you and that you are to wait for him. Can you do that?"

"Mais oui, m'sieu. But what of you?"

"I can look after myself," said Timothy. "These bright boys won't worry about you; they'll stick to me. *Allons, ma chèrie!* I'll be seeing you!"

He saw Corinne slip away from him, wraith-like, and he was

glad, for there were some jobs made only for man, and he was very anxious that Corinne should be safe. He told himself that she would be all right, and made himself believe it. Then he stepped gingerly round the corner, automatic in hand.

The third knife came as he loomed into sight. The ambush had been cleverly placed, for there was a lamp of unusual brilliance at the corner of the street in which the Hôtel Divante was situated. It was impossible to enter the street without offering himself as a target. He swung his body on one side and the knife flashed past his head. As it clanged against the wall, he tightened his finger on the trigger of his gun. A stab of flame shot out, and there came the soft *zutt!* of a silencer; as the bullet winged down the street, Timothy tucked his head down and ran after it, his right hand close to his side.

His trick worked. The knowledge that their quarry had a gun and was not afraid to use it created panic in the minds of the two men who were attacking him. Timothy saw their shadows as they moved from the porch which had sheltered them. He fired to the right of the shadows, and a sudden colourful curse split the near-silence. He fired again, as a fourth knife came. The knife took him in the left shoulder, nicking the skin, but doing no real damage. It was the last throw. The Paris *apache* had courage of a sort, but not the sort to stand against a madman with a gun. Timothy heard the scuttling of their feet as they ran, and he sent a high-pitched, almost hysterical laugh after them. It added wings to their feet.

Timothy Arran felt relief, as if a heavy load had been taken from his chest. The tenseness of the past hour dropped away. He felt exhilarated as he hurried down the street, his eyes open for the house with the red sign—the Hôtel Divante.

As he went, he reasoned. Obviously he had been followed to Paris, and his movements had been watched closely. The reason for his disappearance from the Côte d'Or with Corinne had been guessed, and he had been followed by the brace of *apaches*, who had taken a short cut to the house with the red sign and had waited for him. His trailers, he reasoned with sound sense, had been employed by the same gentry as had twice tried to kill Tony Beresford, and had been chosen because a knife crime in that corner of Paris was not likely to be connected with anything but a robbery motive.

Timothy shivered suddenly. It occurred to him that the knives might easily have been bullets, and bullets travelled at a speed which could not be dodged unless one knew they were on the way. And just as Beresford had come suddenly to the conclusion that the game which had started was very much above the ordinary level, so did Timothy Arran. He realized, too, that he had made a long step forward. The Lavering mystery was connected with the Auveley Street crimes. To think otherwise was to carry the long arm of coincidence too far.

The street was a long one and wider than most through which he had crept with Corinne. Timothy turned with a bend in the road, and saw, a hundred yards in front of him, a stone balustrade and three ornate street lamps. Beyond, he could see the lights of Paris shimmering on the waters of the Seine. That meant he was away from Montmartre now, or at its boundary.

The house with the red sign was on his right, fifty yards from the boulevard and the river. It was poorly lit, but an electric sign proclaimed 'Hôtel Divante'.

It was then that Timothy had a brain-wave. To go alone into the hotel might cause complications and create unwanted danger. He did not know how powerful the *apache* gang which had attacked him was in Paris, but he knew that some of the gangs rivalled the Chicago racketeers. Now that he had his bearings, he could find the hotel easily, and reach it by keeping to the main roads, or the boulevards, where the danger of attack was small. And he remembered that Corinne had said, "M'sieu Lavering is sick."

That might have meant anything, from a knife wound to a bucket of poison, but it showed Timothy Arran a light. What more natural than he should call on his friend with a doctor? And what better doctor than a *Sûreté* official, several of whom Timothy numbered among his acquaintances? Beresford had said 'no police', but he could not have anticipated this urgent development.

Timothy saw a late cab crawling along the boulevard, and whistled it. As he jumped into it, he gave the address of the *Sûreté*, and the words, "*Vitement! Vitement!*"

He reached the *Sûreté* in quick time, and discovered the address of a M'sieu Picot, who in the past had been helped considerably by Timothy as a member of Department Z. Picot, nightshirted and capped, welcomed him effusively. Was there something he could do for *le bon Timothee?*

Timothy explained, quickly, that a friend had become mixed up in an *apache* brawl, a friend who wanted no scandal. He was at the Hôtel Divante, sick and ailing, and Timothy had experienced difficulty in seeing his friend. With the presence of Picot, however, everything would be smoothed out.

Picot flushed at the compliment, and promised to breathe no word of the affair officially. He dressed himself in a uniform and made, Timothy admitted, a fine figure of a man, full-chested, well-preserved, his red face creased with smiles of self-importance, his little beard and moustache perfectly trimmed. The uniform was not connected with the police, for Picot was the French equivalent of a divisional-surgeon. But the uniform was impressive, and every Frenchman liked to look his best.

But Picot's complacency was rudely disturbed when he saw Bob Lavering—a white-faced, unshaven wreck of a man weak with pain. Timothy Arran could hardly recognize him as the spruce young American who had been in London less than a week ago.

"But this is an outrage!" expostulated Picot, after a lengthy examination. "This is a crime, a wicked crime! Your friend is being poisoned, m'sieu, with what you call—er—arsenic, *hein?*"

CHAPTER SEVEN

AND A MURDER IN PARIS

I T was just after one o'clock when Tony Beresford reached the Paris airfield, and it was half past four when he managed to get away. His forbearance where many a man would have raved, shouted or made a break impressed the Customs officials, and his insistence that he would be vouched for by the British Embassy disturbed their peace of mind. Two of them escorted him to the Embassy and were profuse in their apologies when he was acknowledged as a gentleman of the highest repute. M'sieu would fully appreciate that they had done no more than their duty? M'sieu would.

Sir Basil Marshant, the then Ambassador, had known Beresford from the knee upwards, and he looked at the big man, when the officials had gone, with a humorous gleam in his grey eyes. A tall, well-groomed, white-haired aristocrat was Sir Basil, one of the old school and one of the best.

"What the devil have you been up to now?" he demanded.

"I set a trap and got snared in it," said Beresford ruefully. "It'll serve to show me that I'm not so clever as I look."

"On business?" asked Marshant. (Marshant was one of the few

men who was consulted from time to time by Gordon Craigie and who knew many of Z's agents.)

"On a nightmare," grimaced Beresford. "Yes, something's brewing, Sir Basil, and we've an idea that some of it's brewing in France. You remember that note Craigie sent over for Odell?"

"To watch Leopold Gorman? Yes."

"Well, Major Gulliver, darn him, didn't. Gorman made a contact over here with someone or something, and we want to know what it is. Have you seen or heard anything?"

"No," said Marshant. "To tell you the truth, Beresford, we've got more than we can handle over here, and I do nothing but send notes and receive 'em. France, Italy and Germany between 'em will pitch us into a fine mess if we're not careful. The Balkan States aren't helping, either. I wish I could get out of it and spend a couple of months with a line in Scotland," added the Ambassador. "I'd go back to England to-night if I could think of an excuse."

"No, you wouldn't," said Beresford. "You wouldn't leave here until everything was signed and settled and Europe was playing ball all day long. Howso, I've got to be moving. Let me—or Craigie—know if you do get your teeth into anything, will you?"

"Not much chance where Gorman's concerned," said Marshant. "Anything else I can do to help you?"

"You can tell me where the Hôtel Divante is," said the big man, lighting a cigarette.

Marshant looked surprised.

"That place? Your tastes are getting low, young fellow. The Divante's on the fringe of Montmartre, just off the river. And it's more than a brothel."

"I'm not surprised," said Beresford. "Barring accidents, though, I won't be there for long."

The accidents did not happen. The mysterious would-be assassins seemed to have shot their bolt, or else the appearance of Picot scared them. Beresford reached the house with the red sign just after six o'clock, to find an ambulance waiting outside. Timothy Arran was in the hall, skirmishing with a billowy chambermaid. He chucked her under the chin as he saw Beresford, and the girl floated towards the mysterious regions below stairs.

"You've taken your time, haven't you?" complained Timothy, as they shook hands.

"I was delayed," said Tony, without enlarging on the subject. "How's Lavering?"

Timothy Arran looked serious.

"Not so good," he said. "They've been dosing him with arsenic, slow but sure, and it'll be touch and go. We're moving him to a nursing-home now. Incidentally," said Timothy, "I had to get hold of Picot, of the *Sûreté*. He's promised to keep his mouth shut."

"He'll be all right," said the big man. "Has Lavering talked at all?"

"A bit, but he doesn't know much. He says that he went to a show, and then to the Côte d'Or, in the Rue des Coronnes. He must have eaten something there that disagreed with him, because he was taken ill as he started back for the Royale. He was alone, and he can just remember someone bending over him; the next thing he knew was that he was in bed at this place. A doctor told him it was ptomaine poisoning, but when Picot came along he diagnosed arsenic."

Beresford looked grim.

"I hope to the Lord he gets over it. What's Picot say?"

"He might pull through. We've had a couple of specialists here to-day, and we're doing all we can. If you want to see him before they take him out, you'd better hurry."

Beresford had a shock when he saw the yellow-tinged face of the young American. Lavering was sleeping under a drug, but he looked as if he would never wake up. Beresford felt sick. And, unbidden, he saw a mental picture of Adele Fayne, dancing with Leopold Gorman. How much did that couple know of the affair?

The two agents waited until Lavering had been taken from the notorious Hôtel Divante, accompanied by a doctor and two nurses vouched for by the vigilant Picot. Then they made their way towards the Royale. In a private room, Timothy related his adventures in Paris, omitting only the fact that he had been escorted by Corinne. He would introduce the snake-charmer to Beresford later, he told himself.

"I wonder," muttered Beresford, staring at the ceiling, "whether Gorman came over here to arrange for the Lavering business."

Timothy Arran shrugged.

"It's possible. It's even probable. But it isn't likely that he'd come over here for that alone. He could have arranged to get at Lavering by sending an agent."

"Any idea which gang's mixed up in it?" asked Beresford, who knew as well as most people of the strength of the underworld cliques in Paris.

"Nothing definite's come to hand," said Arran. "I've paid a couple of men whom Picot recommends to try to identify the knives that were thrown last night, but they haven't reported yet. Other than that I've done nothing. If we could go to the *Sûreté* we'd get what we want."

Beresford shook his head.

"I don't want to, and Craigie doesn't want to. It's dangerous to bring in the authorities. It'll make Gorman alter a lot of his plans if he realizes he's up against the *Sûreté,* and I'm hugging a fancy that we might get somewhere through the Paris connection. Where are you staying?"

"Here," said Timothy Arran, grinning.

"Then why in blue Hades," demanded Beresford, "did you take a special room when we could have used your apartment?"

"That," said Timothy blandly, "is where I have you. I didn't tell you, son, that it was Corinne who helped me to get at Lavering, did I?"

"No. Who's Corinne?"

"A snake-charmer-cum-dancer," said Arran, closing one eye, "who improves on acquaintance. She led me to the Divante, and she was in a blue funk. So was I," Timothy added frankly.

"Get it all out," urged Beresford.

"That's what I am doing," said Timothy Arran. "I sent her back here before having my shot at the boys with the knives, and she's been here ever since. Since two o'clock this morning, that is."

"In your apartment?"

"In my apartment," confirmed Timothy. "I—here, what are you getting at, you lout?"

"Easy goes," grinned Beresford. "I'll have to tell Toby about you, and you haven't got the excuse that it's the friend of a cousin from America. Has she talked?"

"No." Arran frowned. "I've tried to make her, but she's scared. I don't know what of, but I do know that she was scared when I mentioned Lavering to her, and she's frightened of getting bumped off for leading me to him. I couldn't," he added defensively, "do less than give her food and shelter after she had risked her life for me. Could I?"

"You," said Beresford absently, "have been talking to too many Frenchmen. What's she like to look at?"

"Easy to the eye," said Arran. "She is—or was—the star attraction at the Côte d'Or."

"And she knew where Lavering was?"

"And that he was ill."

"Then she must have a pretty good idea who put him there."

"Bright, aren't you?" drawled Timothy. "I know that, blocknut. She's scared of the boys who tried to get Lavering—all right, got him if you like—but it's the identity of those boys that's puzzling me."

"Have you asked her?"

"Directly, indirectly, and by inference. Money won't make her talk, fair words won't make her talk, romance won't make her talk."

"In fact, she's dumb," said Beresford.

"She's not," claimed Timothy indignantly. "She's a cute kid and she's got brains. But she's dead scared. I got her to show me Lavering because she was more frightened of the *Sûreté* than Bob's boy friends, but now Lavering's safe she won't spill a word. I say, Tony."

"Hm-hum," said Beresford inquisitively, and as he looked at his friend he saw that Timothy Arran's eyes were serious, and his friend's face was set in hard lines.

"Treat her gently, will you? I don't want the *Sûreté* to start mauling her about, and some of those French she-police are vixens. I know we've got to get at the bottom of the business, but——"

Beresford chuckled.

"Idiot," he said. "The police aren't in this, I tell you, and we draw the line at forcing information, even from men. I'll make her as happy as a kitten—but I might have to put the fear of *mon Dieu* into her first."

"Just treat her gently, that's all I ask," said Timothy.

Beresford told himself, as he walked along the sumptuously furnished corridors of the Hôtel Royale with Timothy Arran nearly reaching his chin, that the said Timothy was smitten, perhaps not badly, but certainly a little. The Unholy Twins, Beresford knew, were not ladies' men. Women, to them, meant marriage, and marriage did not appeal. The dancer from the Montmartre cabaret house must be unusual, Beresford told himself.

He was seized suddenly with an idea, and broached it.

"What's going to happen if she's still scared when you leave Paris?" he demanded. "Is she safe?"

Timothy turned troubled eyes towards his friend.

"Honest, old boy," he said, "I don't know. I'm not happy about it. I wish to heaven I'd found Lavering through someone else, and I don't mind admitting it."

Beresford grunted. It was often impossible to reach an objective without the help of a woman, but the agents of Department Z preferred to deal with men. They felt safer, and they were never troubled by qualms such as the qualms which possessed Timothy Arran on the safety of Corinne. If the girl had betrayed one of the Montmartre rats—and she had—her life would be no sinecure.

And then Beresford looked again at the glum face of his friend, and he grinned. To see Timothy Arran blue about the gills over a girl was unusual enough to be amusing, and Timothy, with a little gentle kidding, would see the funny side.

"I'll tell you what," said Beresford, straight-faced.

"What?" demanded Timothy, suspecting a catch.

"Take her home and put her in your harem," said Beresford, "and get Toby to take a half-interest."

Timothy Arran made a comment which was unprintable, and turned a corner in the corridor. As he did so a dinner-jacketed Frenchman turned also. Timothy and the dinner-jacket's middle button collided. Timothy gasped, the Frenchman spluttered, and Beresford soothed both ruffled tempers with a practised hand.

"That just shows you," he chided Timothy, as the latter unlocked the door of his apartment, "to look where you're going and to keep your temper. Hallo," he broke off as he stepped into the apartment. "The bird's flown, has she?"

Arran frowned, and looked round the room, furnished luxuriously as were all the rooms of the Royale. It seemed empty. It *was* empty. . . .

"No, it isn't," said Beresford suddenly, and he placed his large forefinger over his lips. "The maid sleeps, Timothy, in yonder chair. Step softly, son."

The big man went towards a chair, the back of which was turned towards the door and over the top of which he had just seen the top of a head of raven hair, with an exaggerated caution which made Timothy Arran writhe. Beresford kept his companion away, holding him off at the length of his long arm, and thus it was Beresford who was the first to see what there was to see.

Timothy Arran felt Beresford's fingers tighten on his arm. He saw the sudden disappearance of the big man's grin, and the glint in Beresford's eyes. Something that was very near to fear shot through Timothy Arran. His lips went dry. The hair at the back of his neck seemed to stand on end.

"W-what is it?" he demanded hoarsely, cursing the fact that Beresford's height enabled him to see without trouble.

Beresford turned towards him, white-faced.

"It's not nice," he said in a voice that shook. "She's been strangled. I don't think there's much chance, Tim, but hop down and collect a doctor, and have a strong whisky before you come up."

Timothy Arran stared at his friend for a second that seemed an eternity. The Twin's face was pale, his eyes were wide open and unnaturally bright. There was the suspicion of a quiver on his lips and nostrils, which told Beresford more than anything else could have done that in twelve brief hours Timothy had learned of that thing called love.

Then Arran turned on his heel.

"All right," he muttered, "all right." But as he went out of the room, Beresford heard him muttering to himself, and the name on his lips was 'Corinne'.

CHAPTER EIGHT

THE MYSTERIOUS MR. WILLIAMS

As Arran turned away, Beresford hurried round the chair and picked the dainty body of the dancer out of it, carrying her across the room and lying her full length on a settee. The sight of her face made him clench his teeth. It was blue and swollen, horribly distorted, and the tongue and the eyes were protruding. Around her neck was a single silken cord, twisted with fiendish tightness until it had squeezed every atom of breath from her bursting lungs. Round the cord, where it bit into her once-slender but now swollen throat, were the lacerated marks where she had torn pitifully at the cord, trying to ease the awful constriction, trying to breathe.

She was dead. Beresford knew that no doctor in the world could bring her back to life. But he took her elbows in his hands and worked her arms gently, trying artificial respiration in case of the hundredth chance. The rise and fall of her breast sickened him, knowing as he did that it was only caused by the forced movement of her arms and shoulders, and he averted his eyes from her face.

A doctor, happily unofficious and innocent of mannerisms, came up within five minutes, accompanied by a white-faced manager. Timothy Arran, Beresford found with relief, had not been able to steel himself to return.

"No chance, is there?" Beresford asked of the medico.

The man shrugged his shoulders.

"None at all, m'sieu. Life is quite extinct. If you had come ten minutes before, you might have saved her, but even that is doubtful. A terrible crime, m'sieu."

"And in the Hôtel Royale!" groaned the manager, wringing his plump hands. "It will be the ruin, messieurs, it will——"

Beresford barked at him.

"Cut that out, will you? Get downstairs and have every door locked, kitchen quarters as well. Telephone to the *Sûreté* and get M'sieu Picot to come here, and if he's back yet, M'sieu l'Inspecteur Piquet. And ask M'sieu Arran to telephone me on the house line, but not to come up. Do you understand?"

"*Mais oui, m'sieu.*" The manager turned away, cowed by the ferocity of the big man's manner.

Beresford turned to the doctor, who was still trying respiration, although both of them knew it was a matter of form.

"One thing I can't stand," muttered Beresford, "is a ruddy ghoul like that cuss. Ruin be damned, and he with it!"

The doctor gathered the drift and agreed with the sentiment. Moreover, Beresford's knowledge of two of the most respected officials at the *Sûreté* impressed him, and he asked no questions. Beresford, glad to keep away from the still body on the settee, walked across the room and picked up a suitcase—Timothy Arran's only luggage.

The case was unlocked, and Beresford snapped his fingers. A quick glance told him that the contents of the case had been turned over in a hurry, as though someone had been looking for something—something which might have been in it. That meant, the big man told himself, that robbery played a part in the crime. Suddenly, too, he remembered the dinner-jacketed Frenchman.

The man had turned out of the passage; he must have been hurrying, or he would not have banged into Arran.

The telephone burred suddenly, loud and out of place in that chamber of death. Beresford hurried to it and muttered, "Hullo," unconsciously keeping his voice low.

"Want me?" asked Timothy Arran. There was a note of dejection in Timothy's voice and his drawl was missing.

"I was going to ask you to call up Craigie on the long-distance line," said Beresford, "but before you do that, get round the smoking-room and the restaurant and see if you can discover the cove you walloped into just now. Got that?"

"I'll ring you back," said Arran.

But when he rang through again, it was to report that, with the help of the police, who had arrived quickly, he had seen every man in the place, from servants to temporary visitors, and that while he had examined many dinner-jackets, the vital one was not there. Beresford grunted, and promised to go downstairs within five minutes. He turned away from the telephone to Anton Piquet, who had luckily returned to Paris during the afternoon. Picot had arrived too, dressed for the theatre, and as self-conscious as ever. The hotel doctor had gone. The usual camera men and fingerprint experts were working, displaying more physical energy than their English counterparts would have done in the same circumstances, but saving little time, if any.

Piquet was a slight, wiry man, sallow-skinned and shrewd-eyed. He spoke flawless English with only the slightest suggestion of accent, and with little idiomatic effect.

"This is a bad business, Beresford. Do you know much about it?"

"Nothing more than Picot knows," said Beresford. "Listen, Piquet. I've got to get back to England quickly, but I don't want this murder to look like anything but a jealousy crime—*crime passionelle*, if you get me. The last thing I want is to be connected with it myself—or Arran, for that matter."

Piquet pulled his thin lips.

"Well, for you, Beresford, I can do it. You will have to be careful with the newspaper men, *hein?* They are downstairs."

"I'll dodge them," said Beresford. "And if I get anything that will help you, I'll telephone you from London. You know who the girl is, and you can be pretty sure that she's been killed because she knew who poisoned Lavering, the American. Picot's told you about that, hasn't he?"

"I conceived it my duty," said the surgeon stiffly.

Beresford smiled at him amicably.

"Of course—you could have done nothing else."

"Although," said Picot, plucking at a speck on his immaculate waistcoat, "it grieved me to betray my promise to a friend, but what else could I do?"

The detective broke in.

"Were you looking for Lavering, as well as M'sieu Arran?"

"Yes," said Beresford.

There was a grim smile at the corners of the little man's lips. A very human policeman was Anton Piquet.

"One of those dangerous games you play for your fun, eh, Beresford?"

"Exactly," said the big man.

He could have sworn that Piquet winked, for Piquet was understanding, as well as human, and Beresford had played many prominent parts in affairs which had not been confined to England.

"Then," said Piquet, "we will work together, and help each other where we can. *Adieu,* Beresford. I am sorry I did not meet you again in more happy times."

Beresford shook hands with the two Frenchmen, and experienced a queer tremor in his chest. There were times, he told himself philosophically, when nationality mattered little and men were men.

When he reached the lounge, he was surprised to find that

89

Toby Arran was with his brother. Toby had not lost much time in Oxford. Timothy had been drinking more than usual, and his lips were set in a straight line.

"Tim's told you?" asked Beresford of Tobias.

"Yes," said Toby, and swore.

His brother cleared his throat, and Beresford hurried on to another subject.

"What did you find out from Meiklejohn?" he demanded.

"Williams saw him all right," said Toby. "Your scholar got there at two o'clock, and left Trinity at three."

Beresford rubbed his chin.

"But he didn't get back to his flat until two o'clock in the morning. I'd like to find out more about that gentleman."

"You've plenty of opportunity," Toby pointed out. "He lives in the same house."

"He did," said Beresford, "but he might have flown."

Neither of the others appreciated the humour of this remark, and Beresford did not enlighten them. The affair of the 'Air France' trip and the wireless transmitter still rankled. Certainly, he told himself, he would investigate the activities of Mr. Nicholas Williams as soon as he got back to London. Providing that gentleman was still sure that his disguises had not been penetrated, Beresford would be able to turn the tables. When he tackled Mr. Williams he suspected that there would be a variety of odds and ends of information to show for it.

The big man lit a cigarette and pondered the position. Timothy Arran was badly cut-up. He was not in a mental condition which would enable him to tackle any problem but that of the murder of Corinne the dancer; on the other hand, he was not fit to tackle even that problem with a clear mind. Yet he would kick, and naturally, if Beresford wanted him to return to England at that moment.

The big man reached his decision as Timothy said:

"What do you want me to do, Tony? Stay here?"

Beresford noticed the harshness of the twin's voice and the glint in his eyes. It would go hard with any man or woman whom Arran could prove was connected with the brutal murder at the Hôtel Royale.

"Yes," said Beresford, "you'd better stay in Paris, and Toby with you. Don't work against the police. Have a talk with Piquet, upstairs; you'll work well together, and he'll keep it dark while they can. And listen, both of you. Don't forget your big job is to find something on Leopold Gorman. Trace every line with that end in view, and report to Craigie daily anything you hear about him. All right?"

The Arrans nodded.

"Good," said Beresford.

He shook hands with Toby, and then with Timothy, and as he gripped the latter's palm he said awkwardly:

"Sorry, Tim, darned sorry. But don't blame yourself. Blame the Department. It's kill or be killed in our game, and death's always round the corner. But the game must go on, taking rough and smooth together, and once we're in it we can't get out."

A gleam lit up the shadows of Timothy Arran's eyes.

"Thanks," he said, and his voice shook. And then he averted his eyes, and Beresford left him.

Beresford went to London on the night 'plane, and ran his maroon-painted Hispano from the Croydon garage, where he had left it, direct to Whitehall. It was nearing twelve when he reached Craigie's office, but the Chief was still there, working on a mass of figures at his desk.

As Beresford stepped through the door made by a sliding partition, Craigie stood up and walked towards him.

"How's Arran?" he asked quietly, as they shook hands.

"Taking it hard, but taking it well," grunted Beresford. "God! If I could get my hands round the swine who killed that kid I'd ..."

He broke off with a laugh which had no humour in it, and Craigie drew the armchairs up to the fire, saying nothing but fully understanding. Beresford realized the necessity for Craigie knowing every fact available and without loss of time, and he had telephoned Whitehall 63 before he had left the Royale, and had told the Chief that Arran had been hit by the murder. Craigie's first question when they met concerned Arran; it was a typical gesture, but it moved Beresford strangely.

"Well?" asked Craigie, after a pause.

Beresford lit one cigarette from the stub of another.

"I suppose we haven't done so bad," he said. "We've proved pretty well that the Lavering business is the Gorman business. The only thing we want to know is why Gorman tried to put Bob Lavering out of the way."

Craigie drew at his long pipe.

"Did he?" he asked suddenly.

"Well ..." began Beresford; and then his eyes widened. "Damn me for a mutton-head!" he jerked. "Of course he didn't, or he would have done!"

"That's as I see it," said Craigie. "Lavering was in that place——"

"The Hôtel Divante."

"For nearly three days. If Gorman put him there—or Gorman's men—he could have been killed and probably never discovered afterwards. And there's another thing."

"You mean the arsenic?" muttered Beresford. "That puzzled me, Gordon. Why try to poison him, slowly, with arsenic? It didn't run smoothly, somehow. The facts didn't fit."

"They still don't," said Craigie, tapping his pipe against his strong teeth. "You saw Lavering was ill with arsenic. I'd say that if he'd been dosed with the stuff for the first time while he was in

Paris, he'd have died. It doesn't take much to kill a man, *unless he's used to it in small quantities."*

Beresford crushed his cigarette between his fingers.

"But, darn it, that suggests he's been taking the stuff as a dope. I don't think Bob Lavering would——"

"He was probably dosed with it while he was in London, and for some weeks past. Gorman could get at him easily enough through the Fayne woman. I think," added Craigie quietly, "that we can take it as read that Gorman didn't want to kill Lavering, but only to put him out of the way for a while."

Beresford nodded, impressed by the reasoning.

"So now we want to know *why*," he said. "There's another thing to remember. Timothy didn't have a big job getting Lavering out of the mess. A sticky one, yes, but not up to Gorman standard. Why did Gorman go to all the trouble to catch Lavering alive, without taking him to some place more difficult to get at than the Montmartre Boulevard? It was like pinching a dollar and giving it back with interest."

Craigie grunted and rubbed his hawk nose.

"Maybe," he suggested, "Gorman wasn't kept in close touch with the Paris end. Looking at it logically, this hotel in Montmartre was a fairly good hiding-place. You say Lavering wasn't registered there under his own name?"

"Not registered at all, from what I gathered."

"Then the only way of finding Lavering was the way Arran did it. And remember, Gorman probably thought his quarry was safe in Paris. He didn't expect you'd send Arran over there, because he didn't know we were interested in Lavering. I probably wouldn't have connected Lavering up at all if you hadn't noticed his fiancée dancing with Leopold Gorman at the Two-Step."

"There's another thing, too," said Beresford thoughtfully.

He spoke quickly and gave an unvarnished account of his adventure in the air-liner. Craigie chuckled. Beresford scowled, then chuckled too. In retrospect, the trick was as funny as it was clever.

"I fancy," Beresford said, "that Williams didn't altogether expect I'd send him on to Lyons. He probably reckoned on my pinching his wireless, but thought he'd be able to follow me to Paris, where he would have learned that Timothy Arran was already there. And while I was arguing it out with the Customs, he would probably have been working another disguise of sorts."

"He seems a useful man at that job," said Craigie.

"Good, but not perfect. He can't disguise his eyes, except with glasses, and he forgot to alter his voice when I tackled him first time on the liner."

"You didn't tell me about Williams when you telephoned," Craigie said quietly.

Beresford detected a mild note of reproof, and chuckled.

"No. I'd telephoned Tricker at the flat, before speaking to you. Tricker says that Williams hasn't been in since I left London. I told him to telephone Miller at the Yard if Williams returned before I got to the flat, and to tell Miller to hold Nicholas the Learned on some charge or other."

"What kind of charge?" inquired Craigie.

"I left it to Tricker," said Beresford, with a grin. "He sounded well, and he says he's been up to-day. Seriously," he added, "if Williams wasn't at home at half past six, there was a sound chance that I'd get back before he did."

Craigie nodded, and smoked for a few minutes in silence. Beresford, stretching his great legs in front of him, lit another cigarette and told himself that two problems of equal importance were waiting for solution. They were:

1. Why had Gorman tried to hold—in effect kidnap—Robert Lavering?

2. Who was Nicholas Williams, who was he working for, and why had he once used water instead of a knife?

Suddenly:

"I'm beginning to wonder," said Beresford, "whether Williams is working for Gorman. He doesn't fit the part, as Williams, as Ruddy Face, nor as the policeman. I——"

He broke off as the telephone-bell burred. Craigie got up and walked across the office. Beresford heard his occasional words, the sharpness of his voice, and the final: "We'll be right over. Good-bye."

Beresford was already out of his chair.

"Where are we going?" he demanded.

Gordon Craigie looked grim.

"We're going to Ealing," he said. "That was Miller. He's been to Ealing on a murder job, and he says that the dead man's either Nicholas Williams or his double!"

CHAPTER NINE

VALERIE LESTER SPRINGS A SURPRISE

ONLY by shutting out all memory of Ruddy Face and the Paris trip could Beresford bring himself to identify the body of Nicholas Williams. Williams was found in an empty house near Ealing Common, and the police had been called by a tramp who had broken into the house for a night's shelter. The scholar's death had been caused by a bullet wound through the heart—and he had been dead for forty-eight hours!

"And yet," said Craigie, looking grimly at Beresford in the dim light of the empty house, which was illuminated only by half a dozen storm lanterns and the white beams of police torches, "you reckon you saw him, as Ruddy Face, yesterday afternoon. We've gone wrong somewhere, Tony."

Beresford grunted, and looked down on the white face of the unfortunate Williams. Suddenly:

"What's the colour of his eyes?" he demanded.

Miller already had physical particulars.

"Grey," he said.

Beresford banged his palms together, and swung round on the detective.

"I thought so," he grunted. "Both of you saw Williams—or the man who came to Auveley Street on Monday night. But his eyes were blue——"

"Hidden by glasses," said Miller suddenly.

"I remember them," said Craigie. "Thick lenses, but they were blue all right. Which means——"

"That the real Williams had a telegram and went to Oxford to see Meiklejohn. He was killed on his way back, and the pseudo Williams took his place."

"He took a big chance of being recognized by you," said Craigie, rubbing his nose.

"Not so big," protested Beresford. "It was late, and the light was artificial. He was excited—or he aped being excited, and in that light, and at that time, I wasn't likely to notice any differences beyond the display of temperament that he served up. No," he added thoughtfully, "I don't think that he took much of a chance, Gordon. It's not as if he had to keep it up for long."

"Did you see him after that night?" asked Craigie.

"No. But that's nothing unusual. He was often out all day, pottering about in museums or at gatherings of intellectuals, and he was something of a hermit."

"Poor devil," muttered Craigie. "Killed because Gorman's crowd wanted to get into your flat for that night, and take no chances."

Miller cleared his throat, and went across the empty room to talk with his fingerprint man. Beresford thought suddenly of his words to Timothy Arran a few hours before. Anyone might jump into eternity because they crossed the path of those who worked in the Game—and those who worked against it. Death came quickly, from any angle, at any time.

He blinked as a photographer made a flash for a photograph of the dead Williams, and seemed to see the horribly distorted face of Corinne through the blue-white glare. He cursed, suddenly, viciously. Craigie gripped his arm.

"Steady up, Tony."

Beresford forced a grin.

"All right," he said. "It's the outside element that's getting me. Corinne and this poor devil——"

"Work it off," said Craigie, staring hard at the big man. "Work like the devil, Tony. We've got to get at the bottom of it, and the longer we take getting there the more jobs we'll meet like this."

Beresford nodded, and his mind cleared of the cold anger which had filled it. Suddenly:

"We still don't know why the pseudo-Williams didn't put me right out," he said.

"There's a lot," said Craigie, "that we don't know. But there's one big thing we do know, my son."

"Name it," grunted Beresford.

"We know that Gorman's at the back of it all. And we know that he's still buying. He took a controlling share of Eastern Consolidated Oils to-day."

"Orient-Western and Eastern Consolidated together, eh?" Beresford drummed his fingers against his thigh. "That means he's got petrol under his thumb. We'll see a price increase soon, I suppose. Anything else?"

"The rise will be a cautious one when it comes," prophesied Craigie. "Yes, there are half a dozen smaller jobs he's tackling. I was working out some figures when you arrived. I'll finish them to-night, and you can come over in the morning and we'll talk round it again. We've got to keep at it. We can't lay up."

Beresford nodded, his eyes narrowed.

"We'll need more help," he said. "The Arrans will be busy in Paris for a day or two, and there's one big angle that wants working up in London."

"Which one?" asked Craigie.

Beresford's eyes were very hard.

"I don't like it," he said. "Women in this game are the devil. But what's Adele Fayne doing? Can we get anything from her?"

Craigie shrugged his shoulders, but there was a curve at the corners of his lips.

"I'm hoping to," he said, "if only to get a line on some of Gorman's theatre combines. Number Seven is working on Adele Fayne."

"Number Seven?" Beresford looked doubtful. "I thought Timothy Arran was Six and Toby Seven."

"We keep changing," said Craigie, and in his voice there was a note of infinite weariness. "We have to, Tony. I've heard nothing from Nick Carris for six months. He's off the list. So Dodo Trale takes Number Seven, and the Arrans go up a point each. I'll let you have the new list in the morning. Meanwhile, take my tip and borrow a spot of your man's sleeping-powder—and if he's got none at the flat, get some from Doc Little. I don't want you to crack, Tony."

Tony Beresford chuckled. It was not so much that he was amused; he wanted Craigie to feel that he was still a hundred per cent capable, for it was an axiom that if an agent could not laugh he could not work.

"My son," said Beresford, laying his hand heavily on Craigie's shoulder, "you do me wrong. Let's get back to town, Gordon, and gnaw a bone."

Craigie refused to help with the bone, and after dropping the Chief at Whitehall, Tony garaged the car in a tin shed at Shepherd's Market, walking from there to his flat. The cool night air cleared his mind, enabling him to see things in their true perspective, and that perspective was disquieting.

The plain truth, Beresford told himself, was that the only ostensible reason for connecting Leopold Gorman with the crimes in Paris and London was the fact that Diane Chester had seen him betraying an unusual—by appearances—interest in her friend. It was true enough that Gorman was buying on a big scale, but buying was no crime, and it was reasonable to suppose that Gorman was paying for his purchases either on his own bills or the bills of any syndicate backing him. There had come no whisper of trouble from the City, and whispers were usually well ahead of events. On the surface of things, Leopold Gorman was increasing his holdings and potential influence; also on the surface there were no grounds for connecting him with the two murders and the other crimes.

Neither Beresford nor Craigie had spoken of these facts, but both men had realized they existed. It was that, as much if not more than the effect of the murders, which had tended to make both of them view life that night on a basis which Beresford called, for the sake of a better description, slightly morbid.

Both of them believed that Gorman was behind it. Both of them knew that the Adele Fayne and Bob Lavering engagement gave them grounds for suspicion. But there they stopped. And Tony Beresford, turning the key in the lock of his front door, told himself that the thing to do, first, foremost and before anything else could transpire, was to get a direct line between the financier and the Paris incidents. And then he told himself, gloomily, that he had as much chance of getting that line as he had of reaching the moon.

Beresford, then, was depressed. His depression tended to make him forget that Department Z worked in devious ways, and that there was rarely a straight-forward problem to be solved. The essence of Secret Service work was to garner information from all quarters and on all subjects, to sift the wheat from the chaff, and mix what remained together until it made sense. At that stage in the affair which has been variously described, but by Beresford was always looked on as the Lavering Affair, the actual rewards for Department Z's efforts had been substantial. Only the fact that they believed Gorman was at the back of it, and wanted badly to prove it, gave Beresford—and, he knew, Gordon Craigie—that rare feeling of depression.

Beresford felt more cheerful when he reached his flat and discovered Maria sitting in the depths of his pet armchair, steel-rimmed glasses drooping from her nose, and a copy of the *Evening Sun* in front of her. Maria was not attending faithfully to her duties. For all she cared, Beresford thought with a grin, Samuel Tricker might have been gasping his last. Treading softly, Beresford poked his head into Tricker's room. The ex-prizefighter was sleeping the sleep of the just, and although his head was still bandaged, he looked much fitter than he had on the previous day.

Cheered, Beresford crept into the kitchen and brewed himself coffee, which he liked hot and strong, and plied himself with bread and cheese. He enjoyed the snack, and enjoyed his task of keeping the two beauties asleep even more. When, twenty minutes after his arrival at Auveley Street, he slipped between the sheets, he did so with the conscience of the man who has done his day's good deed; and he slept well.

He was awakened at half past eight by a sprucely clad but rather anxious Tricker, with tea and a message.

"Miss Lester telephoned you, Mr. B. Would you please ring her up as soon as poss.?"

"Lester? Lester?" Beresford sat up, yawning, and tried to recall a Miss Lester. "Darn you!" he said suddenly. "Why didn't you wake me, Sam?"

"I 'ave, sir," said Sam truthfully.

Beresford grinned, having connected Lester with Valerie and found the message pleasant. He took his tea, and eyed Sammivel sternly; that worthy, for the first time in Beresford's memory, was looking sheepish.

"Well, Sam?" inquired Beresford.

Tricker shifted his feet, and patted his bandage, as though imploring a light sentence on a sick man.

"Well, Mr. B., it's like this. We 'ad a 'eadache larst night an' took a coupla ashprins, an'——"

Realization dawned on Tony, but his face was set.

"Who," he demanded, "are 'we'?"

"Well, we wasn't expectin' you 'ome, Mr. B.——"

"The same 'we' Sam?"

"Yes, Mr. B. It wasn't 'er fault, though, s'elp me. We—she—I'd 'ave woke up if you'd only give us a shart, Mr. B. Maria would-n'ver let it 'appen fer the worlds, she says, an' she ain't no liar. 'Never before 'ave I slept at me post,' says she, an'——"

"Sam," said Beresford gently.

"Yes, Mr. B."

"You're a born fool, Sam. Tell Maria that I came home drunk last night, and that only her guilty conscience matters. And don't interrupt me, Sam. Tell her that in order to ease my—I mean her —conscience, she ought to grill my bacon. While she is grilling my bacon, you go out and get me a copy of *l'Echo de Paris*—you'll get one at the Circus station—and before you do any of those things, Sam, hand me that telephone."

The beam on Samuel Tricker's face threatened to disturb even the bandage on his forehead.

"O.K., Mr. B.!" he said. "And thanks, Mr. B."

Beresford grimaced at him, and dialled the number of the Chesters' Park Lane house. A mournful-voiced butler promised to contact with Miss Lester, if the gentleman would hold on. Beres-ford, who knew of that near-mausoleum which the Chesters called a home, grinned and did.

Valerie Lester's voice came over the telephone quickly, clearly, and yet with a suggestion of that huskiness which made it so attractive when not impeded by the wires.

"You wanted me, sweet one?" greeted Beresford.

"Yes," said Valerie Lester. "I wanted you yesterday morning, and you weren't in. I wanted you yesterday afternoon and you weren't in. I wanted you last night——"

"I was out last night," said Beresford blandly. "But if I hadn't been I wouldn't have known how badly you longed for me, so your twopences weren't wasted."

Valerie Lester laughed lightly, but when she spoke Beresford noticed the hardening of her voice.

"Tony——"

"Sorry, lass. I'll be serious."

"Are you all right?"

"Am I——" Beresford broke off, and whistled under his breath. Here was a development with a vengeance! At last: "Why in the name of the pink moon shouldn't I be all right?"

There was a pause. Beresford, picturing the vivacious face of the girl at the other end of the wire, wrinkled his nose in perplexity at her question. For there could be no mistaking its meaning. She either knew, or suspected, that he had been doing things not usual in the life of the average man-about-town; and Beresford wondered how she knew or why she suspected.

"I'd rather not say, over the telephone," said Valerie at length. "But I had a—warning—that made me worried."

"About me?"

"Ye-es."

Beresford wanted to say something that would have seemed, afterwards, a little hasty, so he checked himself and asked whether she had had breakfast.

Valerie laughed—Beresford liked the way her laugh came over the telephone—and said that she was about to.

"Is Aub there, or Diane?" asked Tony.

"Diane's on the Row. Aubrey's got a headache."

"How like that man," groaned Beresford. "Howso—you're breakfasting alone, are you?"

"Hm-hm."

"I like the way your voice went up and down when you said that," said Beresford, "but I don't like the sentiment."

"You *are* a fool!" said Valerie Lester. "What's the matter with the sentiment?"

"You're not breakfasting alone," Tony assured her cheerfully. "You're breakfasting with me—I've got Maria here, Queen of Chaperones, so your heart needn't flutter. That's if you can wait half an hour for your breakfast," he added considerately.

"I'll try," said Valerie. "In half an hour?"

"Ten past nine on the dot," said Tony. "Don't keep me waiting!"

He replaced the receiver, and hopped out of bed, slipping into a dressing-gown and invading the kitchen quarters, where Maria, still sharp-featured but definitely nervous, was prepared to grill bacon. Beresford stood in the doorway and said, "Boo!" Maria jumped round and proverbially out of her skin. Her eyes widened when she saw Beresford, and for a moment her lips tightened.

"Did you say that, young man?"

"Yes, I did, young woman, and I don't want any backchat. I'm having a friend in to breakfast, so double the rashers, and don't make a mess of the tomatoes like Sammivel does."

As he spoke, Beresford was smiling, and when he finished he continued to smile and he winked. It was, as Valerie Lester knew, one of the most attractive of smiles, and it broke through the armour of Maria and battered down all her defences.

"You great big fool of a man!" she said, with a shake of her fist. "What time's your friend coming?"

"Ten past nine, and her name's Lester."

"A woman?" Maria's eyes sparked.

"Yes, and if you don't like it I'll come and tickle your conscience. Turn the hot tap on, there's a dear soul, so that I can scrape my stubble."

As Beresford tubbed, he told himself that he would not think of Valerie Lester's warning until he knew just what it was. And he grinned to himself as he remembered that Diane Chester, Valerie Lester and even Maria had called him a fool. Beresford liked being called a fool. It made him, he said, feel clever.

CHAPTER TEN

A SURPRISE AND A SHOCK

VALERIE LESTER appeared, punctual to the minute, and Beresford told her that she looked divine. Actually she looked beautiful. She was dressed in a blue serge tailor-made costume, and the V of the coat revealed a cream-coloured silk creation which in turn showed the white smoothness of her skin. Her eyes were bright, her cheeks glowing after her brisk walk from Regent's Park, and her dark-brown hair was like a flurry of autumn leaves.

Beresford introduced her to Maria, and explained carefully that Maria was Samuel's mother. Samuel said, "'Ere!" and then said, "Sorry," and all four laughed.

"Breakfast before business?" suggested Tony.

"Yes, if you like."

"Fine. And let me tell you, lass, not to worry your head about my goings, comings or stayings. I do those things by habit, and I always get home in the end. What I mean," he added with a quick smile, "is don't worry about me, Valerie. Just at the moment I'm busy, and I hop about all over the place on those rare occasions. Coffee or tea?"

"Coffee, please."

"Share my table, share my tastes," said Tony. "Bacon and toma-toes or grapefruit? First, I mean?"

Valerie rejected grapefruit, which was a thing of habit rather than sustenance, and they commented on many things, not forgetting to praise Maria's cooking. It was a happy meal, the more so because it was unexpected and unorthodox, and Beresford was sorry when Valerie finished her coffee and looked at him squarely. Samuel carried the tray into the kitchen, and the door closed behind him and Maria.

"Well," said Beresford, "I suppose we'd better get down to it, Valerie. What's been worrying you?"

Valerie Lester said, "This," and handed a folded sheet of notepaper across the table. She had kept it in the pocket of her tailor-made, Beresford noticed, and not in her bag. He unfolded the note, prepared, he thought, for anything. But he was not prepared for what he read.

I have reason to believe [the note said] *that you are financially embarrassed. If you will call on the writer to-morrow morning at eleven-thirty o'clock, it is possible that your problems can be partially solved.*

Yours, etc.,
Leopold Gorman.

Beresford read the note twice, automatically registering the fact that the notepaper was of finest texture, and the thick writing sloped backward twenty degrees from vertical. But the message itself left him in a state of near coma. It was a veritable bolt from the blue, in more ways than one, and it made him swallow hard as he looked at the girl.

"When did you get this?" he demanded.

"Yesterday morning," said Valerie Lester.

"And you kept the appointment?"

The girl nodded, and smiled.

"I—I couldn't resist it. It was so extraordinary."

"I'll say it was!" muttered Beresford.

"And coming from a man like Gorman," said Valerie, colouring a little, "I couldn't keep away. Besides, you and Diane had been talking about him——"

"So we had," said Beresford, smiling. "So that was why you went, was it? Because Diane and I had discussed the glares and the glowers at the Two-Step. Thank you, Valerie."

"That was the real reason," admitted the girl. "I—I suppose I ought to say that there's no truth in the——"

"Financial embarrassment," grinned Beresford.

"I'm not rich," said Valerie Lester, "and I lost a lot of money a year ago, when Wall Street went upside-down. But I've enough money to keep me going nicely, and my father isn't a poor man."

"Call that part read," said Beresford, his eyes glinting. "What happened? Did you see Gorman himself?"

"Yes."

"What was his game?"

Valerie Lester took a deep breath, and her eyes showed a mingled uncertainty, amusement and, Beresford thought darkly, a hint of fear.

"Putting it bluntly," she said, "he asked me to keep you from leaving England during the next ten days, and he offered to pay me a hundred pounds a day while I was doing it!"

Beresford stared at her as if she had asked him to marry her! For a few moments silence reigned over the table, while Valerie Lester wondered why the effect of her words had been so devastating. At last:

"Well, well, *well*," gasped Beresford, "that's the coolest piece of work since Noah! What in Hades did you say?"

"I—I didn't say one thing or the other. He didn't approach the subject as bluntly as that, of course. He—he said that he had reason to believe that——"

Valerie broke off, and a red flush mantled her cheeks.

"That you could tie me down," Beresford chuckled. "And then what?"

"And he said that you threatened to interfere with a matter which he wanted to handle in his own way, and that it would be worth my while to—to try it."

Beresford looked at the note again, as though trying to read the secrets of Leopold Gorman's brain in that thick, sloping hand-writing. The thing was absurd. The obvious thing for Valerie Lester to do, unless she was in desperate need of money, was to tell Beresford, just as she had done. And the big man could not bring himself to believe that Leopold Gorman, who was clever if nothing else, would have taken so grave a risk in providing the one thing that Department Z wanted—direct proof that he was behind the attacks on the big man in Auveley Street.

It just didn't, Beresford told himself, ring true. It had happened, of course; he would as soon have doubted the sincerity of Gordon Craigie as the honesty of Valerie Lester. But the motive was not what it seemed to be. Leopold Gorman had written that note to the girl for a very different purpose than he had professed when she had called on him. Damn it, thought Beresford, he'd need no telling when he saw the girl that she wouldn't rise to his bait.

"Well," asked Valerie in a very low voice, "what do you make of it, Tony?"

Beresford grinned.

"I think Gorman's going batchy," he said cheerfully. "He ought to know that you wouldn't take the job——"

"How could he?"

"He's a judge of men," said Beresford, looking at her straightly, "and he's a judge of women. He wouldn't have got where he is if he wasn't. So—it stands to reason."

The girl from America smiled—a slow, grateful, appreciative smile, but Beresford thought there was a shadow in her eyes.

"You have a wonderful way of presenting your compliments," she said.

"It's all a matter of inspiration," said Tony genially, but there was an underlying note of sincerity in his voice. "And it's the source of the inspiration that should take the kudos, my lass. I'm very glad you came to England, Valerie."

The girl's eyes gleamed.

"So am I," she said frankly.

"And one day, in the not too distant future," went on the big man, "I'm going to tell you why, and not leave you to guess. But for the moment——"

"You're busy?"

Was her expression humorous, or quizzical, was it understanding, or was it regret that he should let that moment slide? Beresford didn't know. He told himself that it was a mixture of all four, and he told himself too that she was very, very lovely. But there were things to do.

He hardened his voice perceptibly, and his smile was less in his eyes than usual.

"I'm busy," he agreed. "Mr. Leopold Gorman and I are having a difference of opinion, as he told you, and I've got a lot to do to stop him from having his way."

"I didn't know you dabbled in finance," said the girl.

"That's because you know nothing about me," said Tony, puffing out his chest with mock complacence. "I dabble in all things——"

"Tony!" Valerie leaned across the table, and her slim white hand rested against the brown of Beresford's skin. Her eyes were wide open, and in them was an appeal which he could not fail to read, and her lips were quivering as her voice came slowly: "Tony —don't fool. Gorman told me enough to make me fear that something would happen to you, if—if you went abroad."

The humour, the facetiousness, dropped from Beresford's face, and his body went rigid.

"The devil he did! He frightened you, or tried to, to try and keep me in England. Is that it?"

His voice was rough, harsh almost. His eyes were like unwinking orbs of steel. Just for a moment Valerie Lester saw the Beresford which existed beneath his mask of tolerant good-humour, of genial foolishness. And she was amazed.

"I—I think that was it," she said.

Beresford drummed his fingers on the table.

"I see. That explains why he tackled you, anyhow. And one of these days, my Valerie, I'll wring that lopsided brute's neck to teach him not to drag women into this game." He laughed suddenly, abruptly. "And now we're having a spot of heroics, lass. Will you do something for me?"

"I'll try."

"Forget that you ever went to Gorman. Forget what he told you, and what he hinted. Remember that nothing in the world can stop me from fighting Gorman——"

"But why?" There was anxiety in Valerie's voice.

"I can't tell you." Beresford spoke almost roughly. "It'd be too dangerous for you to know, anyhow. Just forget it."

"I might," said Valerie Lester, quietly but firmly, "just as well try to forget that this is London, not New York. And I think I should know——"

"The devil you do!"

"Yes." The girl's chin went up, and her eyes flashed. "You say it's too dangerous to talk about. Well, I'm in it now. Gorman forced me into it. It's as dangerous for me now as it will ever be. For instance"—she paused for a moment, and drew a deep breath —"I was followed from Regent's Park. I was followed all yesterday afternoon, when I went shopping. I shall be watched all the time— and if I don't try to keep you in England, I shall be in as much danger as you."

Beresford felt cold. He heard her quiet voice, filled with emphasis of tone rather than words, and he knew that there was a great deal of truth in what she said. And he realized the cunning with which Leopold Gorman had made this mood. The financier had reckoned on using the woman to hamper the man, that age-old trick which rarely failed. To himself, Beresford swore, and Valerie Lester saw the moving of his lips and guessed at what was going on behind those hard grey eyes.

"Isn't that right?" she demanded suddenly.

Beresford drew a deep breath.

"H'm. I suppose it is, up to a point. But it doesn't alter facts, Valerie. I can't talk. I can tell you that Gorman's playing a big game and a dangerous one. I can tell you that there's death behind it and death in front of it, and that anything might happen before it finishes. And," the big man added, putting his hand over hers, "I can ask you to do one thing, Valerie."

"And that is?" Her voice was steady, only her eyes showed fear.

"Get back to America," said Beresford. "You're not safe here now. You won't be safe until the job's finished, and I haven't time to look after you as I'd like. Will you go?"

She drew a deep breath, and Beresford grunted to himself when he saw a smile lurking in her eyes.

"No," she said quietly, "I won't go back. Gorman thought that I might be able to—to influence you, and he thought that I was—interested—in you. And, Tony, *I am.* I want to see it through, now I've started."

Beresford stared at her for a moment, uncomprehending. Slowly:

"You really feel like that?"

"Yes—really."

Beresford stood up and went round the table, and gripped her slender shoulders with his great hands. He smiled, chuckled, and in his eyes Valerie Lester saw what she wanted to see.

"All right," said Tony Beresford. "I'll give in. I ought to send you back to America, but I don't think I can, after that. Valerie..."

"Tony?"

"You know what I'm thinking, don't you?"

"I've a pretty good idea."

"Do you mind if we keep it like that, for a while? No words. Just in our minds. Because I've a big job on, Valerie, and I don't think I can tackle two at once—and I can't drop the Gorman one."

"I'd hate it if you wanted to," said Valerie Lester.

Beresford realized that the girl was a weak link in his armour against Gorman, for men do mad things when a woman is the prize. On the other hand, she was level-headed, not likely to take fright easily, and if an emergency did present itself, she would probably handle it well. For the sake of safety, however, he telephoned Superintendent Horace Miller before Valerie left the flat, and arranged with the detective to keep the girl under watch. Valerie grimaced at the precaution, but did not protest.

"Stick to the ordinary rules," Beresford cautioned her. "Don't go anywhere on the strength of letters, wires or telephone calls, and keep in the crowd as often as you can. I think," he added thoughtfully, "that you'd better tell Aubrey that there's a spot of bother in the offing. He had a similar spot of it with Devenish last year.* Aubrey doesn't look much," he said, with a grin, "but he's sound."

"What are you going to do?" asked Valerie, drawing on her gloves.

"I don't know. I'll let you know if I'm going out of England at all, and, other things permitting, I'll hop round to the mausoleum some time to-night. Unless you're booked up?"

"I'll be there," said Valerie.

Beresford sat back in his chair and looked hard at the unproductive ceiling for ten minutes after the girl had gone. It was an unexpected complication, but, looking back to the previous Monday, Beresford could see, now, that it had been coming. The thought of Valerie Lester's glowing eyes, the slimness of her lovely figure, made his lips curve. He felt a deep sense of satisfaction, a gladness different from anything which he had ever experienced before. But it was tempered, as it must be tempered, by the Gorman aspect. He mustn't let up on the Gorman job. He must think as little as possible about anything else. Afterwards . . .

The *Echo de Paris*, London edition, mentioned the murder at the Hôtel Royale, and Beresford saw that Piquet had given a story out to the Press—the French police are better able to control the mouthpieces of public opinion than the English—which made it appear that the brutal murder was a sequel to the dancer's love affairs. For Timothy Arran's sake the big man wished that that had not been necessary, but it was unavoidable. There was no mention in the paper of the discovery of Robert Lavering. Picot and Piquet between them were doing well.

Beresford folded the paper and put it in his pocket before collecting the Hispano and going to Whitehall.

Craigie was waiting for him, and heard the new development without comment until Beresford had finished. Then:

"Gorman must have guessed that she would come to you," he said. "The bribe wasn't big enough."

"It wouldn't have been big enough if it stretched into six figures," grunted Beresford.

Craigie looked at his Number Two thoughtfully.

"Like that, is it? Well, you're probably right. But I think we ought to look up Miss Lester's financial position, Tony. I'll get Miller to find out. Gorman must have had something in his mind before he wrote that letter. Where is the letter, by the way?"

Beresford passed the note across the Chief's desk.

Craigie looked at it for a moment and Beresford saw the frown puckering his forehead. Craigie grunted, and pulled open a drawer in his desk, taking from it a file of papers which Beresford knew covered the whole of the Gorman affair. For a moment the big man failed to understand; but he realized what Craigie was doing suddenly, and his mouth went dry.

"Well?" he snapped, as Craigie looked up from the papers which he had been comparing.

The Chief of Department Z looked worried.

"Sorry, Tony," he said. "But this writing isn't Gorman's. It would pass a quick glance, but not a close inspection. Look for yourself."

Beresford rounded the table and stared down at the note which he had taken from Valerie Lester, and at a second note which Craigie had secured for his file. The thick, slanting writing was certainly similar, but it was not the same.

"She told you that after getting this she saw Gorman, didn't she?"

"Yes," grunted Beresford.

"And she knew what Gorman was to look like—she saw him at the Two-Step the other night."

Beresford grunted, and stared at Craigie's hands without seeing them.

"Well," said the Chief, "she took you in, Tony. If she hadn't known Gorman to look at, she might have been duped herself. *We* know Gorman didn't sign this letter; yet *she* says she went to see him about it; that he discussed it with her."

"Meaning," said Beresford in a dead voice, "that she was lying?"

Craigie shrugged his shoulders.

"I'm afraid so," he said.

CHAPTER ELEVEN

VALERIE LESTER PAYS A VISIT

VALERIE LESTER did not go direct from Beresford's flat to the Chesters' Regent's Park house, called by others as well as Beresford the mausoleum, because of its vastness, the age of its servants and the longevity of its traditions and the Dowager Lady Chester, Lord Aubrey's mother. Aubrey and his wife inhabited a small corner of the great house, which corner was as bright and lively as a charade after the thick drama of the entrance hall and the dining-room through which it was necessary to pass when visiting the Chesters; but Valerie had no wish, then, to see either of them.

She walked quickly towards Bond Street, knowing full well that a detective was trailing her, and deliberating on her best move to shake him off. As she walked, she saw a mental picture of Tony Beresford, and twice she bit her lips as she imagined his reactions if he learned that she had deliberately tricked him.

But, she told herself, he didn't know. It might be possible to get herself out of the tangle of complications in which she was caught before he discovered it.

After ten minutes, she had picked out her trailer, a weedy-looking individual who kept within twenty yards of her as she walked along Bond Street, stopping when she stopped to look in a window, starting in pursuit as soon as she moved. Despite the disadvantage of knowing London only a little, she doubled on her man at the roundabout beneath Eros, and reached the Haymarket subway when the weedy one was breaking his neck to reach the stairs leading to the London Pavilion. She saw the detective hesitate and look about him quickly, and chuckled to herself as he hurried down Shaftesbury Avenue on a false trail.

Taxis were two-a-penny at that hour of the morning, and she hailed one, directing the driver to 15, Cheyne Gardens, Chelsea.

"Do you know them?" she asked.

"Do I know the shape of me nose?" demanded the cabby. "I'll 'ave yer there in no time, miss. 'Op in."

Number 15, Cheyne Gardens, Chelsea, was a large terrace house near the Embankment, one of the many which were split up into a dozen or more flats for those with enough money to live in comfort as well as at an 'address'. Quickly—but not until she had paid and tipped the cabby and seen him drive off—she turned into the house and made with the assurance of familiarity for a flat on the third floor. She knocked twice on the gargoyle-shaped iron knocker, and rang the electric bell three times—short, sharp rings.

There was a shuffle of feet on the other side of the door, which was opened suddenly, after Valerie had heard the click of a released lock. An old woman peered short-sightedly round the door, grunting as she saw the visitor.

"Oh, it's ye back agen, is it? Well, he's out."

"I'll wait for him," said the younger woman, stepping across the threshold.

The other made way reluctantly. At second sight she was more middle-aged than old, but prematurely white hair and a thin, lined face created the latter impression, and only the careful observer would have noticed that her hands were full-fleshed, with none of the blue veins of age, that the whites of her eyes were clear and bold, and that she carried herself upright and with a vigour which few people over fifty could have shown. Her dress was nondescript. A loose-fitting brown frock was tied at the waist with a black leather belt, her brown lisle stockings wrinkled at the ankles, showing what Beresford would have called poor and insufficient suspension, and her flat-heeled button-and-strap shoes were unfastened. Her near-white hair was drawn severely back from her forehead to meet at the nape of the neck in an old-fashioned bun.

"What time do you expect him back?" demanded Valerie.

"The same time as usual—when he comes." The elder woman's voice was sharp, and her lips twitched in bad humour. Valerie Lester told herself that she was looking at a discontented, prematurely aged woman who could not prevent her quarrel with fate from revealing itself in ordinary conversation.

But she knew that the woman was on the right side of forty, that there were times when she could laugh and joke with the best, when her hair was brown, not white, and when the wrinkles on her face were non-existent. She knew that the woman was rehearsing a part which she was to play within the next few days, and that even in her flat, talking with someone who knew her as she was, she maintained that discontented air, the high-pitched, complaining voice, so that when the time came for her to be tested out she would not be found wanting. Valerie dropped wearily into an armchair by the fireplace of the first room which she entered, and watched the other woman walk across the room into the kitchen quarters. Looking round the apartment, the American told herself that it looked what it was supposed to be— the home of a middle-aged bachelor who was rich enough to afford a housekeeper, but well satisfied with the furniture which had lasted him for fifteen or twenty years. Nothing was new in the room, not even the pictures. The only sign of the nineteen-thirties was a wireless set in one corner, an up-to-date and expensive product. For the rest, there was an old oak sideboard, a dining-table of the gate-leg variety, four stiff-backed chairs, two easies, and a large oil-painting set in gilt framework on each wall.

And yet, Valerie Lester knew, it was a room of secrets.

She closed her eyes, wondering how long the man whom she had come to visit would keep her waiting.

It was twelve o'clock when he arrived, and he looked exactly what would have been expected for the owner of that room. A man of rather less than medium height, his hair was greying at the sides and temples, he affected a close-trimmed moustache, nearer white than grey, and his complexion was red, almost florid. He was not fat, but he looked sleek and well-filled. His eyes were light blue in colour, and he blinked rather more than seemed necessary in the poor light of the room, the windows of which were hung with heavy red plush curtains.

His voice was the one thing about him which did not fit in with the room. If Beresford had heard it he would have wrinkled his nose in surprise. For the man's voice was pitched on a high key, and it was a hundred per cent. American!—tough American!

" 'Lo, you," he said. "Yo' back early. Did you see de big fella?"

"Sure I saw him." Valerie Lester's voice would have surprised Beresford too. It was more twangy than that to which he had grown accustomed, and she slurred the vowels more in accordance with New York's West Side than its East.

"Did he bite it?" demanded the man, whose namer as it was known to the postal authorities, was Josiah Long.

"I—I think so."

"Think?" Long blinked quickly, like a nervous man asking for more money from his boss. "We can't think in dis game, sister, we gotta know. Did he bite?"

Valerie Lester drew a deep breath.

"Yes, he bit all right."

"Fine!" Mr. Josiah Long dropped into a chair and lit a Camel cigarette. "Did yuh catch anything?"

"No—only that he's fighting Gorman."

"Sho' thing he's fighting Gorman. I knew dat de day we started dis game, sister. Anything else?"

"Not yet. I didn't ask questions."

Long sprayed grey smoke about the room.

"Better not run him too fast at first," he acknowledged. "But I wanna know all 'bout Big Beresford," Long went on. "When's yo' next date?"

"To-night."

"Lay it on thick and heavy," said Long. "What's he like? Clever?"

"I should think," said Valerie Lester, "that he's very clever. And he's careful. He had a detective put on my trail to make sure that Gorman didn't try to rush me."

Long looked down his nose.

"A dick, eh? Did you shake him off?"

"Yes, at Piccadilly."

Long blinked at her, still with that false impression of nervousness.

"Say, sister, yuh don't seem so keen on dis job as you was on de udder side. What's tickling you?"

The girl stood up suddenly and walked to the window. For a moment she stood there with her back to Josiah Long, and stared out across the sluggishly moving Thames. Long looked at her, but did not move, and he said nothing. She turned round at last, and eyed him frankly.

"No," she said, and her voice was now the voice that Tony Beresford knew, "I don't like the job so much. I wish I hadn't tackled it. There's something about Beresford which—well, there is."

Mr. Josiah Long stared at the girl for a full minute. And when he spoke he echoed, unconsciously, Gordon Craigie's words to Tony Beresford of a few hours before.

"Like that, is it? Well, maybe you're right. But we can't let up now. Beresford's our man, sister. I don't know who he is, but I've a mighty close idea that he's in the Service, and if he is, and he's working against Gorman, he'll be the best man to give us our meat. Pecker up, kid. De woild ain't all black crape, not by a long way. Keep me in touch, and if Beresford's got any idea o' yo' getting at him, skedaddle like a Christmas turkey!"

CHAPTER TWELVE

NOSEY DEAN—DECEASED

THE bullet which had killed the genuine Nicholas Williams was a .32 Webley—an unusual size and pattern—and it had been fired from a revolver whose bore, the experts told Horace Miller at Scotland Yard, had scratched the bullet slightly, and would scratch any other bullet fired from it. There was only one other clue as to the identity of the murderer—a fingerprint on Williams' toe-cap. The print was a good one, although all the others on the shoes had been blurred and unprintable, made when the killer had dragged the scholar into the empty house—or had shifted the body.

The bullet gave Miller little assistance, but the print gave an entirely unexpected result. Its double was found beneath the photograph of a stool-pigeon and small crook named Nosey Dean. Nosey, a rat-faced, undersized individual, was well known as a betrayer of secrets, and he was the last man in the world whom Miller would have suspected of complicity in a murder, unless it was a gang-killing, when Nosey would probably have turned King's Evidence.

Then Miller found Nosey Dean.

Nosey Dean's body was picked out of the Thames at Woolwich. He had been shot through the heart by a bullet from the same revolver as had been used in killing Williams!

"He'd got it coming to him," the Super said when he heard the news. "Find out where he's been seen in the past week, whether he's been flinging money about lately, and if he's shown any big money, get hold of the notes."

He was in his small office at Scotland Yard when he gave these instructions to an assistant-inspector by the name of Rogerson, and Rogerson, who scented big stuff behind these two killings, told himself that he had his chance at last. Miller, worried more than usual, telephoned Craigie; but Craigie for once was out. Miller then tried Beresford, who was in his flat, and the big man visited Scotland Yard.

This was on the afternoon of Valerie Lester's breakfast visit, and Beresford was in no very good humour. He realized, however, that the Nosey Dean element was unusual and might, because Nosey was well known amongst the smaller fry of the criminal classes—provide a line of inquiry.

Rogerson, the Assistant-Inspector, got to work so quickly that before Beresford had left the Yard the telephone burred out in Miller's office, with a call from him.

Miller grunted, and told Rogerson to keep where he was. The red-faced Super's blue eyes were bright as he turned away from the instrument.

"Rogerson's found a woman in Wapping who was with Nosey Dean the night before last. Will you come over with me?"

"Women again," grunted Beresford. "Yes, old son. I'd like to."

The two men travelled in the maroon Hispano to the house in Wapping—Number 79, Frisk Street. The big car excited comment and not a little ribaldry; and Beresford, who had more than a sneaking liking for the born-and-bred Londoner, whatever his morals, was in a much better temper when he reached the place than he had been when he had called on Miller.

Leaving the roadster in Frisk Street, they entered Number 79, which, Beresford said with truth, stank. It was one of the filthiest places that he had ever entered, and he felt sorry for Assistant-Inspector Rogerson, who had been forced to stay there for over an hour. As he walked through the narrow passage, brushing against wallpaper which hung in ribbons from the wall, he saw into the front room, which was furnished with one long bench table and narrow wooden forms.

"A doss-house," Beresford muttered, "and one of the worst."

"You don't know this part of the world as well as you think you do," said Miller dryly. "Ah—here's Rogerson."

The lean-flanked Assistant lost no time in talking. He nodded perfunctorily to Beresford, whom he had not met before, and addressed his superior.

"She's in the back kitchen, sir—throwing a faint. I've got a couple of men in with her."

"Is she known at all?"

"She's new here, sir, but this place has been under observation for some time."

"For hygienic or moral reasons?" asked Beresford, grimacing at the stench from the kitchen as they neared it.

Rogerson shot the big man a suspicious glance. He had no sense of humour, Beresford discovered, but he was a go-ahead graduate from the College.

"Both, Mr. Beresford."

"What's her name?" demanded Miller.

"Higson," said Rogerson. "I don't know her other name."

Beresford snorted at this, but Rogerson was too eager to show his prize catch to notice the snort.

The woman, who was recovering from her faint, was a slattern who looked near the seventy mark. She stared aggrievedly at the three policemen, as though complaining that the world was against her. Lines of discontent ran from her lips almost to her eyes. Her hair was white, and her eyes screwed up to narrow, suspicious slits. Beresford noticed that her vigour, for a woman of her age, was exceptional, and her voice, although mournful, was strong.

"I ain't done nothin' to be ashamed of, mister," she moaned as Miller entered the room. "I'm a n'ard-workin' wumman, an' hit's a crime ter——"

"Did you know Dean well?" Miller asked quietly, motioning the two plain-clothes men out of the kitchen: four was a crowd.

"I don't know no one well," grumbled the slattern; "I 'ad a bit o' luck with the gees, Inspector, an' I bought this plice. I only bin in it a coupla' days——"

"And you didn't know Dean before that?" asked Beresford.

"No, I never!"

"You naughty girl," said the big man waggishly.

The slattern turned on him, quivering with sudden rage.

"Oo the 'ell are you forking to, you big lump? I 'as rooms 'ere to let orf an' I 'as a lot o' beds. Keep yer ruddy marf shut——"

Beresford chuckled, but took the hint and said nothing. It occurred to him, however, that Rogerson's original "a woman who was with Nosey Dean the night before last" seemed—and he afterwards learned was—an exaggeration.

"Dean slept here the night before last, did he?" Miller asked.

"I dunno 'is nime," said the woman, with a scowl, "but yer boy friend showed me a photer——"

Rogerson stepped forward, like a well-trained adjutant, and Miller looked at the photograph of Nosey Dean. It was a good likeness. Beresford, who had known the stool-pigeon slightly, recognized the long nose flattened against the left cheek, the sloping forehead and the weak chin.

"And you're sure he was here?" demanded Miller.

"I wouldn't sye so if I wasn't."

"And the night before?"

"Yus."

"That was the first time you took the house over, was it?"

"Yus." The answer came grudgingly.

"Was he a regular boarder?"

"I—I fink so."

"Don't you keep a register?" snapped Miller.

"Yus," snapped the slattern, "but I ain't 'ad no noo 'uns since I came 'ere."

"Humph," grunted Miller.

He was thinking, and Beresford could almost see the process of his thoughts, that there wasn't a great deal to learn from the doss-house keeper. Nevertheless, Nosey Dean had definitely been at the house since the murder of Williams three days before. Question after question would have to be hurled at the slut whose 'luck with the gees' had enabled her to buy the doss-house; Beresford himself wanted something more substantial than a knowledge of what Nosey Dean looked and acted like the night of the murder in which, it seemed, he had been implicated.

He turned away, and as he moved the woman brushed her hand across her forehead. For a moment her sleeve, which had been dropping over her hand, was pushed back. He saw the firmness of the flesh. Something inside him seemed to crack a warning. Without batting an eye, he said:

"I'm going to get a breath of air, Miller. You'll come out as soon as you've finished?"

Miller grunted, and told himself that Beresford wasn't being so thorough on this job as he had been on others. For the next twenty minutes Miller and Rogerson turned the woman, mentally, inside out. When at last Miller came out of the house, glad to breathe the comparatively clean air of Wapping's Frisk Street, the big man was pretending sleep at the wheel of the Hispano. Miller groused loudly on the subject of over-eating.

"Horace," said Beresford out of the blue, "how old was that woman in there?"

Miller's eyes widened in surprise.

"Sixty—sixty-five, I suppose."

"What's your guess?" Beresford demanded of Rogerson.

"I should say exactly what the Superintendent says," Rogerson answered stiffly.

"Then you're both as blind as bats," said Beresford affably. "Her hair was white and her face lined, but the lines would come out in the wash. Did you notice her hands?"

"The fingers were filthy," said Miller.

"The back of them," said Beresford.

"No-o. Her sleeves hung over them."

"They were the hands of a woman of thirty-five to forty," said Beresford, "and I'll bet you both a night out at the Two-Step that Miss-or-Mrs. Higson knows a darned sight more than she pretends to."

Neither of the policemen spoke for a moment. Rogerson moved suddenly, turning towards the house. Beresford stopped him with a low-voiced:

"Where the blazes are you going, Rogerson?"

The Assistant-Inspector looked offended.

"To look at her hands," he said.

"Don't act like a ruddy goat," snapped Beresford, and Miller chuckled to himself. Rogerson would learn a great deal from Beresford's rough handling—considerably more than the Police College could ever teach him. "Watch her, and watch where she goes. How many men have you got here?"

"Two," said Rogerson frigidly. "They were in the yard at the back of the house."

"Fetch 'em out," said Beresford, "and tell 'em to make sure that woman doesn't go anywhere without being reported."

Rogerson opened his lips, then turned towards his Super.

"Is that your order, sir?"

"Yes," said Miller, his eyes unwinking.

* * *

Three hours later, Tony Beresford picked up the telephone in his flat, and heard the gruff voice of Horace Miller at the other end of the wire.

"The Wapping woman?" demanded Beresford, jerking his thumb at Samuel Tricker, who moved with the deftness of long practice into the kitchen quarters.

"Yes," said Miller. "She went out and telephoned a Chelsea number twenty minutes ago. Rogerson was watching her himself, and when he saw her enter the booth he dived into a shop, borrowed a telephone, and got the Exchange to trace the call from the call-box while it was still engaged."

"A score for Rogerson," chuckled Beresford. "Who was the call to?"

"A Mr. Josiah Long, of Cheyne Gardens. Number fifteen."

"I think," said Beresford, "that I'll go there, son. All right with you?"

"Yes," said Miller, who did not add that he had received instructions from his Commissioner to give Craigie and Beresford every facility, even though they appeared to usurp some of the duties of the regular police.

"Fine," said Tony Beresford. "Listen ..."

He made a selection from his 'gathering of friends' when he had finished talking, told Tricker that if anyone called he would not be back for some time, and walked quickly to his garage. This time he left the Hispano standing in its glory, and borrowed a Lancia belonging to a certain Dodo Trale, who at that moment was entertaining Adele Fayne. The Hispano would have been easily recognized.

Twenty minutes later he was knocking on the door of Josiah Long's flat at 15, Cheyne Gardens, Chelsea. He wondered, as he fingered the cold steel of the automatic in his pocket, what kind of greeting he would get, and what manner of man Josiah Long would be.

And then the door opened, and Tony Beresford started back

into the hall, completely knocked off his mental equilibrium by the sight of Valerie Lester, dressed just as she had been when she had left his flat that morning!

"Well, well, *well*!" drawled Beresford at last. "If this doesn't beat cock-fighting, whether I've seen it or not. You look surprised, my Valerie!"

Valerie Lester stood like a stone image in the doorway. Her eyes were wide open, her lips parted a little to show her glistening teeth, and she was breathing heavily, as dumbfounded as Beresford had been but lacking his power of recovery.

"No welcome?" asked Beresford, after a pause.

A nasal voice from inside the room answered him.

"Sho' yo' welcome. Beresford, ain't it? I thought I reckernized the voice. Come right in, buddy!"

Beresford went in, to meet Mr. Josiah Long—alias Ruddy Face, alias the policeman, alias Nicholas Williams! Those weak, nervous blue eyes had hovered in front of Beresford's mental vision too often for any mistake.

He stepped into the room, but his right hand was in his pocket, round the handle of his gun. At that moment he had nothing but distrust for Mr. Josiah Long.

CHAPTER THIRTEEN

MR. JOSIAH LONG EXPLAINS

T HE American, as befitting his guise of a real old English pillar of the middle classes, was standing in front of the fireplace in that Victorian-furnished room, his hands behind his back, his stomach gently protruding, his greying hair and fresh-complexioned face typifying the part he was playing. Even his blue eyes were part of it; only his voice, harsh and twangy, revealed him for what he was.

Beresford was more than surprised; he was dumb-founded. The appearance of Valerie Lester in that room, where he had expected to find things which would explain the murder of Nosey Dean and Nicholas Williams, kicked him harder even than he admitted to himself. Since he had seen Craigie and had been convinced that the girl from America was playing a part in the affair very different from what Beresford had imagined, he had spent his spare moments in trying to convince himself that she was being forced into her part, that the deception which she had practised had been made under strong compulsion. Yet her appearance in the doorway seemed to knock his carefully built defence of her into thousands of small pieces. Mentally on edge, it needed little to send him into a frame of mind which would make him believe that she was, deliberately and without compulsion, playing against him.

Never before in his life had the big man felt so tempted to express his opinions in words both uncomplimentary and biting. But the sight of the mild-looking Mr. Long, the upward curve of the man's rather full lips, and the attitude of complete self-confidence, made Beresford bite on his words, helped him to grin, and incidentally helped him to regain his mental balance.

The American looked the big man up and down, and his weak eyes addressed themselves, finally, to Beresford's right hand, which was still in his pocket.

"Dat's de style," he said cheerfully. "Alius keep yo' gun handy—yuh never knows when yuh might need it. But yuh don't need it now, buddy. Let's all be friendly."

Beresford grinned, but kept his hands in his pocket.

"You know what to look for, in your home town," he said.

"Why, sho' we do," said Josiah Long, and for the life of him Beresford could not imagine the mild-mannered little man working hand in hand with Leopold Gorman. "But how'd yuh find us, Beresford. I thought we'd covered ourselves dandy."

Beresford shrugged his shoulders.

"There is a doss-house," he said, "and there was a Nosey Dean, and there is a woman called Higson—she said."

Josiah Long's eyes widened.

"Dat's how you got us, eh? Sit down, buddy, sit down. She didn't talk, did she?"

"Of many things and bitter," said Beresford, who for some reason felt in lyrical mood. "Sit down yourself, Mr. Long, and I'll join you. No, she didn't give you away, but her hands did."

"Ah!" Josiah Long looked relieved. "I thought I could trust her. Who spotted her hands? You?"

"Near enough."

"I was told yuh were smart," said Long, dropping into a chair, "and it looks like I was told right. But how'd yuh find dis place?"

"A telephone-call and a bright policeman," said Beresford.

"They sho' got some brains in dis country," said Mr. Long admiringly. "What'll you drink, buddy?"

A gentle smile hovered on Beresford's lips.

"Some other time, when I know you better," he said mildly.

Long eyed him reproachfully.

"Dat means yuh don't trust me?"

"Not by a long, long way I don't," said Beresford, unconscious of the pun. "Is there anything else you'd like to ask before I start, *Mister* Long?"

"Plenty. But maybe there isn't time, so shoot."

Beresford lit a cigarette, after offering one to Josiah Long, who said he preferred his Camel.

"Well," he said gently, "first—there are six good and hearty cops within call, and I've allowed myself an hour for this visit before they start inquiries."

"O.K. wid me," said the American.

"Second," said Beresford, eyeing the man steadily, "those same cops will be only too willing to arrest a man with weak blue eyes —like yours—on a charge of murder in the first degree. Do you follow, Mr. Long?"

Josiah Long blinked.

"Well, now, dat's jus' too bad," he said. "I'd ha' given a lot to be held on a moider charge, Big Boy, but I jus' ain't got de time. Who's been bumped off, did yuh say?"

"One Williams and one Dean."

"Ah!" Long surveyed the lighted end of his cigarette thought-fully. He leaned forward suddenly. "Say, listen! Yuh an' me oughta woik togedda. What say you spill your story an' I spill mine an' we match up?"

Beresford grinned. And for the first time he trusted himself to look round the room to Valerie Lester, who was sitting on a stiff-backed chair watching and listening, and looking, despite the shock from which she was recovering, very lovely. Beresford was not, normally, a man who took things or people on their face value; but he had an inward conviction that before he left the flat he would understand many things which had previously mystified him, and that with them he would be able to retain his earlier faith in Valerie Lester. So:

"I don't know much about your friend," he assured Valerie lightly, "but he's got a nerve."

In the big man's eyes there was a smile which seemed to challenge Valerie Lester's worry, and disperse it. She laughed lightly, and felt hot round the eyes.

"Wait till you know him better," she said.

"Dat's what I call a pal!" enthused Josiah Long. "I——"

"Wait a minute," said Beresford. "Let's get this straight, *Mister* Long. I want a story from you, and I want it inside an hour. Otherwise my friends the cops——"

Long grimaced.

"Meanin' I gotta talk first?"

"And fast," said Beresford grimly. "You've got a lot to explain."

"What's weighing most on yo' mind?"

"The policeman at Auveley Street," said Beresford, "and your bright show as Nicholas Williams."

Josiah Long drew a deep breath, cocked an eye at Valerie Lester, tossed the stub of his cigarette into the empty fireplace, and leaned back in his chair.

"Listen . . ." he said.

Just twenty minutes later, Tony Beresford pushed his hand through his crisp hair and agreed to join his host in a drink. For he no longer questioned the complicity of Josiah Long in the schemes of Leopold Gorman, but he understood many things which had puzzled him during the past two or three days, including the water-weapon and the radio trick; and he had a shrewd idea as to why Nosey Dean, Nicholas Williams and Corinne the dancer had died.

. . .

. . . . .

Mr. Josiah Long, alias Ruddy Face, alias the policeman, alias (although only after his death) Mr. Nicholas Williams, was, as Beresford needed no telling, a gentleman from America. The voice which he used that evening was as near his own as he could remember, although he told the big man that he used it more for the sake of practice than because it came natural to him. He had aped others so often, and spoken in so many languages, dialects and the argot of a dozen underworlds that he could say with truth that he hardly knew which voice to call his own. He was a man who lived by his wits, but that did not mean that he lived dishonestly. It meant, as Valerie Lester knew, that he gained his livelihood by the same means as Tony Beresford, she suspected, earned his fun.

Josiah Long had experienced more ups and down in his forty-odd years than most people would have experienced in as many decades, if they had lived long enough. He had started life on a Kentucky farm, migrated at the early age of three to Chicago, where his only remaining parent, a small-part actor with consumption, had tried to drink his illness away. Instead, drink had combined with a ruined constitution to make Josiah an orphan what time he was eleven.

Child-acting kept him going until he was fifteen, but he was controlled by an avaricious foster-father who gave him what fiction calls a bad break. Josiah Long had walked out on his foster-father and walked by degrees to Boston. He pecked at journalism, and became a crime-reporter, sandwiching an occasional small part on the stage to help his income.

In 1915, when America had realized that there was a war in Europe likely to last, Josiah had crossed the Big Pond and offered himself to the Foreign Battalion. Unfortunately he was half blind in the left eye, and he was turned down. He joined the staff of the

Echo, for able-bodied men were already scarce in England, and a ready-made reporter was a godsend. When the ban on war correspondents was lifted, Josiah Long was amongst the first to go to France. His despatches earned him fame, but gave him no kick. To imbibe the kick, he. borrowed the uniform of a British non-com., and allowed himself to be interned in Germany. At the prison camp he had learned French and Belgian in a dozen varieties, and had managed to pick up a working knowledge of German.

Things still galled him, and he made a spirited protest as an American subject against his captivity, and was allowed to go to the American colony in Berlin. 1917 saw the coming of America into the War. He squeezed out of Berlin before the declaration, and suggested to the American Embassy in London, where he arrived after a circuitous journey through Holland and Belgium, that he was a perfect and ready-made spy.

He was. Josiah Long was the brightest star in the American espionage system during and after the War. But he tired of risking life and limb for the equivalent of a hundred bucks a week. He cared nothing for either; but he liked luxury, and the Secret Service is one of the worst-paid institutions in the world. Under the name of Lambert Hurst he starred in two Hollywood films, and extra'd in a dozen others. That meant money but boredom. He left the City of Broken Hearts and set up a detective agency in New York to rival Pinkertons.

It did not rival Pinkertons, but it made money, and it led Josiah Long on the biggest gamble of his life. The American Service had a long memory, and, being faced at that time with a problem similar to that which faced Craigie and Department Z, it sent for Josiah Long and offered him big money if he would return to the fold.

"What and where's the job?" Long had asked.

"We don't know where, but England probably. We're losing a lot of big men—money-merchants—and there are several of them gone from the Wheat Pool."

(To an Englishman the Wheat Pool was a name. To an American it was the biggest ring of financiers in North America.)

"What do you mean by 'losing'?" Josiah had demanded.

"Some are going out of the Pool—selling out to a syndicate—and others are being bumped off because they won't sell out."

Josiah Long had grunted, because he had made a practice all his life of saying what he thought.

"Dat ain't an English complex. Dat sounds like someone on our side."

"That's what we thought two years ago, but we haven't traced who's backing the syndicate yet, although we've sent two big shots to the chair for snuffing Wheat Pool members. They'd have talked if they could have done to save their skins, but the only thing they knew was that the money was coming from England to pay them."

"Got anyone in mind?" Long had asked.

And then he had first heard of Leopold Gorman.

"Gorman's the only man capable of it, Long, and we know the English Service is watching him. We want *you* to watch him, and to make sure that he's our man. Because we don't want the Wheat Pool to get out of American control. Will you take the job?"

"Sho' thing I will," Josiah Long had said. "I shall want some helpers—coupla dames and a coupla buddies."

"We'll fix it," he had been assured. "There's one girl in particular—Miss Lester. She's done several jobs for us before, and she's going over to England with the Chester couple. You know them?"

"Sho'," Long had agreed. "Chester's de tennis guy, and his wife useter be at de Emblem Theatre. How's she know them?"

"Cousins," he had been told, and he had whistled.

"Say—is dis de *Valerie* Lester, de goil dat useter hang around wid young Lavering?"

"Yes. She threw him over because he changed his mind so often. When can you start, Long?"

"When are the Chesters and the Lester girl going?"

"On the *Hoveric*, next week—Wednesday."

"O.K.," Josiah Long had assured the august gentlemen of the American Intelligence. "I'll go on de *New Star*, to-morrow. Dat'll give me five days' start of her."

* * *

"An' dat, Beresford," said Josiah Long, getting out of his chair and walking across the room to the sideboard, from which he took a decanter and two glasses, "is how I got to yo' li'l country. Someone was buying big in de U.S.A., and dat someone wasn't stoppin' at bumpin' off when dey thought it was necessary. An' de only line I had was—Leopold Gorman."

The American stopped as he filled two glasses, and carried them across to the hearth, near which Beresford was sitting. Valerie Lester was on a couch by the window. She had said nothing during Long's story, and even now she kept silent.

Beresford looked across the room at her, and smiled. Her answering smile held something which the big man couldn't fathom, but there was a warmth in it which made him turn a shade darker beneath his tan.

"Will yuh drink now?" asked Long, with a grin.

Beresford nodded. It was not so much that he was certain that Long was all he said he was that made him take a chance of drinking doped liquor. It was more the thought of the police who would be calling soon, unless he made an appearance, and the knowledge that Long would not take chances while his flat was, in effect, surrounded. The life of a secret agent was perilous enough at all times, and Long would realize that if he 'got in bad' with the English authorities he would have a lean time.

The American tossed neat whisky down his throat without a gasp, and dropped into his chair again.

"Well, buddy, yuh can take it from me I wasn't jus' goin' to walk up to Mr. Gorman an' take his number. Nope. I had a lot o' papers signed up that I was representing de Mid-American

Timber Corporation. The Mid-American Corp.," Long added, "is the biggest timber shout on the odder side. I went an' saw Gorman, an' told him we wass tryin' to get rid o' a big interest—we wanted money.

"Gorman seemed to bite, and promised to write me. He did. He wrote his name on a point-three-two bullet an' sent it through my hat." The American jumped from his chair again, and fetched a hat from the sideboard cupboard, handing it to Beresford. There were two holes neatly drilled by that .32 on either side of the cady. "Howso, buddy," Long went on, "I taped up on a guy who wass behind dat bullet—a guy called Dean."

"Nosey Dean!" Beresford grunted the words, and his eyes narrowed. Long was getting to the vital part of his story now.

"Sho'—Nosey Dean. Nosey an' me wass great friends. I offered him a hundred dollars fer every word he slipped me about Gorman, and did he earn some dough! Beresford, dat guy musta thought I was Rockefeller hisself. He told me so much about Gorman dat I began to wonder whether Gorman was just anudder name for de devil, but it didn't help me much until he told me that Gorman was going to bump *you* off, buddy—an' goin' to get dat Williams cuss out of de way while he did it. Well, I tried to keep on yo' tail, buddy, but yo' tail ain't so easy to sit on. So I started on Williams."

Beresford grunted. He was beginning to see light—and to realize that Josiah Long's story was probably true.

"De day Williams got dat cable I was after him, an' I followed him to Oxford. He went by coach, an' I went on de same one. I waited outside Trinity while he wass inside, an' I followed him when he walked back for his buggy. Do you know Oxford, big boy?"

"Well enough," grunted Beresford.

"Some o' de streets there are jus' made fer killing. I wass a coupla hunnerd yards behind Williams when he was put out wid a bullet from a passing car, an' I wass looking when Nosey Dean an' anudder guy dragged Williams into deir car an' let her go. Well..." Josiah Long stopped again for refreshment, and Beresford took the opportunity of looking at Valerie Lester, whose cheeks were pale and whose breath was coming quickly. "Well," went on the American, "dat kind o' made me squint. Howso, I hired a bus an' went to yo' place. I broke into Williams' flat, pinched some of his clothes, an' den came back here. Things were goin' ter hum, I reckoned, an' dey wasn't goin' ter be so nice fer yuh. Howso, dat was yo' boid. I wass after Gorman's guys."

"Dressed like a policeman?" interjected Beresford, grimly.

Josiah Long blinked nervously—or so it seemed.

"Sho' thing—like a policeman. I was pretty sure buddy, dat a brace of Gorman's pets went in yo'—I mean Williams'—flat, an' I wanted to be handy. I wass. I missed de porch trick, though—a real cop wass round jus' den—an' I didn't come on de scene until after yo' vallee was knocked over. When yuh wass arter de Arrans ... I knew dey wass friends o' yours," Long added, with a grin, "becos dey had called at yo' flat a bit earlier, an' dey told each odder what dey thought of yuh, seein' yuh were out."

For once in a way Beresford's sense of humour was not at its best, and he made no comment.

"When yuh went arter dem an' yo' Doc Little," Long continued, "I called out so's de guys in Williams' flat could hear me, dat I reckoned dey wass in de flat. Did dey bite on dat, buddy? Dey was out o' de back door before I was halfway up de stairs——"

"Why didn't you stop 'em?" Beresford broke in.

"Why should I? Dey couldn't 'ave told me a thing, an' I was reckoning I'd be able to pay afterwards fer what I wanted to know from Nosey Dean. Howso"—there was a glint of humour in the little American's eyes which made Beresford's lips curve—"I poured dat water over yuh an' skedaddled. Den I came back——"

"As Williams."

"Sho' thing. As Williams. I wanted to see yuh better, Beresford, an' I wanted to size up the cop who'd be on de job. Who was de udder guy?" Long added ingenuously.

"You'll learn," said Beresford, thinking of Craigie's likely reaction to this story.

"Canny, eh? Can't say I blame yuh. Well, buddy, yuh know how dat night ended. I came back to Chelsea, when yuh an' Tricker wass in bed, and fer the next coupla days nuthin' happened——"

"Why the blazes didn't you tackle me in the open, then?" Beresford demanded.

"Why should I?" asked Long blandly. "Would yuh, in de same trousis?"

"No-o," admitted Beresford, thinking of the reluctance with which he had spoken even to Piquet in Paris, although he knew the Frenchman well.

"I'll say yuh wouldn't!" snapped Josiah Long. "No, buddy. I said, 'Watch de big guy,' an' wass going to get Miss Lester woikin' on yuh when yuh went to Paris." The American's lips were straight, but his eyes were laughing. "We sho' put it over each udder on dat liner, buddy. I reckoned yuh'd bite for de wireless, an' dat while I wass getting past de Customs' whiskers I'd be in front of yuh, ready to pick up yo' trail. I didn't," Long added, with a chuckle, "reckon yuh'd send me to Lyons."

Beresford grinned.

"I'm glad I had a bite at that apple, anyhow."

"How'd yuh get away?" asked Long.

"By the exercise of tact and patience," said Beresford, winking at Valerie Lester.

"Sho' yuh did," grunted Long. "Howso—dat's all I know, Beresford, take it or leave it."

"No, it isn't," said Beresford, "not by a long way. What about the Wapping place?"

"Oh, dat bug-house!" The American blinked rapidly. "I reckoned Nosey Dean mighta' stopped sellin', an' I reckoned if I noo where he wass, I could force him kinda."

"Did you know he was dead?" snapped Beresford.

Long blinked still faster, but he was grinning.

"Sho' I did. Wassn't I telephoned before yuh came?"

"And that was the first you knew of it, eh?"

"Absolute," affirmed the American. "How wass he killed?"

"He was found in the river," said Beresford.

"Drowned, eh?" Long lit a Camel thoughtfully. "Well, buddy, I reckon we ain't got much against Gorman yet, unless yuh found somepun in Paris."

"Not a thing," said Beresford, "excepting that Lavering was very nearly finished when I got there."

"Young Lavering?" Long grunted, in genuine surprise. "I never . . . Say, what's de trouble? I . . ."

But Beresford wasn't listening. The big man had jumped to his feet and hurried to Valerie Lester, whose face was as white as wax as she sprawled back on the couch in a dead faint.

"Now why in hell," muttered Josiah Long to himself, "did she throw Lavering up if she still feels like dat about him?"

But he did not pass this thought on to Beresford, who was moistening the girl's lips with whisky from his ever-ready flask. For Beresford was looking at her in a way that few men would ever look at a woman, and Josiah Long told himself that there were more complications near at hand which would not be much help to Beresford's peace of mind.

CHAPTER FOURTEEN

NEWS FROM PARIS

B ERESFORD did not ask questions, probably because he was afraid of the answers. He took the girl to Regent's Park, and Diane Chester upbraided him for dragging Valerie into a bad business.

"Not guilty," said Beresford; but his grin was not genuine. "I wish I was."

Diane, who knew of many things, said nothing, but promised to keep Valerie in the house until Beresford called again. The big man hurried away, pleased if not surprised to find Josiah Long still in the Lancia; he had left the American in the car while he arranged with Diane to be cautious and discreet with Valerie Lester.

"Think I'd taken a jump?" grinned Long, as Beresford slipped in the clutch.

"You'd be a fool if you tried it," grunted Beresford. "We were followed from Chelsea, my son, and you'll be followed anywhere you go, until we've passed you O.K."

"Who's 'we'?" asked Long.

"The other 'guy' you met when you were Williams," Beresford answered.

"De hatchet-faced one?" asked Long.

Beresford grunted again. That was a sound description of Gordon Craigie.

"Where are we going?" Long asked, as the Lancia turned into the Marylebone Road.

"My flat," said Beresford. "Our man will come and see us."

The American made no comment, and the short drive was completed in silence. Both men had plenty to think about, and Beresford himself was racking his brains for a way of tying the murders on to Leopold Gorman. Once they could get their hands on that elusive financier, they could move in other directions. But for the moment Gorman held the strings. He was making the pace, and making it a hot one. Williams, Nosey Dean, Corinne the dancer, were all dead; Bob Lavering, for some reason which the big man could not fathom, had been kept alive.

Beresford grew more certain in his mind as he swung the car into Auveley Street that the secret of the affair could be connected with Lavering without leading far from the truth. Gorman, while buying hard, wanted something from the young American, which would complete his plans. What it was Beresford could not even guess, but he told himself that unless something transpired quickly, he could fly over to Paris again to see if Lavering was recovering, and whether he could talk.

And with Bob Lavering, the fiancé of Adele Fayne, the dancer, Beresford was forced, like it or not, to connect Valerie Lester. What part was the Chesters' cousin actually playing in the affair? How much did she know? And why had she fainted when he had mentioned that Lavering had been at death's door?

The big man's train of thought was broken as he brought the car opposite Number 7. He braked and stopped the engine automatically, then stood up.

A split second later he heard Josiah Long bellow a warning, felt the American punch the back of his knees. His legs bent double and he dropped down, banging his elbows on the dashboard, cursing under his breath.

But he stopped cursing suddenly. A foot above his eyes he saw the windscreen of the Lancia riddled with holes! Bullets smashed through it, splitting the safety-glass without splintering it, and above the clatter he heard the grim rat-tat-tat of machine-gun fire!

Next to him, Josiah Long was crouching down in his seat, the lids of his weak eyes moving rapidly up and down, his rather full lips pressed tightly together. He was looking, not at the bullet-holes, but at the closed Daimler car which hummed along Auveley Street, spraying death as it went.

Above the hum of the Daimler's engine, the whir of its wheels, and the wicked rat-tat-tat of the gun, came the agonized screams of two women and a man who had been walking along Auveley Street and unwittingly towards death.

* * *

"What made you guess what was coming?" asked Beresford.

Josiah Long, leaning back in one of the big man's armchairs and smoking his inevitable Camel—which, for the sake of the uninitiated, is an American cigarette equivalent to "Player's Please", but seeming, to the English taste, as pungent as black twist—swallowed an appreciable portion of a bottle of Shortt's XX before he answered.

"If you'd been in Chicago as long as I had," he said, "you'd know that a closed car with drawn curtains was a thing to dodge. And we're neither of us popular, just at the moment."

"No-o." Beresford eyed the smaller man thoughtfully but thankfully. It occurred to him as strange that Long should have lapsed, for a moment, into pure English, instead of maltreated American, but at that moment he was too grateful for that warning to force the point. Long might be—he *was*—a funny cuss. But Long had certainly saved him from being riddled with bullets from the gunman's machine.

Long dropped back into his home tongue.

"Dose poor devils who caught it—are they . . .?"

"Gone right out," muttered Beresford, pale-faced.

A quarter of an hour had passed since the outrage in Auveley Street. In that time, Beresford had telephoned for an ambulance, talked briefly with Horace Miller at Scotland Yard, and left a message with that gentleman, discreetly worded so that Josiah Long should not catch its drift, to ask Gordon Craigie to telephone or call in person at Number 7, Auveley Street. Beresford had no desire for the American agent to know that Gordon Craigie was the Chief of Department Z. In what little private life he led, Craigie was a plain Civil Servant, and as such he wanted to be known, not without cause.

Miller had caught the drift of the request, and hung up. By that time Beresford, looking out of the window of his flat, had seen the ambulance outside the house, and the half a dozen blue helmets amongst the hundred-odd heads which formed a crowd round the victims of the 'accident'. He had gone downstairs to inspect the damage, leaving Josiah Long in charge of the simmering Tricker, and his first question, when he had returned, was to ask Long how he had guessed what the Daimler's advent into Auveley Street had meant. Then Long had asked, and had learned, how the victims of the machine-gun outrage had fared.

"Dead, hey?" Long drew hard at his cigarette. "Hell! More Gorman——"

"If we could only *prove* it!" muttered Beresford.

"It don't need much proof," grunted Long. "I saw de guy, an' half an hour after I'd left him I had a bullet through my cady——"

"But you can't prove Gorman fired it, or was behind the job."

"I know Nosey Dean fired it, buddy, an' I know Nosey Dean wass woikin' wid Gorman."

"How?"

"I saw him go into Gorman's place—Park Place, ain't it?"

"Did anyone else see him go there?"

"Not so's I know it. It wass late." The American lit another cigarette, eyeing Beresford with his weak blue eyes. "Howso, Dean told me enough to——"

Beresford interrupted him with a grunt.

"Use your sense," he snapped. "Nosey Dean's dead. We've only got your word for anything he said or did; you might convince me, but you wouldn't cut any ice with twelve good men and true."

The American rounded his lips.

"Crown me fer a hobo!" he muttered. "Sho' I wouldn't."

"Give us just one direct line on the man," Beresford said half to himself, "and we'd tie him up. But without it——"

"Say!" Long jerked forward, his eyes blinking double time. "Dere's one thing, Beresford. I got Nosey Dean's gun——"

"The gun which shot Williams?"

"Sho'. And what shot my cady." Long grimaced.

Beresford felt a shiver of excitement run through his limbs. He leaned forward eagerly.

"Where is it?" he snapped.

"At Cheyne Gardens."

"Hidden away?"

"No-o. In the middle drawer of the sideboard in dat room, Beresford."

"There are times," said Beresford, with a flash of his real self, "when I wonder that the American Intelligence didn't show some when they picked on you——"

"Easy goes," protested Josiah Long.

Beresford grinned, getting up as he did so and reaching for the telephone.

"Sorry, son, but I ask you! If Gorman's bright pals know you've got that gun, they'll move heaven and earth to get it. Won't they?"

"Maybe," admitted Josiah Long. "What are yuh goin' to do, buddy?"

"Just you listen," grinned Beresford, as a gruff voice at the other end of the wire told him that he was speaking to Scotland Yard. He was switched on to Horace Miller, and gave that stalwart exact information as to where the gun which, Josiah Long believed, had killed Nicholas Williams would be found. "You'll call me when you've got it?" Beresford asked.

"Yes," said Miller, and hung up.

"I don't think he thought he'd find it," said Beresford, returning to his chair. "But if he does, we might trace it back to Gorman——"

"Or his big shots," twanged Long.

"One of these fine days," said Beresford, his chin jutting forward aggressively, "we'll put irons round the wrists of his big shots, and then it won't be long before we get irons on little Leopold."

"Don't yuh mean maybe?" Long grinned.

"I don't," said Beresford, and the American stopped grinning. There was an expression on the big man's face which did not lend itself to humour, direct or reflected.

For five minutes both men were silent. Beresford was not sorry to have time to get his breath back after the lightning-like attack from the Daimler's gunmen, and he let his thoughts run willy-nilly. Josiah Long had explained many things, but there were obvious flaws in his explanation, and Beresford, while admitting that Long seemed genuine, would not be satisfied on that point until he had received confirmation from the American authorities that they had actually sent Long to England. Beresford himself could not get that confirmation, but when Craigie arrived at the flat, and heard what Beresford had heard, he would immediately arrange to contact with America.

Tony looked at his watch. It was seven o'clock, less than four hours since he had visited the doss-house in Wapping and picked up the trail of Josiah Long. Many things had happened in that four hours; how much more would happen in the next twenty-four?

Beresford didn't know, but he felt in his bones that it would be a mad drive now, until the end was reached. And for once in his life he did not feel secure about the end. Leopold Gorman, that sinister figure in the background of the affair, held many cards, some of them aces. The one possible weak link in the care with which the financier had covered all his actions was that revolver which Josiah Long said was at his flat; that might, or might not, prove a valuable contact. The big man could only hope for the best.

There were other more unlikely things, of course. The Arrans might find something in Paris. Bob Lavering might at any time be sufficiently recovered to talk, and in talking he might reveal a reason for Gorman's interest in him, especially the reason why Gorman had kept him alive. Beresford was still convinced, in his own mind, that through Bob Lavering the solution of the mystery would be reached, but he had not dwelt at any length on this subject with Josiah Long; Long was still suspect.

The big man looked at his watch again. Ten past seven. Craigie should arrive at any time, and Beresford was looking forward to his next talk with the Chief.

"When's yo' guy coming?" demanded Long, who was showing commendable patience.

"He'll be here," said Beresford.

Long shrugged his shoulders, and relapsed into silence. In the kitchen, Tricker was moving to and fro between his pots and pans, obviously anticipating sudden calls on his larder and preparing for them. Below the flat, in Auveley Street, the murmur of voices still hovered, floating through the partly open window, for the outrage would be the talk of the day for a long time to come. Beresford wondered grimly what kind of story the Press would run on it. Headlines had been sober-hued during the past few days, and a shooting in London's most exclusive residential district would brighten them up a lot. He wondered, too, whether the Daimler had been traced. It had been driven from Auveley Street without any trouble, and in all probability had got clear away. Beresford was too experienced in the game to think that there was much chance of tracing back from the Daimler. It was probably a hired car, which would be found deserted in a suburban street before the night was out.

The telephone-bell clattered out suddenly. Josiah Long started in his chair. Beresford grinned and went to the instrument. Many a man had been startled out of a reverie by the harshness of that bell.

Horace Miller was at the other end of the line.

"Any luck?" asked Beresford.

"We've found the Daimler," said the Superintendent. "At least, I think it's your bus, and there's a smell of cordite in the back of it."

"Call it ours," grunted Beresford. "Where was it?"

"On Clapham Common. A Daimler hire-service car, taken out yesterday afternoon—by a woman."

"A woman?" Beresford's voice went up.

"A middle-aged woman," affirmed Miller, and Beresford felt absurdly glad. For a moment he had seen the face of Valerie Lester, and his blood had gone cold.

"We can't kick back on that," the Super went on. "She was dressed in black, wore a wig, and paid a deposit in gold sovereigns."

"Gold, did she?"

"Yes—and snubbed the hire people when they remarked on it, so they asked no questions."

"Humph," grunted Beresford. "That's another dead end. Anything else?"

"Rogerson's been over to Chelsea—he's there now, in fact. So is the gun."

148

"There you are!" said Beresford, with a chuckle. "I told you so and you didn't believe me. You'll get that lined up with the bullet?"

"Which bullet?"

"Blockhead!" snapped Beresford. "The one that killed Williams."

Miller hesitated for a moment, and then went on:

"Yes, of course I shall. I'll ring you if the gun and the bullet fit."

"Still think I'm dreaming?" chuckled the big man. Then his voice dropped, and Miller could hardly hear him, while Josiah Long, who had been listening and blinking throughout the conversation, Beresford's end of which conveyed its drift, could hear nothing at all. "Did you ring Craigie?" he demanded finally.

"Yes," said Miller. "He said he'd be over right away. Hasn't he been?"

"No-o." Beresford scowled into the telephone. "He'll be here any minute, I expect. By the way—you're having that Wapping place watched?"

"Yes. But if Long's what you say he is——"

"We'll wait until we hear from U.S.A. before we're sure of that," grunted Beresford. "Meanwhile, keep someone on the tail of the Higson woman. And, Horace——"

"What?" grunted Miller, who was not always impressed when Beresford used his Christian name.

"Be a sweet man," said Beresford, with a grin, "and see that your ugliest and most efficient 'vec keeps an eye on the Chesters' house at Regent's Park. There's a certain young lady there——"

"What am I going to be?" demanded Horace Miller with a rare touch of humour. "Best man?"

"Horace," said Beresford reproachfully, "you have no fine feelings. Good-bye, Horace."

Beresford replaced the receiver thoughtfully, and did not notice Josiah Long's inquiring gaze for several seconds. Beresford was puzzled about Craigie. Twenty minutes should have been ample time for the Chief to have come from Whitehall to Auveley

Street, for Craigie rarely lost time when there was work to do. Moreover, Department Z's Number One was worrying himself grey over the Gorman business.

"Say!" Josiah Long's nasal twang jolted Beresford out of his reverie. "Can I sleep here, buddy, if it comes to it?"

"Rather that," said Beresford bluntly, "than let you out of my sight until I've tested your story."

"Beresford," said Josiah Long with sincerity, "I like yuh better every time yuh talk—say! Do yuh like dat telephone?"

The Englishman scowled. He was suspended between a standing position and his chair, but jerked back to his feet suddenly, and said that he didn't. He lifted the instrument off its platform, and told the Exchange operator that he would certainly hold on for the Paris call that was coming through for him.

"Long-distance?" inquired Josiah Long, blinking.

"How did you know?" demanded Beresford, who had not mentioned the word Paris.

"I kinda guessed," said Long, and Beresford told himself that Josiah Long was clever. In some things perhaps too clever.

A moment later, however, he forgot Josiah Long, and forgot everything but the fact that Timothy Arran was on the other end of the line, speaking from the Hôtel Royale in Paris. There was an urgency about Arran's voice which made Beresford stand by for trouble. The big man's eyes narrowed as he listened.

"I tried to get Craigie," said Timothy Arran rapidly, "but he's not in his office, so I came through to you Tony——"

"Get it out!" snapped Tony Beresford.

Arran paused, and Beresford had an idea that he was swallowing hard at a lump in his throat. At last:

"Lavering's gone," said Arran.

Beresford's fingers tightened round the telephone.

"Gone? You mean disappeared?"

"No." Arran's voice was as cold as death. "I mean he's dead. The nursing-home was burned down, and everybody inside went with it!"

For a moment there was no sound on the line. Beresford's tongue seemed to cleave to his mouth, and his whole body was rigid. From his chair, Josiah Long stared at the big man, wide-eyed, expectant.

CHAPTER FIFTEEN

NO NEWS FROM CRAIGIE

B ERESFORD broke out of the mental paralysis which had gripped him after Arran's bald statement, but his voice was harsh and unnatural, and his limbs were still tensed.

"No chance at all?" he demanded.

"I can't see any," said Arran.

Beresford pulled himself together with a physical effort.

"Listen, Tim," he said. "Go to Marshant at the Embassy, tell him I sent you and that it's the same game as I saw him about yesterday. Tell him to get the *Sûreté* moving quicker than it's ever moved before, and to find the crowd who fired that nursing-home if it's the last thing they do. Got that?"

"All right," said Arran, who sounded lifeless. "Anything else?"

"No, but get back to London, with Toby, on the first 'plane. I've something here to keep you busy."

"All right," said Arran again. "Chin-chin."

Beresford dropped the telephone on to its platform, and turned round towards Josiah Long. Josiah Long was a nuisance now. He was in the way, and for the time being he couldn't be trusted.

"Buddy," said Beresford laconically, "I've got a nasty shock coming for you."

"Yeah?" Long's eyes widened, and for once he did not blink. "Let's have it, big boy."

"I'm going to jail you," said Beresford. "Sorry, but it can't be helped. I'll let you out at once when I get an O.K. from the powers-that-be. Ready?"

Josiah Long, his full lips pursed thoughtfully, heaved himself from his chair and reached for his hat, which was on the table. He was about to speak, but the kitchen door opened suddenly and Tricker, still bandaged, poked his head into the room.

"When'll you eat, Mr. B.?"

"Sam," said Beresford, drawing a deep breath, "I don't know when and I don't know where. Is that guardian angel of yours coming here to-night."

"Wot, Maria, Mr. B.? I——"

"Anyhow," grunted Beresford, "even if she is she isn't. This place isn't likely to be healthy to-night, Sam. Stay here yourself until Horace Miller or one of the Arrans comes, and then take your pet to the pictures. Deliver her afterwards to her home, Sam, and then park yourself at a temperance hotel for the night. Do you get that?"

"You don't want me to stay here to-night, Mr. B.?"

"I don't, Sam, unless you want to take a chance on getting a bigger wallop than you had the other night."

"O.K., Mr. B."

Beresford grinned fleetingly, then slipped into a mackintosh, and escorted Mr. Josiah Long out of the flat. As they climbed into the Lancia, still standing at the kerb, the big man grinned again, but there was a whimsical gleam in his grey eyes.

"You're taking it all very calmly, O Josiah."

The American grunted.

"I got to," he said logically. "If I make a break for it, I'll have a posse of yo' cops on my tail, and dat won't give me my dinner. How long," he added, as the Lancia moved off, "will it be before you can give me a pass out? Days or weeks?"

"Hours, with any luck," said Beresford. "I'll get a call through to Washington and have a talk with your boss—what's his name?"

"Yuh just say who you're asking about," said Long cautiously.

Beresford grunted, and swung the car into Bond Street, turning right towards Piccadilly and zig-zagging through the traffic until he turned into Whitehall. He pulled up outside Scotland Yard, and Josiah Long opened the door and climbed out.

"I ain't never been in here," he started. "I——"

But Beresford didn't hear what he was going to say.

The big man was sliding along the seats to get out of the Lancia on the on-side of the car, and he was looking at the long bonnet. As he looked, the bonnet seemed to bulge outwards. For a split second Beresford saw that crazy bulging, and then with a bellow of warning he dropped below the dashboard, squeezing himself as low as possible. Even as he moved, and as Josiah Long, with astonishing agility, skipped away from the car, the bonnet burst with a deep-toned roar which filled Whitehall with rumbling echoes, making a thousand people stop dead in their tracks. Yellow sheets of flame shot upwards and outwards, and the engine of the Lancia burst into a thousand pieces which went into the air like a cloud of shrapnel.

People shouted, women screamed, men swore. The flames developed into a roaring inferno, gaining a hold with frightening rapidity. About Whitehall, pieces of steel and iron thudded against the pavement, into the macadam-topped surface of the road, against the walls of the great buildings on either side. Windows went inwards, shivering beneath the impact of those pieces. The driver of a London Transport omnibus, turning his head instinctively towards the explosion, was met full face with a flying piece of steel which smashed into his eyes. The man screamed, and his hands left the wheel. The bus skidded, crashing into a small car and squashing it against a wall; of the driver of the car there was nothing but a stomach-turning wreckage. The din of shrieking passengers added to the bedlam, and the bus rocked to and fro, as if it must crash over on one side; but it righted itself miraculously, although its windows were splintered and fire started in its engine.

And all the while the flames about the Lancia grew more vicious, and the front part of the chassis was white-hot metal.

Tony Beresford, squashed down beneath the dashboard, caught between the wood of it and the upholstery of the seats, contracted his muscles all he could, but was ready to see death. It seemed to leer at him, but it passed him by. Head first, he wriggled out of the Lancia, through the door which Josiah Long had left open, and willing hands dragged him to safety in the teeth of the flames.

Superintendent Horace Miller leaned against the window of the Police Commissioner's office at Scotland Yard, while Sir William Fellowes, who until recently had been unique as a Commissioner of Police without a title, sat at his desk and listened grimly to Tony Beresford.

Fellowes was a stony-faced man who looked incapable of humour but was in fact a specialist in dry and caustic wit. At that moment, however, there was no humour on his lips nor in his hard grey eyes.

"We've got to get Gorman on some charge or other," said Beresford, and it seemed to him that he had been saying that at regular intervals for the past four days. It was like a refrain in his mind. If they could only hold Gorman, they would have time to breathe, time to catch up with the man's game, time to smash it.

But while he was free he was two moves ahead of Beresford and Department Z and the police. "Can't you get him on a small count of some kind?" Beresford demanded. "If we could only work without him on our tails for twelve hours we might get through."

Fellowes drummed on his desk with his fingers.

"No," he said. "I can't touch Leopold Gorman. Craigie asked me to this morning, and he saw Mannering——"

(Sir David Mannering was the then Premier.)

"What did Mannering say?" Beresford asked.

"He said," muttered Fellowes, hard-voiced, "that if we tried to hold Gorman on any charge that we couldn't prove up to the hilt, we'd smash ourselves. Gorman's not in this on his own, Beresford; he's got powerful backing, and we can't touch him—yet."

Beresford swore.

"Where is Craigie? Do you know?"

"No idea," said Fellowes.

"I spoke to him when you telephoned," Miller interjected from the window. "That's the last we saw or heard of him. An hour and a half ago now, and he's not been to your flat yet—I telephoned five minutes ago."

Beresford pushed his hand through his hair. He was pale, grimy from his contact with the burning Lancia, and his right hand was badly burned. At that moment he was prepared to believe the worst about anything, and to be pessimistic as to the reason for Craigie's 'disappearance'.

"You can't call it that yet," said Fellowes. "He might have gone over to Paris, after learning about the fire."

"Arran couldn't get at him to tell him," grunted Beresford.

"Craigie learns things from more than one source," said the Commissioner. "God, Tony, you're not getting beaten by it, are you?"

Just for a moment the two men stared at each other, hard-eyed. Fellowes knew his man, and knew, too, that the Valerie Lester element had not helped Beresford to keep his mind clear.

But he expected what he got. Beresford's eyes lost their stoniness, and his lips curved.

"Sez you!" said Beresford. "All right, Bill—thanks."

Fellowes smiled, and proffered cigarettes.

"We ought to get the call through from New York at any time," he said. "If Long's O.K. that'll be a big help."

Beresford said nothing, but thought of the American with mixed feelings. Certainly Long had saved him from the machine-gun affray, but the little (not so little, Beresford corrected himself; Long's guise as a middle-aged and somewhat corpulent bachelor made him look shorter than his five-feet-nine) American was what he would probably have called 'in it bad' with Leopold Gorman and that powerful financier's 'big shots'.

Prior to his visit to Chelsea, Beresford had not been attacked since the first night's escapades in Auveley Street. In the five hours since he had seen Long for the first time to know him as Josiah, there had been the machine-gun outrage and the Lancia trick. That meant, Beresford reasoned, that Gorman was prepared to do anything rather than allow the Englishman and the American to join forces. Singly they were dangerous; together, thought Beresford, Gorman considered them an even greater threat to his immunity from trouble. The big man wondered what would be the result of the wireless-telephone inquiry concerning Josiah Long which had been put through to New York by Sir William Fellowes, and which New York Head-quarters had promised to answer as quickly as they could make inquiries at Washington. Would the result confirm Long's apparent genuineness?

Beresford was waiting for the reply from New York with more anxiety than either of the others realized. The result of that message would explain many things to him, but just then he was not prepared to pass his theories on to Bill Fellowes or the phleg-matic Horace Miller.

A telephone-bell whirred out suddenly, and Beresford's eyes

widened. Fellowes shook his head as he heard the voice at the other end of the wire.

"From Jennings," he said, as he replaced the receiver. (Jennings was a police expert on arson.) "About your Lancia."

"Dodo Trale's Lancia," grinned Beresford. "What's the report?"

"He's coming here to tell us," said Fellowes.

Jennings arrived—a small, sallow-faced man with a wall-eye. A rogue to look at, Beresford grinned to himself, if ever there was one. He spoke with obvious knowledge, however, and even his low-pitched voice demanded respect.

"I don't think there's much doubt as to how the thing started, sir." Jennings spoke to Fellowes while looking every now and again at Beresford. "An asbestos container holding nitro-glycerine was fastened to the inside of the radiator. The container was sealed, but became unsealed after some manipulation, and the heat of the engine—or a spark—sent the engine sky-high. That's all, sir."

"*All!*" muttered Beresford. "I should say it was a whale of a lot! But how was the container opened?"

"I don't know," admitted Jennings. "The container itself is hardly damaged, but the lever or wire which was used to open it is burnt. I'd imagine," he added, taking courage from Fellowes' nod, "that the thing was timed to open after you had applied the foot and handbrakes, sir."

"Not the door?" Miller snapped the question from the window. Horace Miller was frequently wide awake when he looked asleep.

"I shouldn't imagine so," said Jennings, turning towards the Super. "The door might have been opened and closed several times while the car was still standing—I mean, before it was put into motion after the trap had been set. So the container would have opened earlier——"

"Possibly before Mr. Beresford got in," muttered Miller.

"Or the other gentleman," said Jennings, thinking of Josiah

Long, who at that moment was in Jennings' office, waiting patiently for the report from America.

"Ye-es," Beresford said, after a pause. "Besides, the engine wouldn't have been hot enough at the start of the journey, and the door would have been opened and shut before I started the engine —or it might have been."

"Exactly," said Jennings, eyeing Beresford with fresh respect.

"All right, Jennings," the Commissioner said, after a pause. "Keep at it, though. If you can find just how the container was operated it might help a lot."

Jennings did not say that the mechanism of the trap had been blown sky-high, and that even if it had not been burned it was probably littering Whitehall. He went out of the office quietly. Beresford started to speak, but the telephone-bell cut into his words.

Fellowes took the instrument up quickly. The expression on his face told the other two men that it was the New York call. They waited, eager-eyed, for the conversation to finish. Beresford's, "Well?" and Miller's, "Is he all right?" were snapped out simultaneously, before the telephone was replaced.

Fellowes nodded, picked up another receiver and muttered, "Send Mr. Long up here," into the mouthpiece. Then:

"Long's story's true," he said. "He's on a special commission to investigate the source of the Wheat Pool mystery, as well as some killings which New York reckons were planned in England. He's got two men and two women with him—all regular agents. Valerie Lester," he added, with a grin at Beresford, "is one of them. She's been on the Wheat Pool job for some time."

Beresford grinned back, relieved. Miller grunted.

"What Wheat Pool business is it, sir?"

"Someone in England's buying up Wheat Pool interests," said Beresford, "and America doesn't want control of the Pool to leave the country. We'd feel the same," he added.

Bill Fellowes grunted.

"It isn't the financial part that's the trouble," he said. "If Gorman—and they think it's Gorman, because he's the only man big enough to tackle it—wants to buy, no one can stop him. But whoever is buying isn't satisfied with 'no' for an answer. If a man won't sell——"

"He kicks the bucket," muttered Beresford, "and his holdings go to someone who will sell. That's what Long told me. Is that what you got?"

"Yes," said Fellowes, and paused as someone knocked on the door. "Come in," he called.

Mr. Josiah Long, heralded by a uniformed constable, entered the office. He looked, at first, anxious and nervous, but Beresford had learned not to connect his weak, blinking eyes with nerves. A glance at Beresford's face, however, satisfied the American special agent. He grinned, and went through his pockets for his Camels (Beresford guessed), and the big man grinned when he saw a packet of Player's, familiar with their bearded sailor jacket.

"Run out of stock?" asked the big man, and Long grimaced and nodded. "Anyhow—we're going to believe you, O Josiah."

"Dat's good hearing," said Josiah Long cheerfully. "I thought maybe dey wouldn't want to talk on de udder side. Howso—what are yuh buddies goner do?"

"Get Gorman," said Beresford.

"Sho' thing. But how?"

"Listen," said Beresford, and for the next half an hour he talked, interrupted occasionally by Long's nasal questions, or Fellowes' dry, "Don't forget this," or Miller's stolid, "You can try, but ..." Nevertheless, all three men were impressed, and Josiah Long made no bones about saying so.

* * *

There was one way, as Beresford had explained, by which Leopold Gorman might be tripped up and his connection with the murders and attacks proved. But before he put the method to the test, Tony Beresford wanted to see and talk with his Chief. Discipline was strong in Department Z, and Beresford had no desire to break the rules. On the other hand, unless Craigie turned up soon, Beresford would have to put his plan into motion.

It was nearly nine o'clock when the big man left Scotland Yard, unaccompanied by Josiah Long, who was still talking with the Police Commissioner and the Super. Craigie's office had been telephoned several times, his Brook Street flat, as well as the eating-house in Villiers Street which he occasionally patronized for its grill. But there was no trace of Gordon Craigie, no message, no word of any kind.

Beresford was more worried than he had admitted to the policemen. More than they, he realized the extreme care with which Craigie always worked. It was a thousand to one against the possibility of the Chief having gone off on some obscure—or for that matter plain—trail without leaving a message behind for Beresford, who was keeping in constant touch. The big man wondered, not without a tightening of his lips, whether Craigie was safe. Gorman was probably fully aware that the Chief of Department Z was his most dangerous opponent. Craigie had influence, and if it came to a showdown between Gorman's influence and the Chief's, Gorman would probably lose; the financier would go to the absolute limit to clip Craigie's wings—and Gorman's limit was death.

As he walked to his flat, Beresford let his mind run again. The Paris development had been sizzling in his brain from the moment that he had heard from Timothy Arran, but he wanted to keep away from the subject of the nursing-home fire until he had talked with the Arrans, who would be in London before midnight. The incidents in Auveley Street and the remarkable affair of the Lancia demanded a hearing too. The machine-gun episode, while lurid, was understandable. The Lancia affair was not. Beresford tried to puzzle it out as he walked towards the Carilon Club, where he had it in mind to do many things.

The Lancia had been tampered with, almost for certain, while it had been standing outside the flat in Auveley Street. During the three-quarters of an hour that Beresford had been at Number 7, the asbestos container, with its nitro-glycerine contents, had been fastened to the radiator or inside the Lancia's bonnet, and the trap had been rigged up to ensure that the container was opened while Beresford was in the car. All that time, Beresford told himself, there had been crowds outside Number 7, because of the machine-gun sensation, and there had been at least three police-men. Whoever had done the job had done it quickly, and without attracting attention.

Beresford walked along the Mall towards the Carilon Club, twice cursing himself for a fool when he fancied that two pedes-trians seemed to show more interest in him than they should have done. Beresford was—or had been until then—a stranger to nerves. The affair which had started so innocently, so far as Beresford was directly concerned, that night at the Two-Step Club, was playing havoc with him. Things happened, out of the blue. He reminded himself, with a twisted smile, of his little harangue to Timothy Arran. Death was always round the corner ...

The two pedestrians, however, had no designs on him, and Beresford turned into the Carilon, relieved by its sobriety, the dozen or so men who 'halloed' him as he went towards the bar, and glad to see one Dodo Trale, Agent Seven of Department Z, whose job—happily, said Trale—was to follow up the Adele Fayne contact with Leopold Gorman. At that moment he was drinking beer, and he asked Beresford, cheerfully, to join him.

"Tankards—two," said Dodo Trale, as Beresford nodded. "I've been expecting to see you, Tony. I——Now what the blazes is making you so green, drat you?"

That was an exaggeration, but Beresford, who was looking

over a member's shoulder at an *Evening Echo,* was certainly looking grim. For the *Echo's* headline was:

TWOPENCE RISE IN PETROL PRICES

Beresford seemed to see the sloping shoulders, the uneven face of Leopold Gorman as he read the line. The price ramp had started!

CHAPTER SIXTEEN

VALERIE LESTER AND A MAJOR

W HEN Valerie Lester had heard of the illness which had all but killed Bob Lavering she had fainted, and both Josiah Long and Tony Beresford had wondered, with foreboding, why. The girl herself knew the real reason for her swoon; the Lavering incident was the culmination of many since she had first started on what the American Intelligence called 'The Wheat Pool job'. It was true, as Long had told Beresford, that she had once been in close touch with Bob Lavering and—more than Long knew—she had known Lavering all her life, liking him more than a little but stopping at liking. The news that he had been—and still was—in a bad way, had been a shock which she had not been able to shake off, because of her mental perturbation.

These things she told to Diane Chester, slim, lovely Diane, who was as understanding as she was typically English, as typically English as she was beautiful, and who had been called, with truth, the most beautiful woman in London.

"If you'd tried to tell me," Valerie said, as Diane poured out tea, despite the fact that it was after half past six, "that in less than a week I should be—be——"

"In love with Tony Beresford," said Diane calmly, "you'd have laughed at me. Sip it hot, Val—it does you more good."

Valerie coloured but laughed.

"You're taking it coolly," she said, and Diane laughed with her.

"Tony's a man in a thousand," she said, as Valerie sipped tea hot. "Look after him."

The laughter went out of Valerie Lester's eyes.

"I doubt," she said quietly, "whether I shall have the chance, Diane. And I don't know whether I should take it, even if I did."

"Don't you?" Diane kept her voice cool with an effort, and kept her eyes away from Valerie's, to hide the sudden gleam which had jumped into them. "Why?"

Valerie closed her eyes.

"I didn't come over to England just for the trip," she said. "I came over because I'm working—and I don't know where my job's going to end. That's why."

For a second time Diane Chester was hard put to it not to show surprise. It was the first intimation which Lord Aubrey's wife had of the double motive of Valerie's visit.

"You're—working? The same kind of work as Tony?"

"Ye-es."

Diane finished her tea, placed her cup and saucer deliberately on the waggon-tray, and leaned forward, holding the American girl's chin in her white hand.

"You're not working *against* Tony Beresford, are you?"

Valerie shook her head, but tears were very close to the surface of her eyes.

"No—at least, only as much as I'm American and you're—he's English. But we're working against the same thing."

"Hmmm." Diane took her hand away, and smiled. "Well, I'm sorry, Valerie. I don't like Tony's game, and the only thing to be glad about is that he'll have to drop it if he does settle down. But that doesn't help much now."

She stopped, and lit a cigarette, which she rarely did. She knew enough of these things not to ask questions, for there had been an affair in which Aubrey Chester and a certain Hugh Devenish* had been concerned; Diane's memory of it was not pleasant, and she knew that Devenish had been in the 'game' which was now Beresford's. She did not even ask if Valerie could drop out, and Valerie was grateful.

At the same time, the girl from America was worried. She did not know whether others beside Beresford knew of her connection with Josiah Long's work in England. If Gorman or his agents learned of it, she realized, the house at Regent's Park would be a danger spot for her hosts as well as for herself.

"My dear girl," said Diane, when Valerie unloaded this point of view, "if you're with Tony—and in effect you are—I'm with you. You'll be a lot safer here, too, than if you stayed at an hotel or a club."

"I feel—" Valerie looked at the older woman, bright-eyed and flushed—"I feel that I've—taken advantage of you, Diane. You didn't know, when you asked me if I'd come with you, that——"

Diane laughed encouragingly.

"Valerie," she said, "in the 'game' you have to take advantage of every chance and anyone. I know enough of it to know that. Oh, you goose!"

Just one minute later, when Aubrey Chester blundered into the chintz-curtained room which made Diane's boudoir a place of joy in that mausoleum of a house, he saw the two women with their arms round each other, half crying, half laughing. He attempted to make a discreet retreat, but a mat and the half-open door combined to stop him. The women turned round, startled.

"S-sorry," stammered Aubrey Chester.

"Come in and listen," said Diane.

"I-isn't there something I can do to l-lend a h-hand?" demanded Aubrey five minutes afterwards.

Valerie Lester knew then why the Chesters—Diane lovely and Aubrey vacuous of aspect but shrewd—were two of the most popular people in town.

* * *

A liveried and dignified manservant brought Valerie a letter at about half past nine. Aubrey and his wife—for Chester was on the top of the tennis world at that time, having brought back several titles from America—had gone to a celebration party, and the American girl was alone. She slit open the envelope quickly. The message was brief, and, as she expected, from Josiah Long.

Get a line on a Major Gulliver Odell (the note read), *and find out when he last saw Gorman. J.L.*

Major Gulliver Odell. The name seemed familiar, and Valerie frowned as she burned the note, and tried to remember when she had last heard of the Major. She remembered suddenly. On the previous day the Chesters had commented on the increasing friendliness between the autocratic soldier and Adele Fayne, the dancer at the Emblem Theatre. That suggested, Valerie thought, with a frown, that Odell would not be easy to get at. Adele Fayne was ample occupation for one man.

A copy of *Who's Who* gave the girl as much information about Major Odell as she would be likely to need. She telephoned his flat, knowing that a frontal attack with a man of Odell's nature (for the Chesters had commented very freely) was likely to succeed.

Odell was in. It also happened that he was, that night, in an expansive mood, for Adele Fayne had telephoned him to say that she was engaged for supper, and he had consequently dined alone and dined well. He did not, off-hand, remember Valerie Lester during the trip which he had made to America in the previous year, but he was more than ready to admit that his memory was short, for the voice of Valerie Lester over the telephone was low and husky.

"Delighted," said the Major, "delighted you remember me, Miss —er—Miss..."

"Lester."

"Lester. Let me see, weren't you with the—er—the . . ."

"The Laverings, at the Manhattan," said Valerie.

"Of course, of course!" Now that he was on safe ground, the Major felt that he could indulge in his conversational tricks, which were composed of short sentences of little meaning but considerable emphasis. "Remarkable place, the Manhattan, remarkable! But there are one or two places in London"—the Major chuckled meaningly—"which could show it a thing or two."

"Are there?" asked Valerie Lester innocently.

"Astonishing places, astonishing!" asserted Odell. "I—ridiculous of me to imagine it, my dear Miss Lester —I suppose that you can't—I mean you are engaged for to-night? . . . Most fortunate, Miss Lester! Where are you? I'll send my car—yes, I insist! The Chesters'? Of course, of course, I remember reading in the *Tatler*. . . In twenty minutes..."

The Major, resplendent in evening dress and a white carnation, presented himself in person at the Regent's Park house within the twenty minutes. The two detectives who were watching the house, and Valerie Lester, reported the event by means of the recently established wireless telephone service, and the Major's car, an Austin Twenty, was picked up at Marble Arch and followed by a police car to the Silver Slipper, in Haymarket. The Austin was parked in a side street, and the police car parked near it while its occupants kept watch for the revelling Major and his unexpected companion.

CHAPTER SEVENTEEN

THE MAN WHO SHOULD HAVE BEEN DEAD

T ONY BERESFORD discussed many things with Dodo Trale at the Carilon, chiefly that gentleman's success with Adele Fayne. Trale's opinion of the dancer was not high.

"She hasn't got even a suspicion of a brain, Tony. If it wasn't for Solly Lewistein, that girl wouldn't be on the Emblem at all, what about being the star piece. I'll grant you she's got the legs and——"

"We're not concerned with what she's got," grinned Beresford, "but what she knows. Is there a line between her and Gorman?"

Dodo Trale examined the dry bottom of a tankard. He was a small man as men go and puny in comparison with Beresford, while his grey eyes and general bearing suggested indolence out of the ordinary. Certainly Dodo Trale looked lazy, but, Beresford liked to tell him, he also looked beautiful. That night his dress-suit was cut to the peak of fashion, for immaculacy was a religion with that agent of Department Z, and his dark hair was brushed well back from his forehead, revealing his classical profile and emphasizing the perfection of his features. Even as he demanded more beer and more tankards of Petitt, the head-waiter at the Carilon, Dodo Trale looked bored.

Petitt passed the request on to a lesser soul, wished Beresford a frigid good-evening, and passed on himself.

"Well?" demanded Beresford. "Is there?"

Trale deliberated.

"I don't know, Tony. Somehow I think there is. Of course, Gorman's been seen about with our Adele a lot. I don't mean that. I mean I think she's—— Ah, beer!"

"Before you drink that," said Beresford, grabbing both tankards, "you'll talk. She's what?"

"I think she's scared of him," said Trale; "and pass that over quickly, drat you."

Beresford complied for the sake of peace.

"So you think Adele Fayne's scared of Leopold, do you?"

"Yes," said Trale, from the mouth of his tankard. "She hedges like blazes when I start to talk about him. I can't get a word out of her. Ah-h! But I'll tell you one thing, Tony."

"Go on while you've time," said Beresford, who knew Dodo Trale's propensities with beer.

"I think Solly Lewistein's scared too. I happened to mention that I'd met Gorman in the passage outside Adele's dressing-room last night, and Solly seemed to go cold."

"Gorman's money keeps 'em both, remember," muttered Beresford.

"Not that kind of scared," said Trale. "If they were frightened of losing a good billet, they might sulk, but when they had the chance they'd call Gorman everything they could think of—not that it'd be much with Adele, mind you—but they wouldn't shy away when you mentioned his name, and look as if you were poison."

Beresford drank deeply and thoughtfully.

"Who'd you think we could get most out of—the girl or Solly?"

"Solly. If you offered him enough money, I reckon he'd sell Gorman right out. I don't think the girl knows enough. Gorman's got sense if nothing else, and he wouldn't try to put anything in that cold storage plant."

"Obviously," said Beresford gently, "you don't think much of Adele. Did she turn you down, or didn't she think your motives were pure?"

"She hasn't turned me down, and I haven't got any motives. I'm suppering with her again to-night, at the expense of Gulliver Odell—you know that gentleman?"

"Ye-s." Beresford in turn studied the dry bottom of a tankard. "Is there anything between Gorman and Odell, d'you think?"

"I kind of guess so," said Trale. "Solly Lewistein think's Odell's punk, and Adele spits whenever he's mentioned. But he's got influence somewhere, so——"

"It's probably with Gorman?"

"That's my guess," said Trale.

Beresford lit a cigarette and eyed Trale seriously.

"Do you know the size of this job, Dodo?"

"I've got an idea."

"Humph! Well, it's a lot bigger than your ideas. We might catch a packet any day, any time——"

"*Anywhere!*" crooned Dodo suddenly and to the surprise of many members of the Carilon who were telling funny stories and buying the best beer in London.

"Don't be a ruddy ass," grunted Beresford. "I don't think Gorman knows you're one of us—nothing's happened yet, has it?"

"Not even a rough-house," mourned Trale.

"Well, it will," said Beresford. "Feel like taking a chance to-night?"

"Will it cancel that supper engagement?"

"No." Beresford looked grim. "Unless you're too dead to keep it."

Dodo's eyes widened, and he choked at his beer.

"*So-ho!* We're really getting down to it. What's the job, Tony?"

Beresford lowered his voice and spoke without moving his lips, so that only Trale knew he was speaking.

"See Solly Lewistein," said Beresford, "and ask him how much he'll take for the low-down on Gorman."

For a moment Trale seemed too thunderstruck to speak. At last:

"And is that your idea," he demanded, "of a really first-class lead for a spot of trouble? Because I——"

"Son," said Beresford, and Dodo Trale was quietened by the expression in the big man's eye, "if Lewistein doesn't bite, and takes the story to Gorman, I wouldn't give two pins for your chance of seeing morning."

Trale swallowed hard, although his tankard was empty.

"Well, well, *well!*" he exclaimed at last. "Ain't it lucky I wasn't born rich, old son? When do I see Solly? While the show's on?"

"Yes. It's half past nine—no, ten o'clock, within a couple of minutes. You'll catch him all right if you go now."

Dodo Trale stood up, looking for all the world as if he would never be able to outlive the boredom of that evening.

"O.K. with me," he said. "Have I got time to pop round to my place and collar a gun?"

"Better take mine," said Beresford. "I'll join you in the cloak-room in five minutes, and I'll pass it over then. And, Dodo——"

"Sir," said Dodo Trale.

"Watch your step. If Solly seems to jib, go straight round to Fellowes at Scotland Yard and get him to put a man on your tail——"

"The Yard?" Trale whistled under his breath. "What's the matter with seeing Craigie and getting one of our men?"

Beresford looked grim.

"Can't do," he said. "Craigie's not been in for some time, and he made a new list out yesterday. Until we find him I don't know who's with us nor who's dropped out, if any. So——"

"Do you mean," asked Dodo Trale, suddenly very still, "that Craigie's *missing?*"

"I do," said Beresford.

"My God!" breathed Trale, and his face was white.

If he had had time for musing, Tony Beresford would have reflected on the fact that Dodo Trale grinned when he talked of putting his head, figuratively, into Gorman's noose, did not turn a hair when he was convinced that the consequences of his coming interview with Leopold Gorman's theatrical manager were likely to be fatal, or next door to it, but went white when he heard that his Chief was missing. There was no man in the Service who would not willingly have given his life for Gordon Craigie. Craigie contrived to lend a human understanding to a job which was inhuman because of the certainty of death coming in the long run to its agents, and death by violence; by doing so he had made himself, literally, loved by those men, to whom the word 'love' between men was absurd.

Beresford, however, had many things to do. In effect he was O.C. of Department Z, a job which was no easy one, even if he had access to Craigie's papers. But with Craigie missing—the problem of the Chief's disappearance had already been passed on to Very High Officials—Beresford would be badly handicapped until those officials gave him signed permission to take charge.

The most serious handicap was his lack of knowledge as to who was still on Department Z's list of agents. He needed more help, and he needed it badly. And then, suddenly, he cursed himself for a fool. There was help in plenty waiting for the asking; that the men he had in mind were not agents of Z was an advantage rather than a disadvantage; they would not be recognized by Leopold Gorman, or Gorman's mysterious 'big boys'.

Beresford felt cheered. To cheer himself still further, he

hopped into the first telephone-booth and called up the Regent's Park house, hoping for a word with Valerie Lester.

That same solemn-voiced servant answered him.

"Miss Lester left the house, sir, about thirty-five minutes ago."

"Alone?" Beresford snapped the question.

"She was called for, sir, by a gentleman."

"Do you know him?"

"No, sir. Reynolds, who received him, has gone out."

Beresford replaced the receiver, after a muttered thanks. He was worried, although he realized the possibility that Valerie's companion was one of Josiah Long's associates. On the other hand, Gorman *might* have tricked her away from the Regent's Park house.

Beresford cursed, audibly and to the disgust of a spinster who was passing him across the Trafalgar Square roundabout. He did not grin at the lady's 'tcha!' a sure sign that he was worried much more than usual. The possibility of trouble developing with Valerie Lester made his blood chill. Yet, he reasoned, she was in the thick of it; just as Josiah Long had been singled out for special attention, so, probably, would the American girl be spotted.

Fighting back his anxiety, Beresford hurried to the Éclat Hotel, where he hoped to find several gentlemen of his acquaintance who would not shy at trouble. It was not his lucky night, for the only men who would serve his purpose—and who were indulging in a beer-battle at the Éclat's bar—were Robert Montgomery Curtis and Wallace Davidson.

A beer-battle between those august gentlemen was a thing of humour for those in the mood for it. It consisted of a trial of repression on the part of the combatants, for the winner was the man who drank less beer over a prescribed period, throughout which period the beer, in tankards, must be hovering in front of the battlers' nose, frothy with temptation.

"Why," said Bob Curtis, a giant of a man whose ugly face was redeemed by a pair of the most humorous brown eyes in London —"why, here's St. Anthony! Join us, soldier!"

"Beer—tankards, three, quick," drawled Wally Davidson, a man of perpetual weariness, considerable size, although smaller than either Beresford or Curtis, of light-brown, curly hair and undistinguished features but immaculacy on a par with Dodo Trale's. "You look peeved, Tony my son. Would you rather have something with more bite?"

"Bring that stuff to a table," grunted Beresford, "and try to keep your wits clear. I've got a job for you."

Davidson and Curtis* exchanged glances, instructed a waiter to transfer their beer from the bar to a table, and followed Beresford willingly. They did not know, but they guessed that Beresford was a man of strange missions, and they were possessed of a philosophy which proclaimed satisfaction only in action.

"Well?" demanded Bruce hopefully.

"Spill it!" drawled Davidson. "No, drat you, not the beer! Oi! What the blue hades is your trouble, Tony?"

Beresford, who had touched his lips with the tankard of beer, deposited it suddenly on the table, spilling a fair portion in close proximity to Davidson's trousers. He stared for a fraction of a second towards the door of the bar-room, at a man who had just entered and who was looking round the room inquiringly. Davidson and Curtis looked, carefully, with Beresford. They saw the slim, well-dressed figure of a young man whom they knew moderately well, but for the life of them they could not conceive why his appearance had made Tony Beresford go temporarily mad.

They did not know that Robert Lavering was supposed to be dead!

CHAPTER EIGHTEEN

THE REMARKABLE STORY OF BOB LAVERING

L AVERING saw the trio suddenly, and his eyes widened. He
came towards the table, and the three men saw, as he grew
nearer, the dark rings round his eyes and the general appearance
of weariness which suggested an illness from which he had not
fully recovered. Beresford stood up quickly and pushed a chair
into position. Lavering dropped into it thankfully; the trio noticed
that he was breathing hard.

A waiter hovered near. Beresford beckoned him and ordered
brandy. Lavering, when he had let the spirit course through his
veins, looked better.

"Nothing like a nip," said Wally Davidson, who had a bad habit
of improvising couplets, "to make you full of zip. Howdo,
Lavering?"

"Drop it," said Beresford. "These two are all right," he added, as
Lavering looked at his companions doubtfully. "How'd you
manage to get here, Bob?"

Bob Lavering grimaced. He was a broad-shouldered man of
five-feet-eleven, narrow-hipped, lean, and good-looking in a
boyish way. Normally he had the American characteristic of not
looking his age, which was twenty-six, although that evening he

looked considerably older. His features were well moulded, if a little too sharp, and his blue eyes were normally gleaming with good-humour, wide-set beneath his well-developed forehead and flaxen hair.

"I flew over this afternoon," he said. "I didn't lose any time, when I got the chance, you can guess. Where are the Arrans?"

"On the way over," said Beresford.

"I tried to get them on the telephone," said Lavering, "but they weren't at the Royale. How much do you know, Tony?"

"That the last I heard of you you were ill," said Beresford. "More than ill, in fact—you were dead!"

Lavering's eyes widened. Curtis and Davidson stared at him, trying patiently to sort out the situation.

"How did I——" Lavering began, and then stopped, with the ghost of a smile on his lips.

"The nursing-home you were in was burned down," said Beresford, "and you were supposed to be in it. But half a mo'. Take a breather while I talk to these two. And go steady with that," he added, as Lavering poured more Pol Roger into his brandy glass. "It won't take much to make you roll, son, and I want your story first."

Lavering grinned, and listened quietly while Beresford gave a brief résumé of the Arrans' visit to Paris, and the fire at the nursing-home in which Bob Lavering was reputed to have been burned. He did not enlarge on the more important aspect of the case, for he had no desire to scare Lavering, who might or might not know what was happening.

"So that's why you looked as if you'd seen a ghost," muttered Curtis, when Beresford had finished. "All right, soldier."

"Feel fit enough to carry on?" Beresford asked Lavering.

"Why, sure," said the American. "Shall I start right at the beginning?"

"As far back as you can," said Beresford.

Lavering lit a cigarette thoughtfully. There was an expression

in his eyes which might have meant anything, but it held pain—
mental pain—and Beresford felt awkward.

"All right," began Lavering. "It started—well, you know when I
first met Adele Fayne, don't you?"

"Hm-hm." Beresford's eyes gleamed.

"I fell for her," said the American steadily, "and you know I fell
hard. But for a chance word that I got from Lewistein one night—
her manager, I mean——"

"I know Solly. Carry on."

"I'd never have realized there was anything behind it, and I'd
have been well on the way to Reno." Lavering laughed bitterly.
"You see, Tony, Solly was talking with her, and he said in effect:
'You've got to marry him; Gorman says so'."

"The devil he did!" Beresford grunted. Davidson and Curtis
whistled under their breath.

"Sure," went on Lavering, "and you can fancy how I liked that.
Howso, I didn't feel like talking to 'Dele, and I was mighty interested in the Gorman guy who'd told her who to marry. I'd seen
Gorman, and twice I tried to see him again, but he was always out.
The day before I went over to Paris I heard that he was going over
there, and that he was to stay at the Splendide. I parked my grip at
the Royale, then waited outside the Splendide one morning, saw
Gorman go in, and went right after him. I caught him in the
lounge——"

"Did he jump?" asked Beresford.

"No. Gorman doesn't show what he feels much. Anyhow, I
asked him, without mooning, why he was interested in getting me
married. He laughed it off, and told me that if I went to a little
place called the Côte d'Or he'd meet me there and talk."

"And you bit it?" snapped Beresford.

"Yes," said Lavering wearily; "I bit it hard. I went to the place—
it was a pretty good speakeasy, Tony—and I fell hard for a dancer
there——"

"Corinne?"

"Sure." Lavering looked hard at Beresford. "Know her?"

Beresford nodded, without enlarging on the snake-charmer's fate. Bob Lavering had enough to carry that night.

"Well—you know Paris. I was on the loose, and—anyhow, that girl shied right away from me. All she would say was it was not safe for me. I tied that up," Lavering went on with a wan smile, "with Gorman, and I told myself that Paris wasn't healthy. So I made for the gate, but before I'd got a hundred yards away my legs went right under me, and I felt like a pleasure-cruiser on the first day at sea. Someone bent over me, and then I went right out.

"The next thing I can remember clearly," went on the American, lighting another cigarette, "was waking up in the nursing-home and feeling a lot better than I had for a long time. I remembered Tim Arran coming to the first place I'd been parked in, and that uniformed doctor he had with him, but it's all a haze until I got to the nursing-home. I had a room there with a window looking into the street, and this morning, when I was up for the first time, I looked out of the window and saw—well, you can guess."

"Gorman?"

"Yes—Gorman." Lavering's voice hardened as he went on. "That man is poison, Beresford! You don't have to look at him twice. Howso, he grinned up at me with that one-sided mouth of his, and tossed"—Lavering took a letter from his pocket as he went on—"this up. I—I read it, and then I made a break, Tony. I hopped to the Royale, collected my grip, and took the first 'plane over. That's all—only I tried to get the Arrans, once while I was at the Royale and once by telephone, but they were out. So——"

"Here you are," grunted Wally Davidson, his eyes agleam with unusual excitement. "Curtis, my son, does this sound——"

"Like something to keep us out of mischief," said Bob Curtis, slapping his thigh with a vast hand. "Is this the job you were going to talk about, Tony?"

Beresford nodded.

"Then how soon," demanded Davidson, "can we start?"

"Quicker than you expect," grunted Beresford.

As he spoke, and while Davidson and Curtis had been talking, Beresford was watching Bob Lavering. The American was under the weather. His breath was coming quickly, his eyes were unnaturally bright, and his hand, as he handed the letter to Beresford, was trembling.

The note was brief but emphatic, and it explained to Beresford one of the things that had been puzzling him—the reason why Lavering had sought him out immediately on his arrival in London. Davidson and Curtis looked at each other and grimaced as they read the letter over Beresford's shoulder.

It read:

Tell Beresford to keep out of this. Remind him that Nosey Dean died, Williams died, a certain lady is dead. Craigie is going, your delightful friend Valerie Lester is going. Although if you are discreet I may arrange for only a temporary disappearance for that lady.

That was all. It was a blunt statement, cleverly calculated to be more unnerving than a violent tirade of threats. Beresford, as he read 'Valerie Lester is going', felt cold. The others kept silent, knowing that it was not a moment for speech. Suddenly:

"Did Gorman himself give you this?"

"Yes," Lavering nodded.

"And you were by yourself?"

"Yes. No one else was near."

Beresford drummed his fingers on the table, staring straight ahead of him. Slowly he lit a cigarette. Then:

"Did you see anyone with Gorman when you spoke to him at the Splendide?" he demanded.

Lavering closed his eyes.

"I—I don't remember anyone special. Someone had been out with him—a fat little guy with a red face——"

"Odell," Beresford muttered, as though to himself.

"I don't know his name. He looked what you'd probably call military," Lavering said. "I——"

The American broke off suddenly and stared at Beresford like a man seized suddenly with an idea that was going to solve all his problems. Lavering's hand shook as he reached for his cigarettes, and his eyes were more feverish than they had been.

"Jehosophat!" he grunted. "I remember where I saw the fellow again. He was at the Côte d'Or. I can remember him talking to a waiter, the same waiter that served me with my last drink——"

"And you flopped out ten minutes after you'd had that drink," broke in Davidson, no longer looking weary. "Is this Major *Gulliver* Odell, Tony?"

Beresford's eyes were like agate.

"That's the gentleman," he said. "And the quicker we get on to him the better. He's been popping up and down in this job a lot more than I like." The big man looked at Davidson. "Do you know Odell?"

"Fair to middling."

"Well enough to invite him to dinner or a stag party?"

"Well enough to ask him to a little game of *femin de cher,*" said Davidson. "He's a great gambler is the Major."

"Is he then!" Beresford honed the words. "That's worth knowing, Wally. Hop to the telephone and see if the gentleman is at home, will you?"

Wally Davidson hopped, but Major Odell was not at home. Major Odell had left his flat at something after nine, and had told his man that he wasn't likely to be in until late.

Beresford grunted with disappointment when he heard the news, but he comforted himself, not knowing that the Major's companion that evening was Valerie Lester, with the thought that there would be ample time to follow the Major's comings and goings on the morrow. He spoke quickly to Davidson.

"Wally, the Chesters have gone to the Tennis Federation Dinner at the Trivoli. Gate-crash it, will you, and find out whether they know where Valerie Lester was going to-night? O.K.?"

"Sure," said Davidson, getting to his feet.

"Fine. Drop round to Auveley Street when you've got your message. Bob——"

Robert Montgomery Curtis looked hopeful.

"Go round to the Emblem," said Beresford, "and see Dodo Trale. He'll be about the back stage somewhere, on Solly Lewistein's tail. Find out whether he had any luck with Solly, and if he didn't——"

"I'm listening," said Curtis, as his friend paused.

"If he didn't," said Beresford, his eyes glinting, "you get hold of Solly somehow and take him——"

"You mean grab him *bodily?*" Curtis, for once, was surprised, although normally he was a placid and stolid man.

"I mean lure or entice him into a car, cab, or pub," grunted Beresford, "and take him—where the blazes can we keep a couple of boys and girls in hand for a day or two?"

"There's my little place in Kent," said Curtis, his eyes gleaming, for to him it seemed that there was going to be fun in plenty. "It's not big, Tony, but——"

"Your place just outside Farningham?" Beresford muttered. "It's that bungaloid growth, isn't it?"

"That's it," said Curtis equably. "Six rooms and a scullery——"

"It'll do fine," said Beresford. "Get Solly Lewistein down there, Bob, and tell Dodo to get his Adele there too——"

"Adele *Fayne?*" demanded Curtis, his eyes open in great wonder.

"Yes—*La Fayne.* Any objections?"

"Object..." Curtis's homely face split into a beam of delight. He chuckled, stifling his mirth to a rolling thunder in his throat, and as he stood up he quivered. "Lord, Tony! La Fayne and Solly Lewistein, with Dodo and I to keep 'em in order. I——"

"Drop in at your flat as you go to the Emblem," said Beresford, grim-voiced, "and take a gun with you. It won't be one long laugh, if I know anything about it, but it might force Gorman's hand."

Curtis heaved himself to his feet.

"If you get a chance," he said gently, "you might persuade Major Gulliver Odell to join us."

"I will if I can," said Beresford.

Bob Lavering listened to Beresford's instructions and saw the other two men leave the Éclat, yet seemed not to comprehend what was happening. The feverish expression in his eyes was more marked than ever. He was suffering from the natural reaction to his exertions, mental and physical, since he had left Paris, and Beresford knew that unless he was careful, Lavering would crack beneath the strain.

" 'Lo, Bob," said Beresford loudly.

Lavering's eyes widened and he looked startled.

" 'Lo, yourself," he muttered. "I——"

"Feeling a bit rocky in the middle regions," grinned Beresford, levering himself from his chair. "All right, son. We'll have you between the sheets in a brace of shakes, and then——"

Still talking, apparently without meaning, but actually to keep Lavering's mind active, Beresford helped the American up and shepherded him through the lounge and foyer of the Éclat. A commissionaire grinned, believing Lavering to be drunk, and whistled for a cab. He helped Lavering into it and winked at Beresford, who winked back, straight-faced.

Not until the taxi was well away did Beresford give his destination. It was possible, he realized, that the commissionaire would be questioned, and Beresford did not believe in omitting to take ordinary precautions, even though he was only going to his flat.

As the cab turned in Auveley Street, Beresford saw, and grunted with satisfaction at the sight, that two plain-clothes men were waiting near Number 7. Bill Fellowes and Horace Miller between them meant to make as sure as possible that if anything else happened in Auveley Street, their men would be able to get a hot scent.

Inside the flat, Beresford discovered a bewildered and indignant Samuel Tricker confronting two square-jawed gentlemen also of the plain-clothes school. Tricker was protesting that he could come and go in that flat as and when he liked, and the detectives were convincing him that for the time being he could do nothing of the kind.

"Sam," said Tony, as he helped Lavering across the living-room and into his bedroom, "I thought I told you to stay at a temperence hotel for the night."

Sammivel looked unhappy yet pugnacious.

"Yus, an' I booked me room," he said complainingly, "an' then I farnd I'd left me oof behind. Wen I comes to get some, I finds these two—two——"

"Gentlemen," suggested Tony brightly.

Samuel Tricker made a noise which was uncomplimentary.

"Hany'ow, wen I comes I finds I carn't git art, so I 'ad to wite fer you, Mr. B. Give 'em the nod, will yer?"

Beresford grinned, gave the men his assurance that Samuel Tricker was one hundred per cent. O.K., and then pressed the ex-fighter into service. Ten minutes after his arrival at Number 7, Bob Lavering was clad in a suit of Beresford's pyjamas, which were two sizes too large for him, and was between the sheets of Tony's bed.

"Blimey!" said Samuel Tricker, *sotto voce*. "I reckons yer'll want a nursin' 'ome certificate soon, Mr. B. Wot's this gent bin doing?"

"Eating things that didn't agree with him," said Beresford with a fleeting grin. "Sam, hop over and tell your pal Little that I've got another case for him, will you?"

"O.K., Mr. B."

"And, Sam!"

"Yep, Mr. B?"

"Then pop along to Maria—where's she staying, by the way?"

"A flat in Downham Road, Mr. B—back o' Shepherd's Market. She shares it wiv——"

"I don't want to hear about Maria's peccadilloes," said Beresford with severity, and for a moment Sammivel looked thunderstruck, until the grin in the big man's eyes reassured him. "Ask her, Sam, if she thinks she could keep awake for to-night, in case our new invalid wants some attention. Will you do that, Sam?"

"I'm on me way," said Sam.

He glared triumphantly at the plain-clothes men, and stalked past them. Beresford grinned, waited until the door had closed behind his man, and then asked gently for the detectives' identification cards. They were forthcoming, and Beresford was satisfied that they were actually Yard men.

Within ten minutes the mountainous Doc Little arrived, puffing from his exertions and demanding to know of Beresford whether he thought he had an option on his services. Little was a clever physician and surgeon who preferred to make a comfortable livelihood by treating the minor ailments of the rich than to pit his knowledge against the problems of medical science. To ease his conscience, however, Little was on the consulting lists of several large hospitals, and Beresford knew him as a man to be trusted. Six feet high, and fat, he was a Colossus of a man, red-faced, and, unless he was with a patient, lusty-voiced, genial and good-hearted.

"Who's been bashed about now?" demanded Little, as he recovered his breath and looked inquiringly at the two detectives and Beresford. "Your man again?"

"No one," said Beresford, and the doctor saw that he was unusually serious. "It's poisoning, Doc. A man in Paris diagnosed arsenic."

"Arsenic?" Little lowered his voice, as Beresford had done, so that only Beresford heard him. "Let's have a look at him——"

Just twenty minutes later Doc Little dropped into one of Beresford's large armchairs, lit a cigarette and eyed the big man narrowly.

"Sure it was—is—arsenic. Lavering's been slowly poisoned over three or four months, Beresford. The illness you talk about was caused, not by the administration of arsenic, but because Lavering missed his usual dose for a few days. He recovered because the Paris people doped him again—no, don't swear; they had to do it, otherwise he would have dropped right out—but he's tired himself out during the past twelve hours, and he'll take some time to pull round."

Beresford grunted. Little's report was much as he had expected. But there was one thing that he wanted to know, and he put the question quietly.

"When he's picked up again, what's going to happen if he doesn't get supplies of the stuff?"

Little pursed his fat lips.

"He must have supplies. It'll take twelve months to cure that young fellow. He'll have to take the stuff in diminishing doses, not less day by day, but less week by week. Otherwise——"

"What you mean," said Beresford, proffering cigarettes, "is that unless Lavering is kept under strict medical supervision for the next year, he's in danger of dying?"

"Sure. He won't live." Little refused a cigarette, and Beresford remembered that he was a non-smoker. "What are you going to do with him, Beresford?"

"Keep him here for the next few days," said Beresford.

"That'll be all right," said Little, "but you'll want a nurse."

Beresford grinned fleetingly.

"Tricker won't mind that," he said, "and I shan't be here much."

Little eyed his man shrewdly, and offered a word of warning.

"You've got a pretty good tank," he said, "but don't run it too far, Beresford. You're setting a high pace, aren't you?"

"So-so," grunted Beresford.

"Try and cut it down," cautioned Little.

Beresford grinned, and told the fat man to laugh it off. Little waddled across the room, shaking his head and telling himself that Beresford was asking for trouble. But Beresford, as he picked up the telephone, told himself that for a few days to come the pace would get hotter.

He telephoned Scotland Yard, but Horace Miller was out, and the Chief Commissioner had gone home. Rogerson was there, however, and he gave Beresford a message which set the big man cursing.

"Miss Lester," said Rogerson precisely, "was seen to enter the Silver Slipper Club in Bond Street with a Major Odell——"

"Odell?" snapped Beresford, his muscles tensing. "Sure?"

"Perfectly sure," said Rogerson, in whom the matter of Miss-or-Mrs. Higson's hands still rankled.

"Is the Silver Slipper being watched?" Beresford's voice was harsh.

"Yes," said Rogerson coldly.

"Humph. Tell Miller—he's coming back, isn't he?"

"Yes."

"Tell him about this, and tell him that I'll ring him as soon as I can. What time did they go to the Slipper?" he added.

"Just after ten."

"Thanks," said Beresford.

He looked at his watch as he hung up, and was surprised to find that it was nearly half past eleven. That meant that Odell and Valerie Lester had been at the night club for an hour and a half— plenty of time for trouble to develop, if trouble was intended. His recently aroused suspicions of the gallant Major took a decided turn for the worse now that he knew Valerie Lester had been with him that night. For Beresford, who was shrewd above the average, doubted whether Josiah Long had told all that he knew, and the big man guessed that Valerie had not gone with Odell for the sake of his company.

Scowling, Beresford went into his bedroom, satisfied himself that Lavering was asleep, and opened his "gathering of friends", selecting from the armoury a gas-pistol, a mask and an automatic to replace that which he had lent to Dodo Trale. He returned to the living-room as Sam Tricker and his Maria entered, and as the telephone bell burred out.

"How," demanded Tony Beresford of Maria as he went to the instrument, "is your conscience? Get to it, Maria..."

The nurse clucked, more with pretence than real annoyance, and Sam Tricker rubbed his jaw thoughtfully. Beresford put the receiver to his ear, and his eyes brightened as he heard the jerky voice of Toby Arran at the other end of the line.

"We're at Victoria," said Arran. "Anything to do?"

"Yes," said Beresford. "Get to the Silver Slipper, and if you see Odell or Valerie Lester there, keep an eye on them until I arrive. Got that?"

Tobias said that he had.

"Then get this," said Beresford, wishing hard that he could see Toby's face. "Bob Lavering got back to London before that nursing-home was burned down. Yes, *Lavering!* He's at my flat now. Don't drivel, son. He can be, because he is. And make the Silver Slipper slippy, will you?"

Toby Arran said, dazedly, that he would.

CHAPTER NINETEEN

MR. LEOPOLD GORMAN IS WORRIED

A T half past twelve that night, Leopold Gorman, financier, industrialist and director of three times as many large companies as he had fingers, sat in his study at 5, Park Place, W.I, and scowled at a sheet of virgin blotting-paper in front of him. For the first time since the commencement of his campaign against Department Z, as a possible danger to the scheme which he had started five years before and which was fast reaching its maturity, he was worried. Never before had he been met with opposition as varied as it was tenacious. Beresford, the big, innocuous-looking man, had the luck of the devil and a guile which Gorman admitted was far in advance of anything he had anticipated. Craigie too was clever, and Gorman was never sure from which angle the next attack would come.

As the financier leaned back in his chair he looked even bigger across the shoulders than he had done at the Two-Step Club on the evening of his first attacks on Tony Beresford. Beneath the shaded light of the electric chandelier above his desk, the peculiar lopsidedness of his features was more apparent, and the way in which his right brow went above his left was weirdly emphasized by the complete baldness of his head. Beresford's hazard, that night when he had seen the financier for the one and only time of his life, had been right. Gorman's hair had been as unnatural as the redness of Adele Fayne's lips.

Until the Beresford interference, everything had gone right for Leopold Gorman. In England, America, Germany and Japan there had been a slow but sure change of financial control. The combined resources of the five men whom Gorman had met that night after the International Economic Conference had been sufficient to put the virtual control of foodstuffs and raw materials into Gorman's hands. True, he had had trouble with the American Wheat Pool, but he did not anticipate that the trouble would last much longer, and he had already decided, after gaining control of the Orient-Western Oils, to insert the thin edge of his wedge. Petrol was up in price, as Beresford had seen. Other things would go with it.

Leopold Gorman, during the earlier part of that day, had spent several hours visualizing the situation in England and abroad after six months of his manipulations. By pooling the world's resources, he and his partners in the enterprise which had been calculated to adopt the principles of the Economic Conference, without its ideals, could control world prices and force them to whatever level they desired. The strength of the ring which had been formed was now so great that Gorman did not consider failure even a remote possibility. Private ownership was the ruling principle; a man could charge what he liked for what he owned. Admittedly—and Gorman looked well ahead—the price rises would have to be temporary. There would have to be times when they reached a normal level. But they would fluctuate as and when Gorman wanted, and at no time would they be fixed so that Gorman and his associates worked at a loss.

In itself, Gorman's objective was not criminal. It might—and it did—violate every human principle, and it was an abuse of an economic system which, when administered with moral honesty, was efficient and sufficing. Gorman was fully aware that the abuse of it would probably mean its end, but he knew that the end would be a long way off. For ten or even fifteen years Gorman would be able to rig his markets as he liked, and the vastness of his holdings would make any opposition futile. In fact, he told himself, he could break any and all opposition. Already in England he had found help from various unexpected sources. Money was a god which broke down all barriers, and to those people who were in the ring which Gorman had formed, money in the future would be plentiful. Thus the financier had been able to exert considerable influence to prevent too searching inquiries into the nature of some of his activities. As it happened, Gorman had found no trouble at all in England. The American Wheat Pool had been the one big stumbling block, and Gorman had not needed to look far for the reason for that. The Pool itself was a powerful ring, working on similar principles to those on which Gorman worked. It had controlled American—and reacted on world—wheat prices, and the members of the ring had no desire for the control to change hands.

In his efforts to gain control of the Pool, Gorman had been compelled to break the law. To him, the murder of several of America's industrial magnates meant nothing in itself; it did mean, however, that he had left himself open to attack from the law, the one thing which might eventually break his power. Gorman knew perfectly well that if by some freak of chance he was caught, on any one of the charges which Beresford, for instance, was trying to prove against him, the back of the scheme would be broken. In its secrecy lay its safety. Once the rest of the world realized what was happening, those magnates outside Gorman's ring, helpless individually but powerful if united, would join forces. They would have help from most of the Governments, and their opposition would be severe. Any kind of inquiry into Gorman's activities at that time must inevitably lead to failure.

For this reason, Leopold Gorman had left very little of the work against Beresford and Craigie in other hands. Only Nosey

Dean, who had died because he knew too much, and three well-paid general utility men of the gangster variety had ever contributed directly to any of the crimes. There were many who had helped, indirectly, but none of them knew enough to be dangerous. At least, none of them should have known enough.

It was that 'should' which was worrying Gorman on the night of Tony Beresford's great activity in London, the night when Bob Lavering, who should have been dead, had proved himself alive. For amongst Gorman's helpers, Adele Fayne and Solly Lewistein played a large part, at times unwittingly, at others with knowledge. And that night Gorman had reached the Emblem Theatre to see Solly Lewistein and to examine more closely Adele Fayne's recent admirer, the man Trale. Gorman did not know that Trale was one of Craigie's men, but he did know that his only policy was to suspect all and every one who came in contact with the dancer.

For the first time in his life Leopold Gorman had been completely nonplussed. Solly Lewistein and Adele Fayne had left the theatre, although they had received his instructions to wait for him. The discovery had at first annoyed him; then, as he realized the possibilities behind their prolonged absence, it perturbed him. For Gorman had Solly Lewistein in the hollow of his hand, and had counted on his hold over the theatre manager a great deal. Lewistein had worked for him for years; Lewistein knew more, probably, than any other man, how often and in what directions Leopold Gorman had broken the law. If by some chance a charge was ever levelled against Gorman, Solly Lewistein would be the most dangerous witness who could be put on oath in court. In a lesser way, Adele Fayne could be dangerous. There was one thing in particular which she had done and which might put her, with Gorman, in the dock on a capital charge, but Gorman was less worried by that possibility than by the chance that many of the secrets of his financial *coup d'état* would leak out, via Lewistein.

At one o'clock Gorman called the manager's flat, only to find that Lewistein was still missing. He called Adele Fayne, with the same result. As he replaced the receiver after the second call, Gorman sat dead still, his misshapen body hunched in his chair, his curious jade-green eyes narrowed to mere slits. He told himself that it would mean failure if he took any more chances. Beresford had been lucky, but he would have to go now. He was too dangerous while he was alive. The Arrans must go too, with the man Trale, and with Craigie—Craigie.

Gorman, as he sat back in his chair, told himself, and for the first time, that he was afraid of Gordon Craigie. The Chief of Department Z knew a great deal and guessed more. Hitherto Gorman had been afraid that if he tried to get at Craigie he would jeopardize the support of those powerful influences which had made his task comparatively easy over the past five years. Craigie was big meat...

"But he must go." Gorman muttered the words between his tight lips, and his face twisted in an expression which would have made even Tony Beresford afraid. "And there's that damned American too, and Valerie Lester. Valerie Lester!"

Gorman laughed harshly, and for the third time reached for the telephone.

As Adele Fayne had been taking her curtain at the Emblem Theatre that night, a large-limbed, genial-looking man had called on Solly Lewistein and suggested, in a rich, mellow voice which indicated that he had dined well and supped better, that they should drink. Solly was in a better humour that night than he had been for some time past. Major Gulliver Odell was not at the theatre, and to Solly Lewistein, Major Gulliver Odell was much worse than a red rag to an enraged bull. Consequently, the theatre-manager was not so curt with Robert Montgomery Curtis as he might have been, and he even humoured that happy young man inasmuch as he promised to go with him, some night in the near future, to a place which Curtis promised would open his eyes to many a star-to-be in the theatrical business.

From good-tempered indulgence, Solly Lewistein's attention grew to keen interest. Curtis's manner suggested that he was interested in some dancer or other in a two-by-four cabaret show or café, and Lewistein knew that when men were interested in that way, business often resulted. Solly, although knowing that nine times out of ten the budding genius would never rise from the chorus ranks, often 'took an interest' in the lady in question, and received a pleasant fee for his services—before they were rendered.

It was a knowledge of this sideline on the fat man's part which had persuaded Curtis to try his trick. He tried, heavily, to cajole Solly into making his visit that night, but Lewistein was adamant. He had a supper engagement which he must keep. Much as he would like to oblige Mr.——

"Brown," lied Curtis. "But listen, Solly old scout, you really must, she's——"

Solly began to lose patience.

"I haff not the time," he said curtly. "Some odder night, Mr. Brown, mit pleasure, but to-night, no."

Bob Curtis reared himself up to his full height and looked down on the little Jew with extreme displeasure. At that moment the two men were about ten yards from the stage-door, and fifteen yards from the stage itself. From the auditorium the low-voiced hum of applause which invariably accompanied Adele Fayne's last bow came dully to the listeners' ears, and Curtis knew that if he was to have any luck he would have to hurry. His one object, although Solly knew nothing of it, was to get the theatre-manager into the street, and thence into his Bentley.

"All right," said Bob Curtis, with well-aped drunken dignity. "You will not see her, but at least, Mishter—Mr. Lewistoll, you will see her photograph?"

Lewistein groaned to himself, but avarice, and the fact that this man's clothes and manner suggested that he was full of money but empty of sense, persuaded him to see the photograph.

"In my car," said Curtis, with Napoleonic grandeur.

Solly lifted his hands and his brows expressively, but followed the big man out of the stage-door. An attendant watched them, grinning, and Solly snapped out:

"I vill not be two minutes. Tell Miss Fayne——"

The attendant nodded, and turned away from the street. Only a dozen fans, eager-eyed and waiting for *La Fayne*, saw the tall man and the little fat man hurry across the pavement. None of them heard the sudden change of tone in the big man's voice, nor saw the sudden expression of alarm dart across Lewistein's features.

Something hard jabbed into the fat of Solly's back.

"That's a gun," snapped Curtis, *sotto voce*. "Step right into that seat, son. We're going for a little ride, but if you behave yourself you'll be all right!"

In Adele Fayne's dressing-room Dodo Trale, a coloured visitor, was asking himself whether Curtis had any luck with Solly Lewistein, and wondering whether he would have much trouble with the dancer. He did not anticipate any, and he felt at peace with the world. So far as he was concerned, the affair on which Department Z was working had fallen a lot short of the usual in the way of excitement, and Dodo Trale liked his life in high colours. The kidnapping (for the message and instructions which Curtis had brought from Beresford were little short of instructions to kidnap Adele Fayne and her manager) promised that it was about to liven up.

La Fayne swept in, and as the door opened the roar of applause from the auditorium filled the room. Adele was as excited as usual. The plaudits of the people were her meat and drink, and the drink went to her head.

Dodo held her wrap for her. She slipped into it, and rested her slim body against his for a moment, looking up into his face with a smile which should have been (and to Odell would have been) captivating and intriguing. Dodo, who was not in love, told her that she had been more wonderful than ever that night.

"Do you really think so, Dodo?"

"Would I lie to you?" asked Trale impressively.

"All men are liars," said Adele Fayne, with a moué which created the impression that she was delivering a truism at once unique and devastating.

"That proves," said Dodo, with the same impressiveness, "that you haven't met the right men, 'Dele. I say——"

"Hm-hm?" *La Fayne* slipped away from him, into a smaller room which ensured her privacy while allowing her to talk with whoever was paying court. Trale could hear the low-voiced French maid asking *madame* what dress she would wear.

"Make it something warmish," said Trale, "so that we can have a spin out of London and stop at a road-side house. I know several tasty little places."

There was a shriek of delight from the smaller room, and Trale told himself that his job was easy. A moment later, however, he suffered a reverse.

"Dodo—what a divine idea! But I must wait for—for a friend, and then after we have had supper——"

"You're seeing him again, are you?" Dodo Trale's voice sounded grim, and Adele Fayne pictured to herself the scowl on his face. "Who is it?" he demanded.

"It is business——" began the dancer.

"You mean Gorman?"

"But, Dodo—he owns the theatre——"

"He doesn't own you," said Trale roughly, and then, for the sake of effect, added "yet."

There was a brief silence. For a moment Dodo Trale called himself a fool for having gone too far, but the scowl, this time genuine, disappeared from his face as *La Fayne* snapped an order to her maid.

"Hurry, Antoinette, hurry! That blue frock—no, idiot, not for dinner, for the country—and those heavy shoes——"

"You're coming with me?" Dodo put every ounce of expression that he could into the words.

"Yes—I am tired of Gorman! But we must hurry—before he comes."

Dodo Trale lit a cigarette and smiled happily to himself.

At twenty past one, Greenwich time, the telephone bell in the office of M'sieu Franchot, manager of the Côte d'Or, burred out insistently, and Franchot lifted the receiver with a curse. Since Corinne had been murdered, Franchot was an uneasy man at heart. It was not so much that he had arranged for Corinne to be strangled; Franchot was too experienced a rogue to be squeamish on that score. It was not even because the murder had stirred up more trouble than any case which Franchot could remember; Piquet, of the *Sûreté,* was putting all his energy into solving the mystery of the murder in the Hotel Royale, and he had questioned Franchot closely several times, but the Frenchman was not worried about the police; true, Piquet could not be bought, but if Piquet grew too dangerous he could be taken off the case by those in higher authority. Thus it was neither conscience nor fear of the police which had made the manager bad-tempered. It was simply that he had earned a rebuke from Leopold Gorman—and Franchot was very much afraid of the financier. Gorman had the ear of those in higher authority.

Franchot considered that he had a justifiable grievance. He had arranged for the American, Lavering, to be drugged while he had been at the café, and he had had the American taken to the Hôtel Divante. He had, moreover, told Corinne to acquaint him at once if anyone made inquiries about Lavering. Franchot did not see that it was his sin if Corinne had been treacherous, and had tried —indeed *had*—shown the other madman, the Englishman, where Lavering was being kept a prisoner. In fact, being suspicious of Corinne that night, Franchot had taken the trouble to send two of his best street rats after her. It could not be laid at Franchot's door that the Englishman had avoided death, and had cunningly arranged for Lavering to be removed. After all, Franchot in turn *had* arranged for Corinne to die.

Instead of congratulating Franchot on the astuteness with which he had countered Corinne's treachery, Gorman had raged because the mad Englishman had escaped from the *apaches'* knives. Gorman did not pay Franchot *to try* to do things. He paid him to *do* them.

Franchot would have liked to have told the Englishman with the green eyes just where he could go, but there were reasons why he could do nothing of the kind. For one thing, Gorman owned the Côte d'Or. For another, his money and influence sheltered Franchot from many troubles. Without Gorman's support, Franchot knew that he would have a very short journey to make to the guillotine. Franchot *knew* that Leopold Gorman was behind many a murder, and of recent months the murders of Englishmen in Paris on mysterious business; but he could not prove it. Gorman was as clever as he was powerful.

In consequence of these things, Franchot picked up the telephone with no very good grace. The sound of the harsh voice at the other end of the wire made him go tense, however, and his voice was suave as he spoke.

"It is I, Franchot, M'sieu Gorman."

Leopold Gorman, speaking from his Park Place house, after his deliberations over the case of Tony Beresford and others, grunted and snapped:

"I want three more men, in London. Can you get them here by the morning, Franchot?"

"Three?" The Frenchman's voice went up. "Already you have two, M'sieu——"

"Already they've failed to do everything that I've told them." Gorman's voice came over the wires, cold and brutal. "You have had too many failures, Franchot. Do you want to suffer for them?"

"But M'sieu!" Franchot's voice quivered, and at the pit of his stomach there was a peculiar coldness. "I——"

"Send them over before morning," said Gorman coldly. "They need not know London, but they must speak good English."

"Mais oui, mais oui!"

The line went dead. Franchot, sweating as though he had been running, sat for a moment looking at the telephone as if it was an agent of the devil. Then, with a curse, he hurried out of the office. He dared not refuse Gorman—but Franchot did not like sending men to England. There was a ruthlessness about English justice which made him afraid.

CHAPTER TWENTY

ANOTHER GATHERING OF FRIENDS

I T was half past four when Tony Beresford, weary but sustained by a fierce anxiety to find Valerie Lester, turned into Scotland Yard on the offchance of seeing either Miller or Sir William Fellowes. The murders of Williams and Nosey Dean provided work in plenty for Scotland Yard, and Beresford knew that the police would spare no effort to put their hands on the murderers. Moreover, both Fellowes and Horace Miller knew of the probable connection between the murders and the mysterious business which Leopold Gorman was running, and they were as anxious as Beresford to put a spoke into Gorman's wheel. At that time none of them knew the goal for which the financier was aiming, but Beresford and Craigie had already told them something of what they suspected, and those suspicions were very near the truth.

The Super was in, weary but wide-eyed. As Beresford entered the small office, he looked up anxiously.

"Any luck with Craigie?"

"None at all," grunted Beresford, dropping into a chair. "He's disappeared as completely as——"

"Miss Lester," suggested Miller quietly.

Beresford looked haggard.

"Ye-s. She went to the Silver Slipper with Odell——"

"I know," said Miller. "Rogerson told me."

Beresford forced his mind away from thoughts of Valerie Lester. Since he had left Doc Little at Auveley Street, he had been to several places in the hope of finding some clue to the whereabouts of Craigie, Gulliver Odell or the girl. He had learned nothing; but he had found one thing which had given him mingled hope and fear.

His last call had been to the Silver Slipper, where he had sent the Arrans on their return from Paris. Neither of the twins had been at the club, although a waiter had told Beresford that they *had* been there for an hour earlier in the evening. The waiter, however, had known neither Major Odell nor Valerie Lester. Whether the Arrans had gone in pursuit of them, or whether they had been beguiled away from the club by Gorman's agents, the big man did not know. He could only hope for the best.

He passed a brief résumé of his activities to Miller. Finally:

"So the Arrans might be anywhere, Craigie's lost, and —and the girl. Against that, I've got Adele Fayne and Solly Lewistein down at Curtis's place near Farningham. I don't know how important those two are, but I think it'll make Gorman go carefully. There's only one other line——"

"Josiah Long?" suggested Miller.

"Yes. Where did he go, after leaving here?"

"Back to Chelsea. He promised to ring through if he found anything."

Beresford grunted.

"I don't think that clever little devil has told us all that he could do," he said. "I'll have another talk with him. Hand me that telephone, will you, Horace?"

There was a sudden sparkle in the big man's eyes, and from the curve of his lips Horace Miller guessed that Beresford had been seized with what he would have called an idea. Miller pushed the telephone across the desk and waited hopefully. He was a firm believer in the efficacy of Tony Beresford's ideas.

Valerie Lester knew that the general opinion of Major Gulliver Odell was that he was a muttonhead. She was inclined to share that opinion of the soldier for the first hour of her acquaintance with him, but afterwards she began to realize that he was shrewd, if not clever. The man who danced with her and affected a bombastic manner of speech and expression seemed to have guessed immediately that she was baiting him, and the answers he made to her carefully-wrapped-up questions told her that he was skilfully parrying her thrusts.

It was after a fox-trot, which the Major danced with more vigour than grace, that he challenged her.

"Remarkable!" he said. "Astonishing how fatiguing these modern dances are, my dear Miss Lester. Nearly as—er—nearly as fatiguing as asking questions, aren't they?"

For a moment the girl from America stared at him in astonishment. Not for a moment had she expected that he would come out into the open. A dozen thoughts rushed pell-mell through her mind as she stared at his red face, at his eyes, grey and cool, contradicting, somehow, the bombast of his manner. He was smiling at her, and she noticed, as one does notice small things at a time of crisis, that his teeth looked very sound and firm, yet were actually false.

For his part, the man whom Valerie Lester and others knew as Major Gulliver Odell saw a girl of exceptional loveliness, heightened by the flush which was then mantling her cheeks, a girl whom a gown of beige marocaine suited to perfection; it occurred to him as more than strange that she should be mixed up, willingly, in an affair which had carried death and destruction with it, and in which danger was always close at hand. Quietly:

"Was it Long who sent you after me?" he demanded.

Valerie Lester told herself that it was useless to try subterfuge. She would stand a better chance of getting information if she accepted the man's challenge. She took a deep breath, and for some reason seemed to see the comely face of Tony Beresford smiling at her from behind the Major's back.

"Yes," she said, after a pause.

Her companion nodded thoughtfully.

"A very interesting gentleman is Mr. Josiah Long. You think so, Miss Lester?"

"A very clever one," said Valerie quietly.

"You still have faith in him?" There was an edge to the Major's voice, and a hardness in his smile.

"Yes—why not?"

"My dear"—Odell leaned forward a little, and his face was very close to the girl's—"Mr. Josiah Long picked the wrong side when he accepted the American Intelligence offer. If he had worked for Leopold Gorman instead of against him, he might have profited considerably. You might have profited too——"

Odell paused. Valerie Lester felt her pulse quickening. She knew that her companion was suggesting that she changed sides, and for a moment she wanted to throw his suggestion, figuratively, into his face. Caution stopped her, and, following caution, she became obsessed with an idea. So far the job against Leopold Gorman, always approached from the outside, had been a complete failure. She felt, rather than knew, that the affair was reaching its end. Before many days were past Gorman would have lost or won—and at the moment the odds were heavily on him winning.

If she could get at him from the inside, if she could learn something which she could communicate to Tony Beresford or Josiah Long, she would be playing a part more than worth the effort.

Doubt and uncertainty chased each other across her face. The man on the other side of the table waited, but she saw that he was waiting impatiently. Suddenly:

"What is it you want from me?" she demanded.

Odell pursed his lips, letting the air through them with a soft hiss.

"Ahhhh! So you are not averse to helping me—and Leopold Gorman?"

"What do you want?" Valerie insisted.

Odell laughed suddenly.

"My dear, I have no idea. Gorman will certainly be very pleased to see you, and to have you on his side. And after all, Miss Lester, he is only doing what many others are doing, but on a larger scale."

Valerie smiled, but she was thinking fast. That single sentence might mean a great deal to the authorities. She repeated it until she was sure that she would be able to remember it when she wanted, and all the time she was forcing herself to keep cool, forcing herself to stop from saying what she thought. She would have loved to have struck the Major across his red, grinning face; but for the moment she must play a waiting game.

"Where shall I see him?" she demanded, low-voiced.

"I will arrange that," said Odell, lighting a cigarette with jerky, almost nervous movements. Again the girl's heightened sense of perception told her that he was not enjoying the smoke; he was used to a pipe or a cigar, and the cigarette was a poor substitute.

"Yes," said Odell, "I will——"

He broke off suddenly, and for a moment his eyes narrowed. Only for an instant he stared across the crowded floor of the Silver Slipper; then he looked away quickly. The smile had gone from his face when he spoke.

"We have some friends, Miss Lester..."

Valerie went cold inside. For a moment she thought that Odell was talking of Tony Beresford, and at that moment Beresford was the last man whom she wanted to see. She turned her head a little, looking towards the door, and as she saw the newcomers she heaved a little sigh of relief.

Timothy and Tobias Arran were making straight for their table.

Timothy reached them first. He looked, Valerie thought, pale and less self-confident than when she had seen him before, but she told herself that it might be merely the silvery light coming from the walls of the room—the light of the Silver Slipper was in keeping with its name. For Timothy, who was at all times immaculate, a trifle weary to look at and slow in speech, smiled down on her cheerfully.

"Miss Lester, isn't it?" he drawled. "I met you at the Chesters' last week. Howdo, Major?" Timothy lifted his hand lethargically, and Odell grunted. "Enjoying England, Miss Lester?"

"Very much indeed." Valerie forced herself to speak lightly, but inwardly she was seething with anxiety. She guessed that the Arrans were messengers from Beresford, and she guessed that they had been warned to keep her well away from the suspected influence and potential danger of Major Gulliver Odell. But the last thing she wanted, then, was her embryo plot to be broken. She knew that she could, if she chose, rebuff the Arrans in such a way as to ensure that they left the table hurriedly, but if she did that they would carry a report back to Beresford which she knew would make the big man feel that she was definitely against him. She felt herself between two stools.

"Mind if we sit down?" Toby Arran, who had been talking to a waiter, came up to them. "Darned place is always crowded—ain't it, Major?"

Odell grunted and said that they could sit down. He did it with little good grace, and Valerie saw the smile lurking in the eyes of Timothy Arran. And then she had to keep her body rigid, to bite at her lips to stop herself from shouting a warning.

For there was a glint in the Major's eyes which suggested that he was prepared to make full use of the Arrans' untimely interference.

A dozen mad thoughts rushed through the girl's mind. There was—there *must* be—some way of warning the Arrans. But try as she might, she could find no way of warning them without letting Odell see it; and the thing of paramount importance was to convince the Major that she was sincere in her promise to see Leopold Gorman, and to work for him if necessary.

Robert Montgomery Curtis possessed his little place in Kent more by accident than for convenience. Resthaven was a bungalow of the modern stucco variety, built for an aunt who had preferred to die in the country than in London, and Curtis, always a generous soul and willing to oblige, had provided the wherewithal to build to the ornament to Kent. The relative, however, had changed her mind, married into money, and decided to die in London after all. Curtis kept the bungalow in good repair, paying a gardener and odd-job man from the neighbouring village of Lindean to keep it in some sort of order.

Thus it was that the garden was presentable and the rooms habitable when Curtis, with Solly Lewistein in tow, reached the bungalow. Curtis had stopped at a wayside café and purchased a variety of eatables, pointing out cheerfully to Lewistein that it was better to die full than die empty.

Lewistein was still frightened, but he had not said a word during the journey. Curtis's size, apart from the gun in the big man's pocket, was argument enough to keep Solly from threatening violence or trying to attract attention.

"Sorry you don't feel so well," said Curtis, as he turned his Bentley into the short drive leading to the bungalow, and pulled up with a screeching of brakes outside the stucco-work porch. "I was hoping you'd start getting nice and chatty... Right in, old soldier."

He shepherded Lewistein into the first room, which led from the right of the small hall, and pushed the fat one into an armchair, commenting meanwhile on the tightness of the fit. Then he demanded, solemnly, to knew whether Solly liked beer.

"Beer?" Lewistein squeaked the word, and the expression on his greasy face made Curtis grin. Lewistein was slowly recovering from his fright. Something in Curtis's manner told him that he had little to fear.

"Don't say 'beer' as if it was poison," said Curtis. "I'm going to drink some, and I thought maybe you'd join me."

Lewistein made a noise in his throat. He screwed up his courage and banged his clenched, podgy fist on the arm of his chair.

"Vot matness is this?" he demanded. "Vot outrage vould you be doing to vorce me avay vrom London like —like——"

"A bit sudden, I know," said Curtis sympathetically. "But I only wanted a little chat, old Sol. Will you——"

"Take your vilthy stuff avay vrom my dose," snapped Lewistein, taking courage from Curtis's wide smile. "I tell you I demant to know——"

Curtis thoughtfully drank Four XXXX ale, a crate of which, by order, was always kept in the bungalow. He knew that Beresford was anxious to get a line on Gorman, and it occurred to him that it would be wiser to tackle the theatre-manager while he was still suffering, in part, from the effect of the hold-up.

"Solly," he said, and the Jew's body went taut at the change of expression in his captor's voice. "I want a little information from you..."

Lewistein leaned forward in his chair, staring at Curtis in fascination. There was a whitish tinge round his mouth, and his body was quivering. He seemed to sense what was coming.

"I want to know," said Curtis softly, "just what Gorman's got on you?"

For a moment Lewistein gaped at him, as though paralysed. And then he shrank back in his chair, covering his eyes with his hands, and his voice was high-pitched, like that of a man in mortal agony.

"I can't tell you!" he screeched. "Not that—not that——"

Curtis stared down at him, surprised by the vehemence of the Jew's reaction, knowing that Beresford had been right when he had said that he suspected Lewistein could tell many things. He felt, not disgust, but pity for Lewistein. The man had obviously been living on his nerves for months.

"Steady up," said Curtis, after a short, tense pause. "I shan't eat you—and Gorman's not here."

Lewistein pulled his hands away from his eyes. He had gone pale, and the pallor of his face made him look a dirty white. His thick lips quivered, like his fat body.

"Gorman is alvays near," he muttered, as if talking to himself. "He is too strong vor you—alvays too strong..."

Curtis, for no physical reason, felt cold. He tightened his lips for a moment, staring down at Lewistein, and then he walked across the room and thoughtfully opened a second bottle of Four XXXX. There were times when liquid refreshment was more of a necessity than a pleasure.

As the stopper came out with a hiss of escaping gas, a different sound came from outside the bungalow. Curtis lifted his head and waited. Suddenly he heard the swish of wheels on the gravel of the drive, and a moment later the cheerful voice of Dodo Trale.

"Here we are," said Dodo, and Curtis grinned when he realized that Adele Fayne was with him. "All merry and bright, 'Dele, but mind that stone..."

Adele Fayne's voice, raised impatiently, came through the air. Solly Lewistein started up, his face working, his eyes widening with mingled fear and astonishment.

"Where are we?" demanded the dancer. "This isn't a road-house. Dodo, I——"

"Now then," warned Dodo Trale with mock gravity, "don't you go thinking things that aren't. I'm a well-intentioned young man, 'Dele, but a friend of mine wants a little chat with you."

Two minutes later Adele Fayne stepped into the front room, her normally pretty face distorted with anger, an anger which was partly fear. She saw Curtis first, and failed to recognize him, but a moment later she saw Solly Lewistein's plump body squeezed into his chair.

For a moment the dancer and her manager stared at each other, the one stupefied and the other feeling like death. Even Curtis and Trale felt the effect of that silence. There was something here which they did not understand.

Curtis spoke suddenly, his voice harsh in spite of his words.

"'Lo, folks!" he said with forced cheerfulness. "We don't seem so happy as we might be, and all because I said to Solly something about friend Gorman."

"Gorman!" Adele Fayne shrieked the name, swinging round towards Curtis. Like Lewistein, she was afraid, deathly afraid.

CHAPTER TWENTY-ONE

DEATH AT THE BUNGALOW

A T half past eight on the following morning, Tony Beresford swung out of Auveley Street in his maroon-painted Hispano, and headed for Farningham, in Kent. The only development since he had left Scotland Yard at five o'clock was confirmation, from Curtis, that the two prisoners were comfortable, but that mention of Gorman set them screeching. Beresford determined to have a shot at extracting information.

As he spun through Vauxhall, then cut across London towards the Kentish borders, he felt the reaction of the previous day's events. The fact that Valerie Lester was missing made him feel that he could not prevent himself from going to Gorman's Park Place house and facing the financier with a direct accusation. But he realized that he would be serving no purpose by so doing. He would not even help Valerie Lester.

The green fields of Kent, fresh after a light rainfall overnight, did nothing to ease the big man's frame of mind. There was one thing, and one thing only, that would do that—the sight of Valerie Lester safe and unhurt.

Beresford told himself that he was a fool, a thousand times a fool, for letting his thoughts centre round the girl. It was more important by far to find Craigie, even more important to force information which might help against Gorman from the two prisoners at Curtis's bungalow. But the fact remained that Beresford's chief interest was the girl. The possibility that she was not all that Long had said tormented him. She might be playing a double game, with and against Josiah Long at the same time. She might be...

"Don't be a ruddy fool!" Beresford snapped aloud. "You're losing sight of the big stuff, and if you're not careful you'll miss something that matters—now what the hell was that?"

'That' was something which pinged against the side of the Hispano, and it says a great deal for the state of Beresford's mind that he assumed it was a stone thrown up by the wheels. A second ping, fast upon the first, made him grunt and look quickly on either side of the road. There was no one in sight, but on the left side of the road a wooded tract of countryside might have hidden a small army. On the right the fields were bare of everything but the first shoots of the hops, and the network of poles for training them ready for the autumn picking.

But Beresford was not concerned with hops nor their eventual state at that moment. He was telling himself that it would be touch and go if he got out of this spot of bother!

Unconsciously, he was glad that it was happening. It cleared his mind, and forced him out of the comparative state of lethargy into which he had fallen. It was no time for thinking; it was time for doing.

He sized the situation up quickly. The woods ran close to the road, and stretched further than he could see, for the road turned sharply to the right about two hundred yards further on. That acute bend prevented him from following his first inclination and sending the Hispano hurtling along the road, trusting to sheer speed to avoid being hit. For Beresford knew there were two or more gunmen in the woods, and the Hispano made a good target, if a moving one.

Beresford slouched down as far as he could in his seat while retaining full control of the roadster, and took one hand off the wheel. An automatic slipped between his fingers, taken from his pocket, and he kept a hold of the gun while peering into the woods. Twice again those shots came, hitting against the side of the car, but there was no sound before they found their mark, no stab of flame visible through the trees.

Beresford clenched his teeth as the Hispano went forward. The speedometer touched fifty before he began to slow down ready for the bend. He was no fool, and he reckoned that it was better to make sure of the corner and then let the engine have its full run. A smash at the bend would end all the chance he had of getting away from the ambush.

He did not call it an ambush, but he would have been justified in so doing. In the woods, he knew, the gunmen were taking their time as they fired at the Hispano. And they were firing well. By the time he reached the first bend of the corner seven shots had struck the side of the car.

It was the seventh which gave him the split-second of warning that he needed to avert disaster. It sent a shiver of foreknowledge through him, for he realized suddenly that the marksmen were firing well, that seven times they had hit the car, but not once had a bullet gone over his head! In short, Beresford thought as he swung his wheel, *they were firing to panic him, not to kill!*

Beresford knew the reason as he turned the bend!

In the centre of the road a Daimler limousine was at a stand-still, drawn up so that only a small car could have passed on either side. There was no chance at all of Beresford in the Hispano missing the Daimler, and if he had taken the obvious course, by treading on his accelerator and taking the bend hell-for-leather, he must have crashed into perdition. As it was, Beresford was going at little more than twenty-five miles per hour as he started to turn, and that split-second of warning, intuitive rather than actual, had made him fasten on to his brakes desperately. The Hispano skidded as its driver braked and turned the wheel at the same time. For a moment Beresford thought that he must go broadside into the Daimler, but another skid took the Hispano round, and Beresford let his muscles go loose as the radiator of his car crashed against the offside wheel of the Daimler.

The crash sent Beresford's big body jolting sideways, but the worst of the impact had been avoided. The only damage, Beresford thought with a grunt, was to the two cars...

And then he had a shock. For the first time he saw that the Daimler was not empty. A man was sitting at the wheel, sitting with absurd stillness after the smash, and staring at Beresford with eyes opened wide in terror! Beresford swallowed hard, and stared unbelievingly at the man. He needed no telling who it was.

"Odell!" Beresford breathed.

Beresford felt automatically in his pocket for his cigarettes, and lit one as he approached the big car, feeling in need of the narcotic. As he drew near he saw the reason for the Major's stillness, and knew why he had not shouted a warning. And Beresford saw a red mist in front of his eyes as the full devilishness of the trick came home to him!

The man was tied to the seat so that he could not move. His hands were fastened to the wheels, and he was gagged effectively, so that he could not cry out. Beresford needed no telling of the plan which had been conceived. After the smash, which would have killed both men if he had not taken the corner carefully, the men (or one of them) from the woods would have hurried down to the scene of it, cut away the tell-tale cords binding Odell, taken the gag from his mouth, and left the wreck of the two big cars for anyone to find. Nothing in the world would have convinced any sane man that the smash had been anything but an accident caused by reckless driving.

"And that," Beresford muttered to himself, "was why they fired at the car and not at me. And," he added, with a glint in his eyes, "it speaks volumes for the breeze which is floating behind Leopold Gorman. He daren't take a chance at open killing."

That surmise was only partly true, but it was true enough for the moment. Beresford kept his eyes open and his gun handy, but he did not anticipate any trouble from the gunmen who had tried to make him take the bend at a high speed. Nor did he get any trouble from them.

He cut through the cords at Odell's wrists, following with those which fastened the man to the seat. Odell, glaring and a fiery red from forehead to collar, tried to speak but failed, and tried to get the gag from his mouth but failed.

"Allow me," said Beresford with a sudden smile. In spite of the circumstances, the near-apoplexy which was possessing Odell had its humour, and laughter was an easy thing to Tony Beresford.

He inserted his large forefinger into the Major's mouth and eased out a small rubber ball. Odell retched.

"Try a spot of this," said Beresford a couple of minutes later, proffering his ever ready flask to Odell. The man sipped the whisky, sipped again and muttered "Thanks—thanks. My God, but I thought I'd finished for good an' all dat time, buddy!"

As he heard the words, Beresford's body went rigid, and his mind went cold. The humour went from his eyes and he stared at the man as if he could not believe the evidence of his sight. It wasn't Odell...

"You!" muttered Beresford. *"You..."*

"Sho' thing," said Josiah Long cheerfully, "an' my opinion of yuh is getting better an' better!"

It took Beresford several minutes to recover from the shock of his discovery. He had convinced himself that Josiah Long was not all that he seemed. Several things had pointed to Long's association with Gorman, despite the confirmation from America of the agent's official capacity, but the discovery of Josiah, trussed up and ready for killing in an 'accident', was ample confirmation of the enmity which Gorman had for him.

Fast upon this thought was his realization that events suggested that Major Odell was in the affair much deeper than it had seemed—and the last time Valerie Lester had been seen she had been with the Major.

Beresford swore, then forced his thoughts into different channels. He jerked his thumb at the two cars, scowling the while.

"They won't help us much," he grunted; "but we've got to get back to London, and get back quickly."

"Maybe we'll get a ride," suggested Josiah Long cheerfully. "There's a fork turning up de road—let's walk."

As the two men swung along the road, Josiah Long told his story. Beresford listened, grim-eyed. The more he heard, the less he liked of Major Gulliver Odell's part in the affair.

Briefly, Josiah Long had left Scotland Yard on the previous night, free to do what he liked, but for the two detectives who had been trailing him. He had slipped his men, and had decided that the most likely source of information was Major Odell, or Major Odell's friends. Consequently he had decided to visit one or two of the Major's ports of call, dressed and looking like Odell.

His first call had been at Adele Fayne's flat, for he knew nothing of Beresford's preparation for that lady's sudden change of address. The door of the flat had been opened by a man whom he had not recognized...

"An' de guy let me in, buddy, an' den brought de butt of a gun down on me head. I didn't stand a chance——"

"It was about all you deserved," grunted Beresford. "Impersonating Odell was asking for trouble."

Josiah Long shrugged his shoulders.

"Maybe, maybe not. If it'd woiked de udder way, an' I'd gotta line somewheres, it'd been genius."

Beresford grunted.

"Anyways," said Long, "de next thing I knew I wass in de Daimler, trussed like you found me. I wass drugged until den, an' when I came round I reckoned I wouldn't be on dis li'l woild much longer. I sure owe yuh a lot, Beresford."

Beresford grunted again.

"A bit back for the Lancia business," he said. He laughed. "And I'd reckoned you worked those tricks, somehow."

"Did you?" Josiah Long blinked. "Can't say I blame yuh, buddy. Wass dere any udder things you had on me?"

Beresford nodded. He was fully convinced now that Josiah Long was genuine, and it was a relief to talk.

"I told you," he said, "that Nosey Dean was drowned. He wasn't —he was shot, with the same gun that shot Williams. But you had the gun——"

"So it looked like I shot Dean?"

"It did," said Beresford. "How'd you get the gun?"

"Through the post," said Josiah Long simply. "I should have told yuh, Beresford, but it slipped my mind, kind of."

Beresford whistled.

"So it was an effort to make us suspicious of you?"

"That's what I reckon," admitted Long, "an' it did." He grinned. "Howso—dat car looks as if it might have room for us, buddy. Yuh call it. I can't raise a proper shout yet."

At twenty past nine that morning, Curtis weary-eyed because he had been forcing himself to keep awake for the past three hours, although he was tired to the point of exhaustion, swore mildly as the telephone-bell rang. He dragged himself out of his chair, staring enviously at the other three people in the room. Adele Fayne, he already knew, slept with her mouth open. It made her look as vacuous as she really was, and did little to increase her prettiness. Solly Lewistein, on a chair next to the couch which had been hastily made up for the dancer, slept noisily, and as he breathed so the sides of his chair bulged slightly outwards. Dodo Trale, who had won the toss for the first man for sleep, slept as he lived—immaculately.

Curtis lifted the receiver from its hook, halloed, told a sharp-tongued operator that he would complain to a Mr. Belisha if she wasn't careful, which remark seemed to amuse the operator, and inquired of her what she wanted.

"A man called your number from a call-box," he was told, "but he hadn't enough change to pay for the call. He said his name was B-E-R-E——"

"Get me that call-box," snapped Curtis, and the girl sensed the seriousness behind the change of his tone.

Two minutes later Curtis heard Beresford's voice.

"I had a packet of trouble on the way to you," said Beresford, "and I got something that makes me want to get back to London pretty snappy. But, Bob——"

"I'm listening," muttered Curtis.

"Keep your eyes wide open," said Beresford urgently. "I was held up on the road, which means that whoever it was knew I was coming to see you—or, at least, the way I was held up does. So——"

"They know we're here," said Curtis, wide-eyed, "and that means something'll hum. All right, Tony. But send some others when you can—I'm yawning twice a minute."

"With any luck," said Beresford, who had had something under eight hours' sleep, in the last forty-eight, "I'll be there myself."

Curtis hung up, and turned towards the three sleeping beauties. The warning from Beresford had sharpened his wits for the moment, and he was able to grin again at Adele Fayne's open mouth, although even as she rested on the couch he was forced to admit that to many her superb figure would have more than recompensed them for the doll-like prettiness of her face and the comparative vacuity of her mind.

From *La Fayne,* whose back was towards the window, Curtis looked to Solly Lewistein, who was sideways to the window, which window Curtis had opened as wide as possible, for the room was small and the four people made it stuffy. It occurred to him at one and the same time that Dodo should be awakened, for his period of rest was up, and that the open window was another way of asking for trouble. He stepped over Dodo's long legs (Trale was opposite Lewistein) to close the window, a precaution which he would not have taken but for Beresford's warning.

And then, just as Timothy Arran had seen it a few days earlier, Curtis saw something glisten in the light of the morning sun. He swore loudly, and swung away, seeing the handle of the knife, which whistled through the open window. Curtis saw where it was going a fraction of a second too late to stop it!

The knife stabbed through Solly Lewistein's throat, with its blood-red tip protruding on the one side and the handle the other! Curtis saw it, and knew that it had cut through the jugular vein, and felt sick. But he slammed the window close before doing anything else, and a second knife cracked against the glass, splintering it, but dropping outside the house.

Dodo Trale seemed to jump from sleep into full consciousness in a split second. As the second knife cracked against the window he leapt out of his chair, dipping into his pocket for the gun which Beresford had given him. Through the window he could see two vague figures, men on the far side of a clump of bushes in the garden—Franchot's *apaches,* if he had but known it—and he levelled his gun.

"Hold it!" snapped Curtis.

The big man bent down and picked Adele Fayne from the couch as easily as picking apples from a tree. The dancer, who had been struggling to a sitting position, screamed. Then she saw Solly Lewistein, the knife in his throat and the blood coming from it. She went rigid in Curtis's arms, and fainted.

"That's the best thing she could have done," grunted Curtis, hurrying to the door. "All right, Dodo—let 'em have it now."

Trale grunted, and dropped on one knee behind the armchair in which he had been sleeping. He realized why Curtis had stopped him. If he had fired before the dancer had been taken out of the room, the men outside would have had a better chance of wounding her, for the window would be splintered completely by a bullet shot, and the knife could have come through. For the time being Adele Fayne was very precious.

Trale waited for a moment, staring into the garden. He saw a bush move, and fancied there was a man behind it. His finger touched the trigger of his gun, and the bullet smashed through the window, humming towards the bush. A man shouted and cursed, and the vague form disappeared.

Trale told himself two things as he waited for the next opportunity to fire. First, that Beresford had been right when he had reasoned that if he abducted Adele Fayne and Lewistein, Gorman would get rattled and come into the open. Secondly, that the curse which he had heard from the man whom he had shot was not in English, nor American. It was French, and an argot common in Montmartre in the bargain!

CHAPTER TWENTY-TWO

ALL ROADS LEAD TO KENT

Beresford and Long had reached the forked roads when Josiah Long pointed at a low-lying Talbot Sports coming towards them and going towards London. Beresford hailed the driver, who obligingly put on his brakes. While the Talbot was slowing down, Beresford noticed the thoroughness of the preparations which had been made to prevent the smash of the Daimler and the Hispano from being prevented by outside interference. At the fork, a 'Road Closed' notice was supported on two trestles; the short bypass along which Beresford had travelled was blocked.

"Clever, de Gorman guy," said Josiah Long, who seemed at peace with the world.

Beresford gave his attention to the driver of the Talbot, a lean, elegant young man who looked bored.

"Going to London?" asked Beresford.

"Weather and other things permitting," said the elegant young man. "Can I give you a lift?"

"We'd be glad if you will," said Beresford. "And you might stop at the first telephone-kiosk or A.A. box."

The young man agreed affably, and five minutes later the Talbot stopped at a telephone booth on the outskirts of a small village. Beresford had some trouble in getting through to Curtis at Resthaven, but when he had given his message to that genial young man, he asked the operator for Scotland Yard, and the operator asked for no money.

Miller was not at the Yard, but Fellowes was there.

"There's no time for talking," said the big man quickly, "but get half a dozen of your good-and-hearty ones down to Curtis's bungalow—Resthaven, near Lindean, near Farningham."

"All right," said Fellowes. "Anything else?"

"Discovered anything about Odell?" asked Beresford, and his voice was tense.

Fellowes' answer disappointed him.

"Nothing at all, nor of the others."

Beresford scowled into the mouthpiece.

"All right," he said. "I'll be with you in an hour, with any luck. Meanwhile, Odell's our pigeon."

"I'll do everything I can," said Fellowes.

The line went dead. Beresford hurried back to the Talbot, and the obliging driver slipped in his clutch.

"Any special part of London you'd like?" asked the young man politely.

Beresford chuckled. There was something likeable about the driver of the Talbot.

"Whitehall," he said. "Parliament Square end. All right?"

"Always ready to help," said the young man.

Beresford's opinion of their Good Samaritan was even better when the Talbot pulled up outside Scotland Yard, and the young man motioned towards the building, still looking bored.

"I take it," he said politely, "that this is where you want. Any other time I can be of service..."

Beresford was still chuckling to himself when he hurried up the steps of the Yard, and Josiah Long was smiling. The speed of the run from Kent had been considerable, and the young man had been a veritable knight-errant.

"Who are we going to see?" Long demanded.

"Fellowes," said Beresford.

The Commissioner, however, was closeted with some Very High Officials, but he sent a message to tell Beresford that he would be finished within ten minutes. Beresford confounded the officials, but lit a cigarette and spent the period of waiting in trying to put the affair on which he was working into some kind of order.

There were several things clear. Having finally accepted Josiah Long for what he was, the many minor mysteries arising out of the American's part in the business were settled. Nevertheless, there was plenty to sort out, and many things seemed inexplicable. For instance, there was the mystery of Bob Lavering. Why had he been allowed to escape? Why had he been poisoned, although not fatally, by Leopold Gorman? Why had the nursing-home in Paris been burned down *after* Lavering had left for London?

Tony Beresford needed no telling that the Police Commissioner had news, and important news, when he saw that stony-faced gentleman hurry into his office, his stiff right leg thrown forward more than usual. Fellowes looked full of information, but he stopped short as he saw Josiah Long, looking for all the world like Gulliver Odell.

"It wasn't *you* who went to Paris, was it?" he demanded.

Long shook his head.

"No—an' if yuh think hard enough, yuh'll know why."

Fellowes grunted. Certainly Josiah Long had been busy enough in London during the time that Leopold Gorman and Major Odell had been in Paris.

"We can pass Long now," said Beresford. "What have you got hold of, Bill?"

Sir William Fellowes drew a deep breath.

"We've heard from America," he said, "about the Wheat Pool job. Lavering's father is in control of the Pool——"

"The devil he is!" Beresford pushed his hand through his hair, looking keenly at the Commissioner, and realizing that the mystery of Bob Lavering would very soon be explained. He felt tense with a mental excitement, which made him drum his fingers against his thigh.

"And when he dies," said Fellowes, "young Lavering will take over that control. There are two things which we haven't known before: first, that Lavering is behind the Pool—his interest in it has been kept a close secret for years—and secondly, that he's suffering from an incurable disease..."

Fellowes paused. Beresford's lips shaped a soundless whistle.

"So-ho! He's likely to die at any time, is he?"

"Yes," Fellowes agreed, and as he went on his voice was low-pitched. "That's why Gorman wanted to *control* Lavering. He tried first to marry him to Adele Fayne, but in case that didn't work— and it didn't—he had him dosed with arsenic; physically and mentally, Bob Lavering would—or could—have been controlled by Gorman. I fancy that Gorman didn't want to murder either of the Laverings—they're big men on the other side——"

"I'll say dey are!" interpolated Josiah Long.

"Because," went on the Commissioner, "he wanted complete control of the Wheat Pool, together with the influence of the Lavering family behind him. I don't think," Fellowes added grimly, "that we'll have much trouble in tying the Lavering affair on to Gorman."

"All yuh gotta do," said Josiah Long mildly, "is to get de guy."

"We'll get him," muttered Beresford. "That's your lot, is it, Bill?"

"Isn't it enough?" asked Fellowes.

"Plenty," said Beresford, with the ghost of a grin. "Did you send anyone to Resthaven?"

"Two car-loads of men, all armed, and with Rogerson in charge."

"Curtis and Rogerson ought to get on well together," said Beresford. "Anything from Craigie?"

"Not a word," said Fellowes.

"Nor"—Beresford forced himself to speak calmly, but both Fellowes and Josiah Long noticed the tightening of his features and the narrowing of his eyes—"nor of Valerie Lester?"

Fellowes shook his head. For a moment Beresford kept silent, trying to imagine where the girl was, and how she was reacting to the circumstances which had led to her disappearance. For the hundredth time he reasoned that if Josiah Long had been considered a vital danger to Gorman, then the girl, as Long's assistant, was in a tight corner. She would be more dangerous to Leopold Gorman than anyone else, or so Beresford thought, but for a second time that day his hazard was only half the truth.

Fellowes broke the awkward silence which ensued.

"By the way," he said, and Beresford opened his eyes suddenly, "have you heard from the Arrans to-day? Since last night, that is?"

Beresford grunted "No."

"But I haven't had much chance," he added, reaching for a telephone, one of three standing on the Commissioner's desk. "Anything you want them for?"

"I had a call through from Paris just after nine," said Fellowes. "Piquet reckons that he's on to something about that hotel murder. He wanted confirmation of something from Timothy Arran."

Beresford nodded as he listened to the ringing sound on the wire. Either the Arrans weren't at their flat, he told himself, or they were sleeping hard.

"Try the Carilon Club," suggested Fellowes, "or Arran *pater*—no, I'll take the Club, you make the other call."

Within five minutes, however, the two men were convinced that the Arrans had followed the trail of Gordon Craigie and Valerie Lester, and Beresford shuddered as he thought of the end which had been prepared for Josiah Long, as Gulliver Odell, when he had been caught. It was asking too much to believe that the others would escape as luckily.

Fellowes lit a cigarette. He was more worried than he admitted, for his talk with the Very High Authorities convinced him that he would have to find very definite proof before he could make any charge against Leopold Gorman. The cunning of the financier seemed to have covered all possibilities. His financial interests were so varied, and his associates on the boards of his companies so numerous, and socially and politically influential, that any attack against him would be hopeless unless it was well— in fact overwhelmingly—substantiated.

"There's one thing," Fellowes muttered. "We can at least keep our eyes on Gorman, even if we can't touch him. If he leaves London we'll get after him."

"He isn't likely to do anything which will connect him with this ruddy business." As he spoke, Beresford reminded himself of Long's evidence that he had last been conscious, prior to his predicament on the Farningham road, while with Gorman at Park Place. But when the American's story was examined coldly, it left so many loopholes, and in some ways was so fantastic, that a clever counsel could have torn it to bits. Long's evidence would be useful, if the chance did come to put Gorman in dock, but only in a minor key.

"If he's getting worried about Adele Fayne and Solly Lewistein," said Fellowes, "he might slip up—ah!"

The "Ah!" came as a telephone rang, and simultaneously a second bell burred out. Fellowes took one and Beresford the other. Beresford's eyes hardened, and his chin went forward aggressively. Fellowes' eyes glistened.

At the other end of Beresford's line Dodo Trale was speaking urgently, anxiously.

"We're having a tough spot, Tony. Solly's dead... yes, a knife through the window... and there are half a dozen swine outside—

all French, I think... Yes, French... I can see one of them after the telephone wires. Hur——"

The line went dead, and Beresford could almost see the wires leading to Curtis's bungalow falling to the ground. He dropped the instrument quickly, as Fellowes muttered, "You're sure he's heading for Kent... Rotherhithe Tunnel route?... Right."

"Gorman left Park Place," said Fellowes tersely, "and is going across London towards Kent."

"Lewistein's dead," said Beresford, and there was no expression in his voice. "Are you coming with me?"

"Yes," said Fellowes, and gripped Beresford's arm. "We're getting near the end," he added.

"But what's it going to be?" demanded the big man, and his voice cracked.

Leopold Gorman left his Park Place house at half past ten, driving himself, and heading for the Kentish village of Lindean. His odd-shaped shoulders were hunched as he sent the big Daimler through the traffic, and his green eyes were narrowed. He had been worried on the previous night, but now he realized that a smash was inevitable, unless he made sure that Adele Fayne and Solly Lewistein died before they could talk, and that Beresford and his accursed friends followed them quickly. They must go. No matter how many chances he took while getting rid of them, they must go.

The financier had learned, from a man who had trailed Dodo Trale and Adele Fayne, that the dancer and manager were in the bungalow near Farningham. He had sent Franchot's men to the bungalow, and given them instructions to kill. Taking advantage of the then chaotic state of France's officialdom, Gorman had used the Frenchmen, believing that he could more easily prevent the discovery of the fact that his money had paid them, than he could have prevented trouble if he had employed those three gunmen from London who worked for him. Nevertheless, Gorman had little confidence in the Frenchmen. He had used them because they were the lesser of two evils.

The one thing above all others which had persuaded Gorman to travel to Kent was the fact that Beresford and Long had escaped from the crash on the road. When he had discovered that Long was posing as Major Gulliver Odell, Gorman had conceived the scheme to get rid of Beresford and Long without arousing suspicion in minds other than those which already knew of the affair. He had sent his three gunmen to Kent, Long had been made ready for the slaughter—and then Beresford had squeezed out of the crash. The news of the escape had been like a physical shock to Leopold Gorman. From possibility, the chance of his plans failing leapt into probability. He knew then that it would be touch and go before the end was reached.

The Daimler went on, eating the miles, with Gorman unaware that a mile or two in front of him police cars were tearing towards the same village, and that as he finished the drive through Rotherhithe Tunnel, Sir William Fellowes and another were hurtling after him in the Commissioner's Sunbeam, although it would have been a slight salve to his sorely tried mind if he had known that Josiah Long had been unable to join Fellowes; the American agent had collapsed before leaving Scotland Yard.

CHAPTER TWENTY-THREE

ATTACK AND COUNTER-ATTACK

THE twenty minutes following his telephone call to Scotland Yard was one of the worst periods that Dodo Trale had ever experienced. He had seen and shot at a man pulling at the telegraph wires leading to the bungalow while he had been talking, but since that first shot the attackers had learned cunning, and they were breaking the telephone-line at a point out of range of revolver-fire. Trale had, for a moment, comforted himself with the thought that if they were afraid of the revolvers they would give little trouble, but he had no knowledge, then, of the garden at the rear of the building.

Resthaven was situated about thirty yards from a third-class road which led from the Farningham road. The nearest village— Lindean—was a mile away, on the way to Farningham, and apart from several small bungalows, there were no buildings in between. Resthaven was, in fact, isolated. Its long front garden, luckily, was only sparsely shrubbed, and was composed mainly of a green lawn. The Frenchmen outside, as Trale reasoned, could not get within knife-throwing distance without finding themselves within shooting range. But it was a different matter at the rear of the bungalow.

Trale, watching from the front, saw the wires go down and heard his line go dead. He swore, and put the receiver on its hook, glancing as he did so at the horrible figure of Solly Lewistein in the chair. Lewistein's face was bloodless now, his eyes were wide open and glazed, and the knife stuck there, a horrible messenger of death.

Trale's stomach turned. He looked round the room, saw a tablecover over a small table, and biting hard on his teeth, draped the cloth over Lewistein's head and shoulders. Hardly had he done so when he heard a bellow of warning from the rear of Resthaven.

"They're getting on the roof!" bellowed Bob Curtis. "Lock that door and get round here!"

Dodo Trale swung round, slamming the door as he ran out of the room. The key was in the lock, and he turned it quickly, then looked round in the small hall for something which he could push against it as a barricade. An oak chest served his purpose. He tugged at it, dragging it across the doorway, confident that the door could not be broken down without ample warning being given.

In the kitchen, where Bob Curtis was pressing himself against a wall while squinting out of a small window, Trale saw Adele Fayne, still unconscious, lying in a huddled heap. The usually genial Robert Montgomery was cursing softly, fluently and steadily, and his jaw was thrust out. Dwarfed in his great hand was an automatic, and he was saying how much he would like to be able to use it, and he was saying it colourfully.

"The roof, you said?" asked Trale.

Curtis nodded without turning his head.

"Yes, may their sides split! Take a peek outside there, Dodo, and ask yourself..."

Trale looked outside, and his heart sank. There was a short stretch of garden hedged by thick bushes, and those bushes would have given shelter to a couple of dozen men. The hedge was set square, boxing the garden carefully, and enclosing a space of something under twenty square feet. There were, Curtis knew, two gaps in the hedge leading to a larger garden, but the potent factor was that the Frenchmen—providing all the men outside were French—could move right up to the walls of the bungalow without being seen.

"How'd you know they're on the roof?" Trale asked.

"Heard 'em climbing up," said Curtis grimly. "You see that hedge, Dodo?"

"Of course I do, drat you."

"My perishing relative—hell scorch her!—had that put there. Nice and thick, she said, so that the neighbours couldn't see into her garden. Next time I see that unmentionable sexagenarian I'll... Neighbours, mind you, neighbours, and there isn't a rabbit-hutch within a quarter of a mile! Damn! Did you hear that?"

Dodo Trale went pale. Habit sent him rooting in his pocket for cigarettes, and as he rooted, the sound which had made Curtis break off came again—the unmistakable din of breaking stones or slates.

"They're busting a hole through the roof," said Curtis, whose worst habit was that of stating the obvious. "I wonder which room they'll break into."

"If you keep quiet for a moment," snapped Trale, "we might be able to locate them."

Curtis lit a cigarette as he lapsed into silence. For a full minute the two men listened, straining their ears to locate the exact spot in the roof which was being damaged.

"At the front," muttered Curtis at last.

"The hall, or the room we—we slept in," Trale agreed. "What's our counter?"

"Keep at the door leading from here into the hall," said Curtis, "and snipe anything that shows through the hole. It won't do any harm in the front room if you've barricaded it. Have you?"

Trale said that he had, and then he swung round towards the

corner where Adele Fayne was lying. He saw the dancer open her eyes, saw her look round, startled, and then he saw the terrified recollection of what she had last seen flood back to her mind. *La Fayne's* lips opened. She screamed.

"God!" muttered Trale. "I can't stand *that!*"

"Nor me," said Curtis. "For the love of Heaven," he said more loudly, "keep quiet, woman! I——"

Adele Fayne screamed again, and Curtis knew that no amount of talking would quieten her. She was hysterical, all her self-control gone. She stared at the two men yet seemed not to see them, and as she stared she screamed, high-pitched, shuddering screams which set the men shivering. There was something horrible about the sight of that half-demented creature, the dancer who had sent half London frantic, and Trale swore.

"Stuff something in her mouth," he muttered. "It's—anyhow, we can't hear what's happening on the roof if she doesn't stop."

"If we gag her she'll suffocate," said Curtis, "and if she keeps yelling we're in a fix. Only one thing for it..."

Curtis stepped across the small room and shook the writhing, screaming dancer roughly. It had no effect. Grim-faced, he bent down and brought the side of his hand down sharply on the back of her neck. Adele Fayne gave a little choking gurgle and went still.

"Foul!" muttered Curtis. "Still—tarnation, son! *They're through!*"

As he spoke, part of the ceiling in the hall crashed down!

Trale was nearest the door. He swung round, gun in hand, as something splashed into the hall through the hole in the roof. Trale stared dully at it, wondering why the Frenchmen outside should pour water...

"Bless my soul!" said Curtis, in a peculiar, high-pitched tone. "How pleasant they are, Dodo. That's——"

"*Petrol!*" gasped Trale.

* * *

231

"Petrol," agreed Curtis, in the same thin voice. "Now I wonder—put that cigarette out, idiot!"

Just for a moment, Curtis said afterwards, the realization of the Frenchmen's move turned him light in the head. And when, a fraction of a second after he had told Trale to squash his cigarette, he saw something strangely like a foot and leg drop through the hole in the roof, he was sure that it was an illusion.

But it was not. The boot dropped lower, and was suspended at the end of a man's leg from ankle to thigh. At the same time there was a crash overhead, a second, a third. Dimly, the sound of men's voices, raised in alarm, came into the kitchen.

"Does that mean...?" Trale broke off, staring at his companion.

"Reinforcements," said Curtis, with a wide grin. "Oh, boy, this is our lucky morning! *Hallo, there!*"

He bellowed as someone thundered on the front door, and hurried through the hall. Caution made him peer through a small insert of coloured glass before he opened the door, but the sight of half a dozen men in the garden, and two police-cars—open tourers, anyhow, he said to Trale—convinced him that it was safe to let the newcomers in.

A fresh-complexioned man of thirty-odd was the first man to enter the hall. He looked inquiringly at Curtis as he said precisely:

"My name is Rogerson—Assistant-Inspector Rogerson, of Scotland Yard. I——"

"There never was," said Curtis, linking his arm in Rogerson's and drawing that serious-minded officer towards the front room, "a more handsome, efficient or welcome inspector in all of Scotland, never mind the Yard. Do you drink beer?"

Rogerson drew his arm away coldly.

"I beg your pardon," he said with dignity, "and I do not drink beer. I was given to understand that——"

What Rogerson was given to understand was never passed on to Robert Montgomery Curtis, who afterwards said that he seemed to recover his senses when Rogerson proclaimed that he did not drink beer.

"Better have a look at our French beauties," Curtis said suddenly to Trale. "And at Adele Fayne too." He looked at Rogerson and grinned. "Sorry, son. I've had a bit of a tough time, and it went to my head, so to speak. How many of the johnnies did you see on the roof?"

"Two," said Rogerson, thawing a little.

"Any on the ground?"

"Yes—four, I think."

"They hopped off before you got 'em?"

"Ye-es." Honesty compelled Rogerson to admit it, but he did so reluctantly.

Curtis swore mildly.

"That means they're hopping around somewhere, and that a message is going back to London, or wherever they sprang from. How many men have you got with you?"

"Seven," said Rogerson.

"That means we can spare three couples," said Curtis thoughtfully. "Don't mind me making the suggestion, do you? If you'll push three separate and distinct braces of your boys round the garden to look for the bright ones we've lost, it'd help."

Rogerson swallowed hard, and told himself that only on one previous occasion had he felt so much like murder, and that had been when the man Beresford had told him not to be a fool. But there was sound sense in Curtis's plan. Rogerson swung round towards his men, three of whom were in the hall.

"Search round in twos," he said, "and report here inside half an hour."

"I take it they're armed," murmured Curtis.

"Every necessary precaution," said Assistant-Inspector Rogerson frigidly, "has been taken to ensure a satisfactory conclusion, Mr.——"

Robert Montgomery Curtis opened his lips and said "Ah!"

closed his lips and thought many things, but restrained himself from voicing his thoughts, because he knew that he would have been in Queer Street but for the timely arrival of the police squad.

"Then," he said weakly, "that ought to be all right, didn't it? Thank you, Inspector, thank you. Do you mind if I have a look at the lads you pushed off the roof?"

Rogerson grunted, telling himself that the man was mad. Nevertheless he followed Curtis out of the hall, and watched the big man bending over the one Frenchman who had been shot when the police had arrived, and who had fallen to the ground. The man was dead. The bullet had splintered his knee, and in falling he had hit the ground head first.

"Broken neck," muttered Curtis. "The other man's up on the roof, half in and half out, isn't he?"

Rogerson said that he was.

"I'll go up and see if he's conscious," said Curtis.

He looked round the well-kept garden of the bungalow which was called Resthaven, and saw the ladder leaning against the wall, which the attackers had used to reach the roof. By the wall was a tin of petrol, and a second tin was on the ground, open and half empty. Obviously, Curtis thought, it had dropped from the roof when the man who had been pouring the stuff through the hole had been shot.

Curtis reached the roof, and saw the Frenchman who had slipped, and whose right leg was poking through the hole which had been made in the roof. There was an ugly gash in the man's head where he had struck against a broken tile, but he was still alive, although unconscious.

"Doubt if I can get him out by myself," said Curtis thoughtfully. "I think I'd better..."

And then he stopped, for he looked about him, across the countryside, several acres of which he could see from the top of the bungalow. For a moment he stared round him, petrified. His mouth stopped open, and he widened his eyes, as though trying to make sure that he was awake.

About a hundred yards away from the bungalow Curtis saw six men, those plain-clothes men whom Rogerson had sent out to search for the four missing Frenchmen. They were stretched out on the ground, huddled, shapeless heaps, and they were all very still. Further away still, Curtis saw a car which he believed was Sir William Fellowes' Sunbeam, drawn up on the road leading to Resthaven, its nose pointing into a ditch. The driver—it *was* Fellowes, Curtis told himself—was sprawling back in his car, and next to him was Tony Beresford—a Beresford whose features were not in the line of vision—hunched up against the dashboard!

Curtis swallowed hard, and slid his hand towards his pocket for his gun. But the unnatural stillness of those men told him that an automatic would avail him little. The paralysis which had overcome him eased. He shouted down, his voice hoarse with tension.

"Oi, there! Rogerson—Trale!..."

There was no answering sound, and Curtis felt suddenly afraid. He leaned over the edge of the roof, looking down at the garden. He saw Rogerson sprawling across the dead body of the Frenchman, and a second policeman stretched out near by. No one else was in sight.

"Ain't there, though!" Curtis muttered suddenly.

As he spoke, he saw four men approaching Resthaven from four different directions. They looked hideous, but not frightening. Each man wore a mask, complete with respirator.

"*Gas!*" muttered Curtis, putting into words the knowledge which had come to him when he had first seen the strangely still bodies of the men. "Gas, and neatly done..."

As he spoke, he crouched low against the tiles of the roof, hoping against hope that he would not be seen by those approaching men. He did not know who they were, but he guessed, and afterwards he claimed that his guesses were not far wrong. In his mind he reasoned out the manner of the attack. The alarm which he and Trale had sent to Scotland Yard had brought the police, even the Commissioner himself; Gorman, with his three gunmen, had reckoned to make a full haul with the one attack.

And they had succeeded, at least in part. Curtis groaned to himself. He could see no way—unless luck helped him a great deal —of getting away from the spot and warning Horace Miller, or someone else at Scotland Yard, of the belt of poison fog surrounding Resthaven. But there was just a chance, he told himself, that he could pick the approaching men off one by one.

Curtis pulled his automatic from his pocket and levelled it towards the nearest one of the four. He felt, as he took aim, a slight burning about his lips and eyes, but he hardly noticed it in his anxiety to get his man. His finger was actually touching the trigger when the burning increased with a suddenness which made the big man gasp! One moment it had been nothing, the next it was a white-hot pain, searing through the delicate membranes of his eyes, his nose, his mouth! Curtis coughed, a slight, hacking cough—and then the gun dropped from his nerveless hand, clattering down the tiles of the roof and dropping to the ground with a dull thud. Curtis, his mouth wide open, fell back against the unconscious Frenchman, dead to the world!

CHAPTER TWENTY-FOUR

OF A RUSE WHICH SUCCEEDED

C URTIS had made one mistake when he had identified in his mind the men who were near Resthaven. He had fancied it was Tony Beresford next to the Police Commissioner, whereas it was, in fact, Wally Davidson, who had returned from a wild-goose chase after the Arran Twins ("I could have sworn it was those devils!" Wally had told Beresford) late on the previous night, dropped asleep at his flat and, awakening with a guilty conscience, had telephoned to various places and located Beresford at Scotland Yard.

Davidson's story of his trailing of two men whom he had thought to be the Arrans made Beresford thoughtful, but it was not until the Commissioner's Sunbeam was speeding along the Strand that Beresford suddenly decided to delay his visit to the bungalow near Farningham.

Fellowes grunted as the big man climbed out of the car.

"What are you going to do?" he demanded.

"I don't know," said Beresford truthfully, "but I've got a hunch."

"Do you mind if we get after Gorman?" asked Fellowes, "while you follow your hunch?"

"Go steady in Kent," said Beresford, suddenly serious. "Look after him, Wally. He's not used to travelling about without a body-guard of flatfoots."

Fellowes grunted, and released the brakes. The Sunbeam slid along the road, and for a moment Beresford watched it. Then he hailed a passing taxi, and gave the address of a large house in a road leading off Shaftesbury Avenue.

As he leaned back in the cab, he told himself that he would probably wish that he had completed the run with Fellowes. But there had been times before when an idea had forced itself into his mind, and he had been suddenly convinced that he must act on it. This time, he had told himself that it was possible that a call on Major Gulliver Odell's flat (No. 5 of the Shaftesbury Avenue turning) would show profit. For the Major had been to the Silver Slipper, and so had the Arrans, who were missing.

As the taxi swung out of the Avenue, Beresford was looking out of the window, and as he watched his eyes glistened. The one thing which he had wanted to happen was happening. A Daimler saloon was moving slowly away from outside the house for which Beresford was making—and Beresford caught a glimpse of Major Gulliver Odell's florid countenance!

The Daimler was moving away from the taxi, and for a moment Beresford was afraid that he would lose his man. He swore, suddenly opened the door of the cab and swung on to the running-board.

"'Ere!" protested the cabby. "Wot's this lark, Mister——"

"Can you get past that Daimler," snapped Beresford, "and run it into the side of the road?"

The cabby swore luridly.

"Shore, an' then I kin buy meself a noo keb——"

"That'll buy your cab," grunted Beresford.

As he spoke, he pulled his wallet from his pocket and dropped it on to the driver's knees. He knew the easy way to action without questions was *via* money, and habitually carried a substantial wad of notes with him. The cabby saw the wad, and while there was not enough to buy a new taxi, there was more than enough to show earnest. The man stopped swearing and trod hard on his accelerator. The cab gathered speed, passed the Daimler before its engine had started properly, then swung across the big car's nose.

Beresford heard a curse from the driver of the Daimler, and out of the corners of his eyes he saw Gulliver Odell poking his head out of the window. The Daimler stopped dead, its radiator touching the back of the cab. At the moment of the impact Beresford jumped to the pavement, swinging round towards Odell.

The Major's eyes widened, and in that moment Beresford knew that his hunch had been right! For Odell was afraid...

Odell's voice was raised suddenly, high-pitched with fear.

"Get that man—the big man!"

Beresford heard the shout, and saw the driver of the Daimler move his right hand towards his pocket. He saw the driver's little eyes narrow, and for a moment seemed to see death.

But the man's gun jammed for a vital fraction of a second. Beresford leapt forward, his fist clenched, his arm swinging. Every ounce of strength in his great body was behind the blow, which caught his man dead on the point. The man gasped, and then lolled back, his mouth agape, his eyes closed.

At the same moment Tony Beresford bent his knees. He heard the soft zutt! of Odell's silenced automatic, and saw the spurt of flame accompanying it. A bullet whirred over his head, smacking into the wall of a house. A second followed it, a third tore through Beresford's coat, scratching his ribs. He hardly noticed the sharp twinge of pain as he took a chance which was a hundred-to-one against, and launched himself at Odell—Major Gulliver Odell, whose red face was twisted with rage and whose pudgy right hand was holding the automatic.

Odell, inside the Daimler, jerked backwards. The fourth shot from his gun whistled close to Beresford's head, but there was no fifth shot. Beresford slammed his right fist into Odell's thick neck. Odell gasped and swayed. Beresford, forced to hit straight through the open window, followed his right with a left which sent Odell smacking against the far door. The Major's head hit against the framework. Beresford saw his eyes roll, and knew that he would sleep for a long time to come.

Beresford stood still for a moment, breathing hard. As he looked round, he saw a dozen scared pedestrians rushing towards the car. Two blue helmets towered above the crowd, and a policeman's gruff voice demanded to know what this was.

"Ask yourself," grunted Beresford, "and put the handcuffs round those two men. They're liable to be bad-tempered when they wake up. And, Robert——"

"Sir?" Beresford's manner made the man attentive.

"Get one of your pals to telephone for Miller at the Yard—yes, the Super. Tell him Beresford's on something, and for God's sake tell him quick!"

Beresford had realized that the best way of getting quick action was to have Horace Miller, or one of his juniors, on the scene. It was Miller himself who arrived a quarter of an hour later—a Miller who was refreshed by six hours' sound sleep, and who was ready for anything.

Beresford saw the Superintendent turn into the street, and hurried towards him. A few graphic sentences sufficed to convince Miller that the 'something' was big.

"So," said Beresford, "the quicker we get into Odell's flat the better. He'll have some keys in his pockets, but I didn't want to try your Robert's patience too much——"

"It won't take long now," said Miller.

He rapped instructions to a detective who had accompanied him, and within five minutes of his arrival Miller and Tony

Beresford were stepping across the threshold of Major Odell's flat.

The first room was empty, but as the two men opened the door of the second room, Tony Beresford stopped dead, staring at the four people inside, staring at one in particular, and conscious of a tremendous lightness in his chest.

Valerie Lester, bound and gagged, was lying on a settee! The Arrans and Gordon Craigie, trussed so that they could neither move nor speak, were in the room too!

Beresford muttered a prayer of thanks as he hurried across the room, opening a knife as he went, ready to cut the cords from Valerie Lester's arms and legs.

When Robert Curtis regained consciousness, he found that he was sitting in a large armchair in one of the rooms of Resthaven. The chair was apparently dancing a fandango on its own. Apart from the giddiness and a soreness about his eyes and mouth, however, Curtis felt little the worse for the gassing. But as the room—or his head—steadied, and the vague forms in front of him took definite shape and became men, he felt a thickness in his throat, and when he tried to speak the words would not come.

He stared in dumb defiance at the men. One of them he recognized, and his eyes narrowed. Leopold Gorman had come into the open at last!

The second man was, to Curtis, a complete stranger, but for the moment at least he was a good friend.

"Drink this," he said tersely, proffering a glass filled with something which looked like water.

Curtis drank eagerly. There was a bitter taste about the liquid, but it served its main purpose. The genial Robert's throat cleared as if by magic. He grinned.

"That's a pal!" he said gratefully.

JOHN CREASEY

The little man scowled, and there was no answering smile on his lips; Curtis noticed Gorman was glaring——

"Where's Beresford?" snapped the second man.

Curtis frowned. He remembered seeing—or thinking he saw—Tony Beresford in the Sunbeam with Fellowes. He said as much.

"That wasn't Beresford," Gorman said harshly. "If you want to get out of this with a whole skin, Curtis, you'll have to talk."

Curtis forced back a biting retort, telling himself that he was as anxious to know where Beresford was as the others were, and that it would serve no purpose if he told Leopold Gorman that he knew perfectly well that his chance of getting out of the bungalow at all was small, if it rested with the man with the jade-green eyes.

"Talk about what?" Curtis demanded. "How the hell can I talk, anyhow? I——"

"Don't try that trick," snapped the second man, and Curtis swore silently. Time wasted was time saved, in effect, and he had hoped to gain a few precious minutes. "Where's Beresford?" the man demanded again.

Curtis forced a grin.

"I don't know any more than you do," he said. "I telephoned Beresford, and I expected him to be here. Unless——"

He broke off suddenly, and Gorman jumped into the opening.

"Unless what?" he grated, and Curtis felt the fascination of his green eyes.

"Unless nothing," said Curtis, looking at his feet.

The second man snapped suddenly at Gorman, and Curtis was surprised that the financier accepted the other's attitude without a complaint. He could not know that Gorman's companion was the man who had arranged the first attacks on Beresford, had worked both tricks with the Lancia, and had led the attack on Beresford on the Kent road; but he did realize that the man was one of that rare species in England—the killer.

"He's stalling," the gunman snapped. "We've got to get out of here, and get Beresford later."

"Beresford's bound to come," protested Gorman.

"Yes, and to bring plenty with him," snapped the other. "We can't take the chance. We'll be lucky now if we save our necks."

He swung out of the room, and Curtis heard him barking instructions to the others—including the Frenchmen—of the raiding party. Gorman stood by the window, looking across the lawn, and Curtis wondered what was going on behind those green eyes.

But the big man forgot Gorman as he realized what was happening. Three times he saw the raiders enter the bungalow, each time heavily burdened. After the third trip, Curtis knew that they had been carrying the unconscious policemen from the garden into the bungalow. That meant, Curtis told himself, that he had been dosed but lightly with the gas, probably because he had been fifteen yards above the ground; most poisonous gases were heavier than air.

It was a sudden question from one of the men which made Curtis's body go rigid.

"That's de lot," said the man. "Where shall we start it, Boss?"

The man with Gorman spoke callously, and Curtis saw a red mist float in front of his eyes. It was then that the prisoner discovered that although his hands were free, he was fastened to the armchair by a rope round his waist, and the chair in turn was fast to the floor.

"In the kitchen," snapped the man.

"Leaving them all?"

"Yes—not forgetting the girl..."

Curtis closed his eyes, and as he did so heard for a second time within an hour the sound of splashing. He needed no telling that the splashing was of petrol. The cold-bloodedness of the thing was incredible! Gorman and the other man were planning to destroy the bungalow, and all its occupants, by fire! For a moment that seemed like an age, Curtis gritted his teeth and kept his eyes closed. And then he opened his mouth...

But he choked the words back—mad words that he was planning to hurl at Gorman, and that cold-blooded devil in the other room. He heard Gorman cry out, and saw a man running across the lawn—a man who seemed as if he was being chased by the devil.

"Don't fire it!" shouted Gorman. "Here's Odell—Odell!"

The second man cursed and hurried into the room. He watched the figure of the man he thought was Major Gulliver Odell, and it was not until the newcomer was within a few yards of the window that he realized the trap.

"That's not Odell!" He swore, dropping his hand to his pocket. *"That's Craigie—Gordon Craigie!"*

As he spoke, there came the sudden zutt! of a silenced automatic. Curtis, staring wide-eyed at the newcomer, thought for a terrible moment that Craigie—could it be Craigie?—had been shot, but as the thought flashed through Curtis's mind, the man with Gorman staggered, and pirouetted on his feet. Curtis saw the ugly patch of red on his shirt, saw Gorman, his dark, misshapen face a sickly pallor, swing away from the window, and saw the window splinter into a thousand pieces as the man who looked like Major Odell fired for a second time. The bullet took the financier on the knee. Gorman shrieked in agony, and crashed down.

And through a haze, Curtis saw not one man but a dozen racing across the grass towards the bungalow. He saw Tony Beresford, and the dapper figures of the Unholy Twins, and further back a small army of men, moving quickly towards the bungalow. Craigie had taken no chances of being outnumbered in the final assault on Resthaven!

Craigie's voice came urgently.

"Are the others all right, Curtis?"

"I—I think so." Curtis swallowed hard, and noticed that the room was beginning to float about him again. He saw Craigie hurry through to the rear of the bungalow, and was conscious when he heard the Chief's voice raised to say:

"Trale's all right, Beresford—and *La Fayne*."

At which moment Robert Montgomery Curtis fainted, not to know until later that the Frenchmen and Gorman's gunmen had been too cowed by their leader's fall to give fight.

CHAPTER TWENTY-FIVE

OF A CONVERSATION AND A PLACARD

F OR the fifth time since they had first met, Tony Beresford and Valerie Lester were dining—or at least being—*tête-à-tête*. It was two days after the affair at the bungalow, two days which had been full ones for Beresford, and even fuller for Valerie Lester, who had been preparing hurriedly for a journey.

In those two days Beresford had learned many things. He had been told by Craigie how that gentleman had been completely hood-winked by Major Gulliver Odell, whom he had thought to be a fool and little else. The Major, complaining that he had been involved in an accident and was confined to his room, had telephoned Craigie, *via* his flat, saying that he believed he knew something about Leopold Gorman which Craigie should know. The Chief had sent a man to investigate the truth of Odell's 'accident', and the man had confirmed that Odell was at his flat, alone, and with a heavily bandaged leg. Craigie had consequently visited the flat, to suffer, as Long had suffered at Adele Fayne's rooms on the following day.

Major Odell, having caught the biggest fish, had then trapped Valerie Lester, and, with her, the Arrans. Valerie had 'fallen' with her eyes open. The Arrans, believing that Odell might lead to Gorman, had visited that gentleman shortly after he had left the Silver Slipper, and a minor gas-attack had finished them. Not until Beresford and Miller had arrived at the flat had any one of the four seriously thought that they would escape alive.

They had been kept at Odell's flat, Craigie reasoned, because Gorman had no other rendezvous in England, apart from his own house. The financier's anxiety to keep his connection with the outrages hidden had, Craigie knew, caused him to make his head-quarters at the Côte d'Or with Franchot as his chief lieutenant. With the exception of the three Englishmen who had surrendered at Resthaven, and the deceased Nosey Dean, Gorman had no agents in England. Major Odell—who had been short of money for a long time—had been 'bought' by Gorman, but until the last few days of the affair Odell had operated from Paris. He had been the connecting link between Gorman and Franchot for some months.

The French connection, Craigie reasoned, explained why Lavering had been lured to France (Gorman had deliberately gone to Paris to entice the American across the Channel). Corinne the dancer had been intended as a decoy for Lavering, but the threat from Department Z had made Gorman change his plans and rely on the 'arsenic treatment' to keep Lavering under his control. Thus he had been safe in allowing the American to leave the nursing-home in Paris. At any time Lavering's supply (unknown to Lavering himself) could have been withdrawn. (That Bob Lavering would have been the power behind the Wheat Pool was evidenced less than a month later, when his father died suddenly from natural causes.) Craigie could discover no reason for the destruction by fire of the nursing-home; Beresford suggested, reasonably, that in the home was ample evidence of the poisoning to which Lavering had been subjected, and the fire was intended to destroy that evidence.

"Maybe yuh're right," admitted Josiah Long, who was one of the four people present at the conversation when these things were explained.

"What was Solly Lewistein so scared of?" Fellowes asked.

"He knew that Adele Fayne had been poisoning Lavering," said Craigie, "and he knew about the murder of Williams too. Both of them were completely under Gorman's thumb, and were frightened to death that they would be charged as accomplices after the fact of Williams' murder."

Beresford grinned, then scowled. He had seen the knife in Solly Lewistein's throat, and it had not been pleasant.

"Odell was up to his neck in it, was he?" asked Long.

"Yes," said Beresford. "I suspected that gentleman was deeper than we thought when I heard that he was a gambler, and short of money."

"It was lucky you had that last-minute idea," said the Chief Commissioner.

"It was luckier that Craigie thought of going to the bungalow looking, at a distance, like Odell," said Beresford. "If Gorman hadn't been caught out by that, there would have been the devil to pay at Resthaven."

"*Would* have been?" asked Josiah Long mildly.

"You be quiet," Beresford grinned, "or we'll have you deported."

Josiah Long blinked. He was feeling the effects of his encounter with Gorman, and the stuff with which he had been doped had weakened him to such an extent that he had been unable to be in at the death, a fact which rankled deeply. Beresford cheered him, and drank his health in Gordon Craigie's whisky (for the conversation took place in the holy of holies, Department Z) and then departed, for he had an appointment with five young and hearty gentlemen, being the Arran Twins,

Dodo Trale, Wally Davidson and Robert Curtis. The meeting of those five and Beresford was hilarious, and was a celebration continued a long time after Beresford had left.

Beresford thereafter cleared up several jobs which needed doing, assured himself that Bob Lavering was in good hands, and, when he reached his flat, suggested in so many words to Sam Tricker that Maria would be a necessity at the flat in the future.

"And as," he said very seriously, "we haven't got room for more than two bedrooms, Sam, you'd better be popping the question. I'll be your best man——"

Sammivel's face split into the widest beam that Beresford had ever seen on it.

After these things, Beresford called on the Chesters to see Valerie, and for a while they talked. In consequence of the things they said, Valerie had spent a hectic twelve hours buying many things, and out of her experience Diane Chester helped her.

Soon afterwards Valerie and Tony Beresford dined together in the restaurant-car of the Dover boat-train. The last placard that Beresford saw in England proclaimed a fall in petrol prices.

"And that," smiled the big man, "is a very pleasant wedding present."

His wife smiled, for the future looked very bright.

Leopold Gorman was taken to Farningham Hospital, and after an operation on his damaged knee, was transferred to a police nursing-home. The third day after his arrival he was found dead from arsenic poisoning. Gordon Craigie knew that the men who had sheltered the financier during his career had not dared to face the consequences of his trial and the subsequent revelations.

Craigie was pleased rather than sorry. He knew that the plot to control world markets had failed, that Governments were taking precautions against any panic reactions, and that those men who had supported Gorman with their money would crash, financially, soon after Gorman died.

It so happened that within a month of that death four suicides shook the stock markets of the world. Only Miccowiski, in Russia, faced the consequences of his failure, and he suffered as most men suffered who failed not only themselves but also the Soviet.

But the affair which had started with the International Economic Conference had other repercussions. Major Gulliver Odell was hung for the murder of Nosey Dean and Nicholas Williams, although throughout his trial he kept silent about Gorman, hoping that he would gain a reprieve. Adele Fayne left the stage; without Solly Lewistein she was like a rudderless ship, but after her hysteria at Resthaven she altered, mentally, for the better. No charge was pressed against her; Craigie knew that she had been nothing but a tool, and that there was nothing to fear from her by herself.

Craigie thought of these things, and then of the Arrans, who were soon to start on another job of work. Timothy was quieter than before the Lavering affair. The death of Corinne had affected him deeply. Craigie knew, however, that a steadier Timothy would be a better agent; he would be able to replace Beresford, whose marriage automatically cut him off from Department Z's list of agents. Curtis and Davidson, moreover, joined that select list, two men who were likely to do well.

It had been a bad beginning, Craigie told himself, but it had cleaned up well. Gorman's French assassins had been deported, and Piquet would look after them, together with Franchot, at the Côte d'Or. The three English gunmen would hang, although their trial had not yet started—Odell's had come first, for as little sensation as possible was wanted by the Men Who Mattered.

Craigie thought, suddenly, of the registry office marriage at which he had been a witness, and smiled when he recalled the slim, calm loveliness of Valerie Lester. And then he knocked the tobacco from the bowl of his pipe and leaned back in his armchair.

ABOUT THE AUTHOR

John Creasey, born in 1908, was a paramount English crime and science fiction writer who used myriad pseudonyms for more than six hundred novels. He founded the UK Crime Writers' Association in 1953. In 1962, his book *Gideon's Fire* received the Edgar Award for Best Novel from the Mystery Writers of America. Many of the characters featured in Creasey's titles became popular, including George Gideon of Scotland Yard, who was the basis for a subsequent television series and film. Creasey died in Salisbury, UK, in 1973.

DEPARTMENT Z

FROM OPEN ROAD MEDIA

OPEN ROAD

INTEGRATED MEDIA

OPEN ROAD

INTEGRATED MEDIA

Find a full list of our authors and
titles at www.openroadmedia.com

FOLLOW US
@OpenRoadMedia

www.ingramcontent.com/pod-product-compliance
Lightning Source LLC
Chambersburg PA
CBHW020358030726
47496CB00007B/2193